ARCHIE COMIC PU INC.

co-ceo
JONATHAN GOLDWATER

co-ceo
NANCY SILBERKLEIT

co-president/editor-in-chief
VICTOR GORELICK

co-president/director of circulation
FRED MAUSSER

vice president/managing editor
MIKE PELLERITO

assistant editor
PAUL KAMINSKI

cover
PAT SPAZIANTE

production
STEPHEN OSWALD
TITO PEÑA
JOE MORCIGLIO
SUZANNAH ROWNTREE
IAN FLYNN

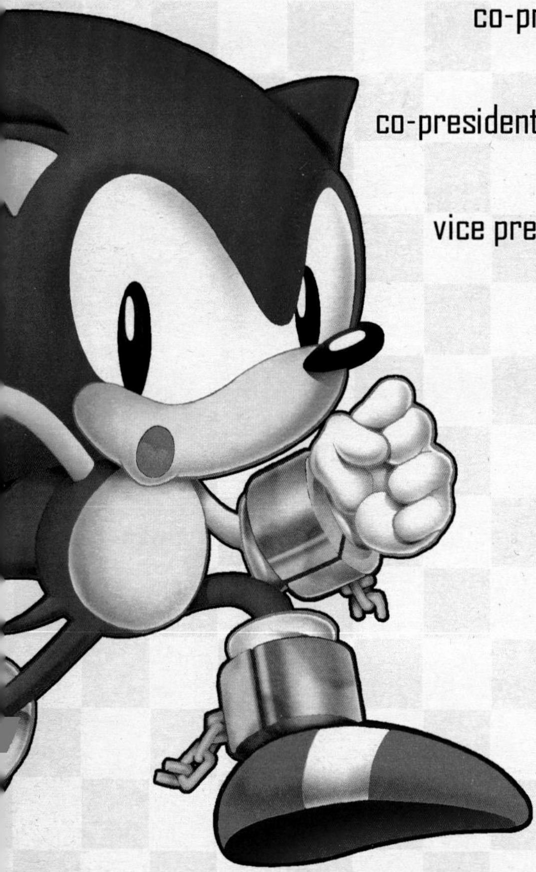

archiecomics.com sega.com

NIC THE HEDGEHOG ARCHIVES, Volume 12. Printed in Canada. Published by Archie Comic Publications, Inc., 325 Fayette Avenue, Mamaroneck, 0543-2318.

ISBN: 978-1-879794-53-5

TABLE OF CONTENTS

"KNUCKLES' QUEST pt4"
The long road to the Sword of Acorns draws to a close as Knuckles, with the help of his mentor Archimedes, takes on the maniacal magic of Mathias Poe! Will the Paladin's advice be enough? Or has Knuckles hit another dead end?

Sonic the Hedgehog #47:
"ENDGAME pt1"
The Ultimate battle begins here!
Sonic and the Freedom Fighters, with the help of Lupe and the wolfpack, launch what may very well prove to be their final assault on the evil Dr. Robotnik. Lines are drawn, trust is shattered, and the casualties mount. All of Mobius stands on the very brink in this pulse pounding first act to the most epic Sonic tale of them all!

Sonic the Hedgehog #48:
"ENDGAME pt2"
Sonic the Hedgehog: MURDERER?!
When Sonic is put on trial for the murder of Sally Acorn, a suspiciously merciless King Acorn sentences True Blue to a life of horror in the DEVIL'S GULAG. Upon escape the hunt is on as Geoffrey St. John and the newly formed Royal Guard must track down the fugitive Sonic! All this and a betrayer revealed in part two of ENDGAME!

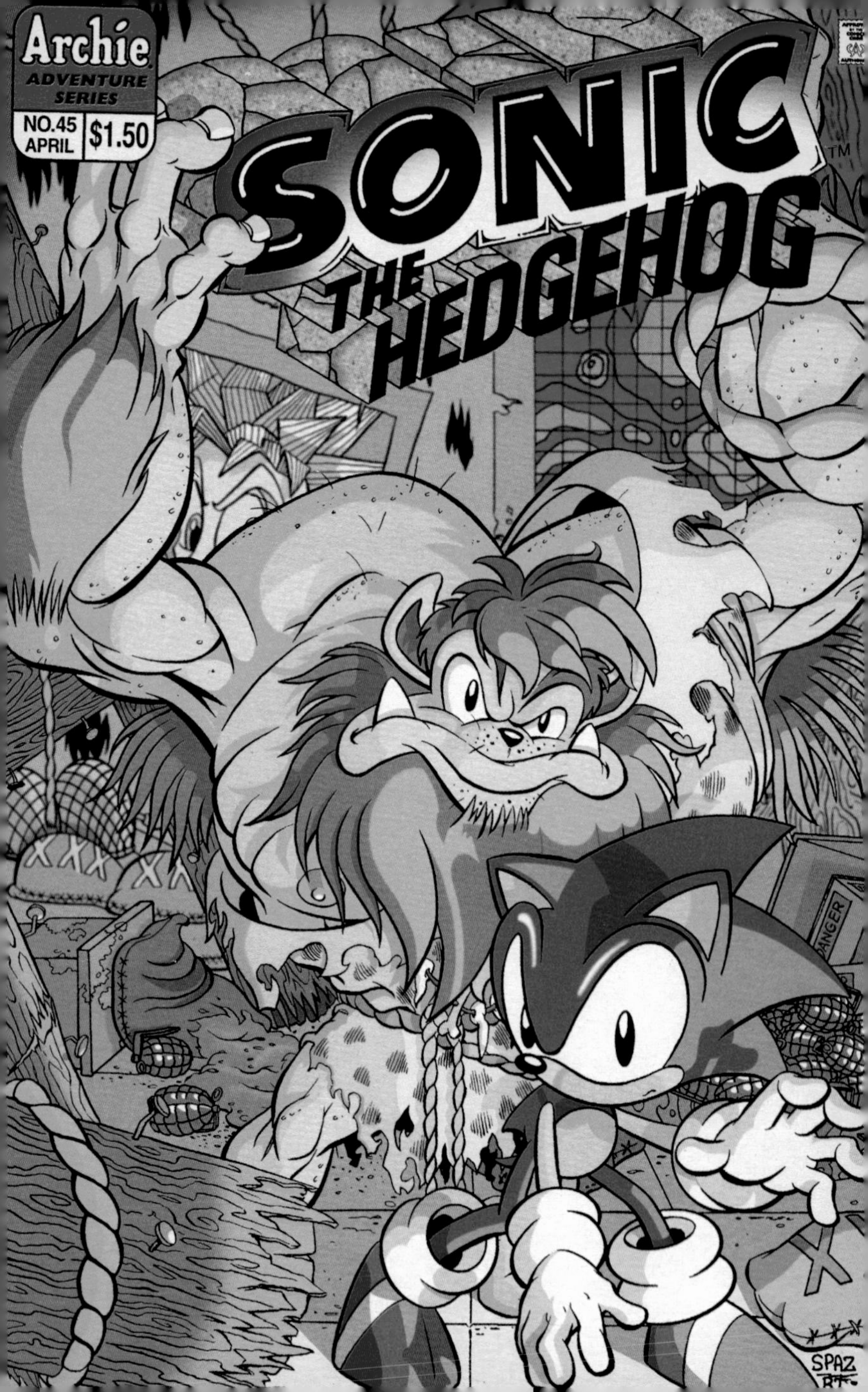
Archie
ADVENTURE SERIES
NO.45 APRIL
$1.50
SONIC THE HEDGEHOG
TM
DANGER
SPAZ

SOME TIME AGO, THE FREEDOM FIGHTERS DISCOVERED AN ANCIENT MOBIAN ENCASED IN ICE,

THEY BROUGHT HIM BACK TO KNOTHOLE VILLAGE AND REVIVED HIM...BUT "MOBIE", AS THEY CALLED HIM, WAS A BEING OUT OF TIME!

GRROWR

SMASH!

REALIZING THAT "MOBIE" WAS AN ARTIST, THE FREEDOM FIGHTERS LEARNED HOW TO COMMUNICATE WITH HIM...

SEE? WE'RE FRIENDS!

...AND FOUND A HOME FOR THEIR NEW-FOUND FRIEND IN THE MOBIAN JUNGLE! HERE HE'S LIVED HAPPILY...

...BUT NOW, THAT'S ABOUT TO CHANGE...

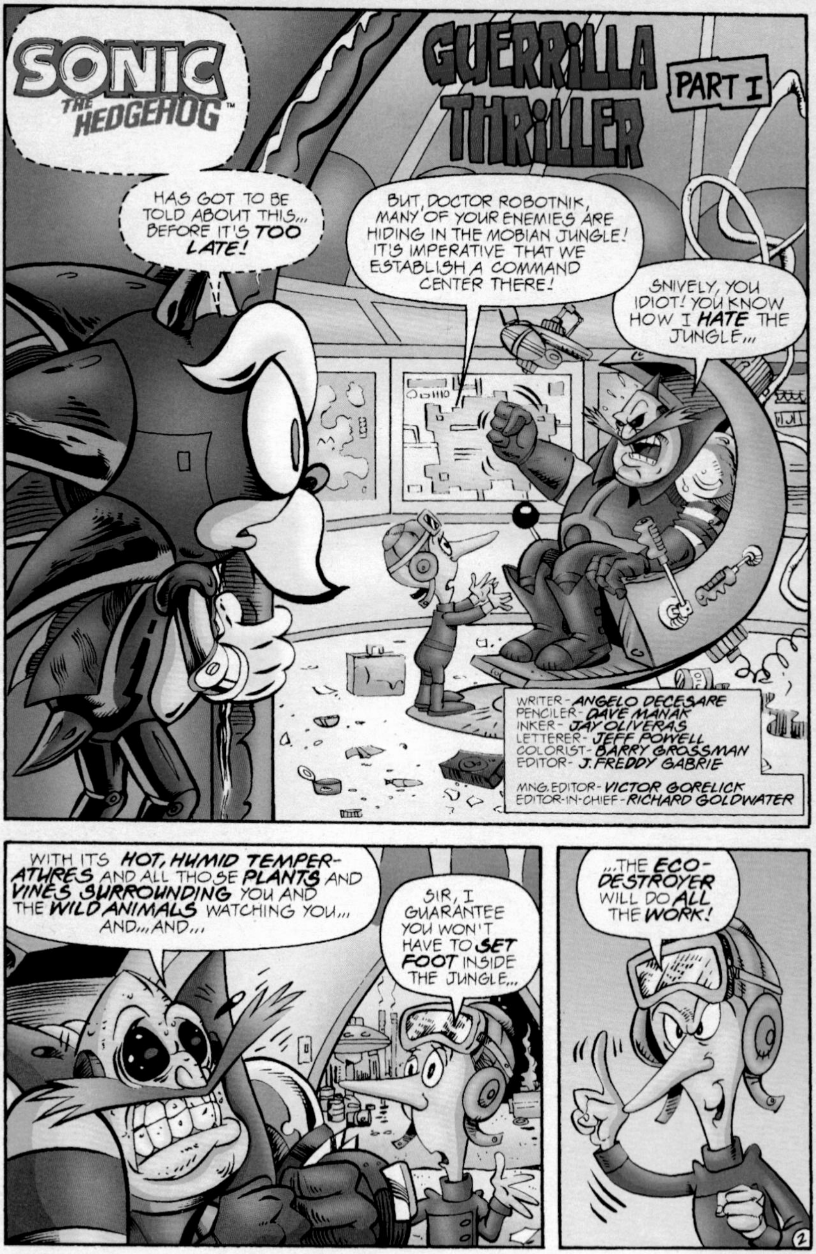
SONIC THE HEDGEHOG™
GUERRILLA THRILLER PART I
HAS GOT TO BE TOLD ABOUT THIS... BEFORE IT'S TOO LATE!
BUT, DOCTOR ROBOTNIK, MANY OF YOUR ENEMIES ARE HIDING IN THE MOBIAN JUNGLE! IT'S IMPERATIVE THAT WE ESTABLISH A COMMAND CENTER THERE!
SNIVELY, YOU IDIOT! YOU KNOW HOW I HATE THE JUNGLE...
WRITER- ANGELO DECESARE
PENCILER- DAVE MANAK
INKER- JAY OLIVERAS
LETTERER- JEFF POWELL
COLORIST- BARRY GROSSMAN
EDITOR- J. FREDDY GABRIE
MNG. EDITOR- VICTOR GORELICK
EDITOR-IN-CHIEF- RICHARD GOLDWATER
WITH ITS HOT, HUMID TEMPERATURES AND ALL THOSE PLANTS AND VINES SURROUNDING YOU AND THE WILD ANIMALS WATCHING YOU... AND... AND...
SIR, I GUARANTEE YOU WON'T HAVE TO SET FOOT INSIDE THE JUNGLE...
...THE ECO-DESTROYER WILL DO ALL THE WORK!
2

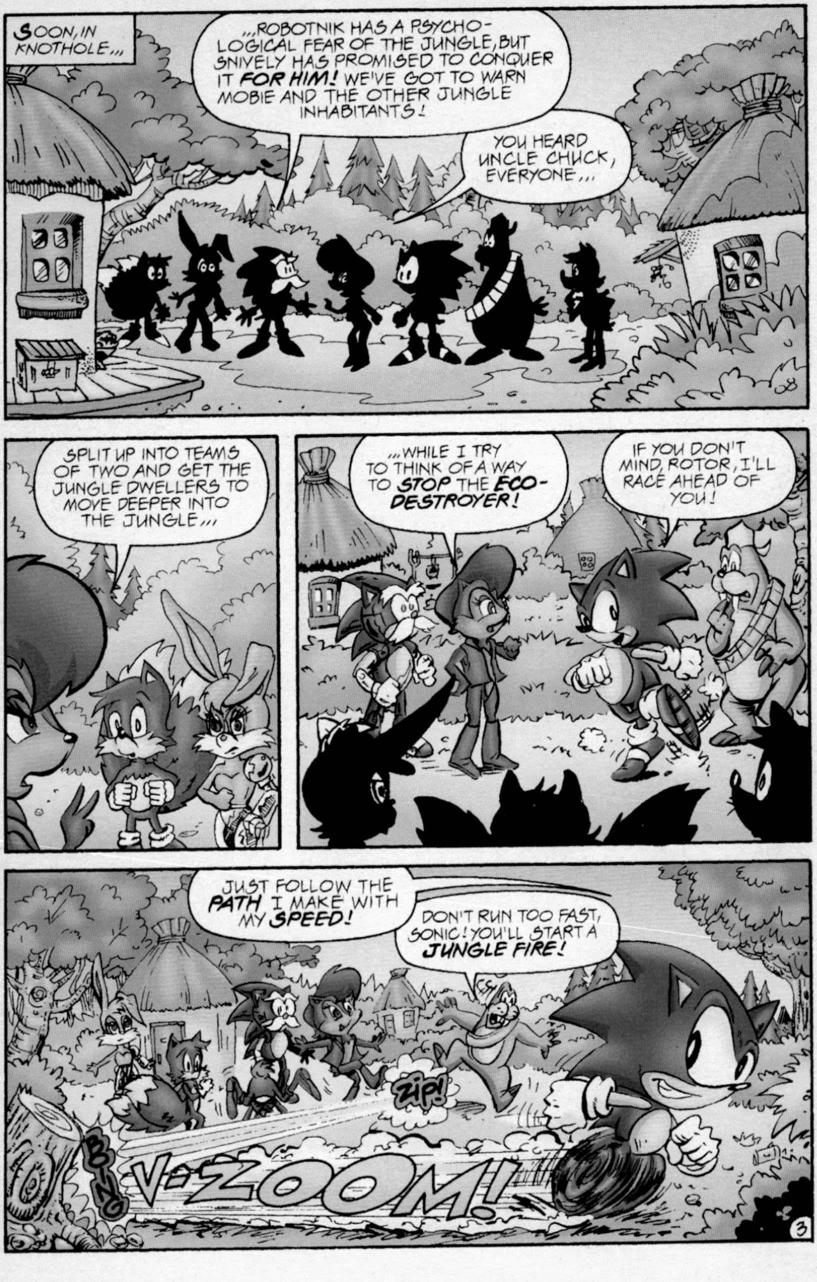
SOON, IN KNOTHOLE...
...ROBOTNIK HAS A PSYCHOLOGICAL FEAR OF THE JUNGLE, BUT SNIVELY HAS PROMISED TO CONQUER IT FOR HIM! WE'VE GOT TO WARN MOBIE AND THE OTHER JUNGLE INHABITANTS!
YOU HEARD UNCLE CHUCK, EVERYONE...
SPLIT UP INTO TEAMS OF TWO AND GET THE JUNGLE DWELLERS TO MOVE DEEPER INTO THE JUNGLE...
...WHILE I TRY TO THINK OF A WAY TO STOP THE ECO-DESTROYER!
IF YOU DON'T MIND, ROTOR, I'LL RACE AHEAD OF YOU!
JUST FOLLOW THE PATH I MAKE WITH MY SPEED!
DON'T RUN TOO FAST, SONIC! YOU'LL START A JUNGLE FIRE!
ZIP!
BOING
V-ZOOM!

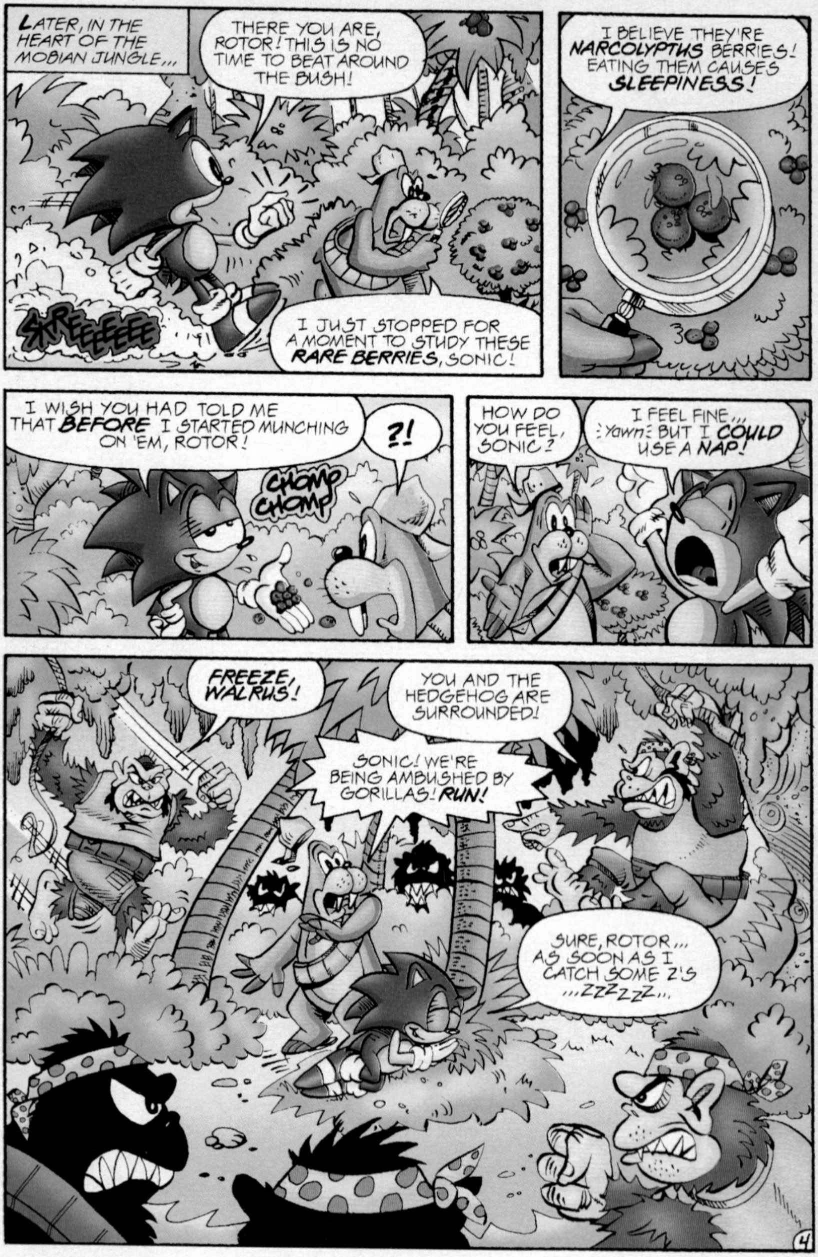
LATER, IN THE HEART OF THE MOBIAN JUNGLE...
THERE YOU ARE, ROTOR! THIS IS NO TIME TO BEAT AROUND THE BUSH!
SKREEEEEEE
I JUST STOPPED FOR A MOMENT TO STUDY THESE RARE BERRIES, SONIC!
I BELIEVE THEY'RE NARCOLYPTUS BERRIES! EATING THEM CAUSES SLEEPINESS!
I WISH YOU HAD TOLD ME THAT BEFORE I STARTED MUNCHING ON 'EM, ROTOR!
CHOMP CHOMP
?!
HOW DO YOU FEEL, SONIC?
I FEEL FINE... Yawn BUT I COULD USE A NAP!
FREEZE, WALRUS!
YOU AND THE HEDGEHOG ARE SURROUNDED!
SONIC! WE'RE BEING AMBUSHED BY GORILLAS! RUN!
SURE, ROTOR... AS SOON AS I CATCH SOME Z'S ...ZZZZZZ...

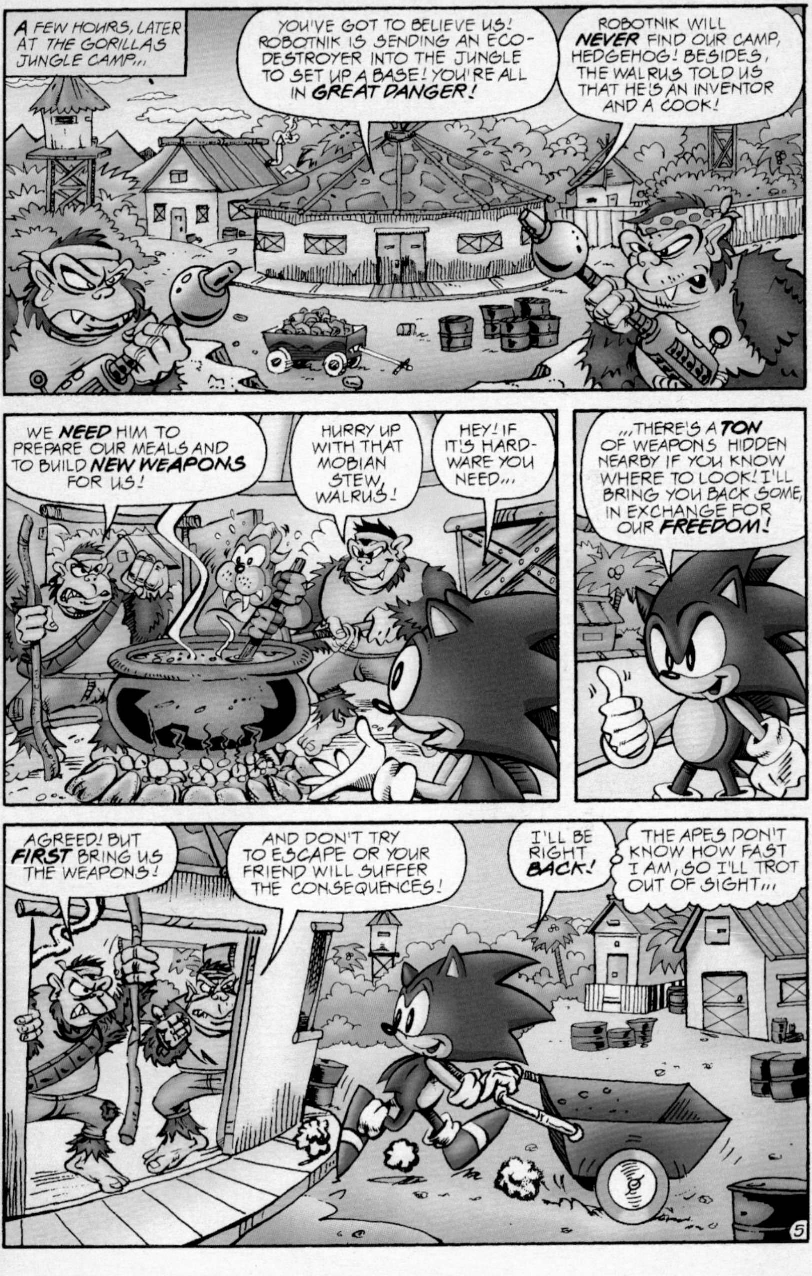
A FEW HOURS, LATER AT THE GORILLAS JUNGLE CAMP...
YOU'VE GOT TO BELIEVE US! ROBOTNIK IS SENDING AN ECO-DESTROYER INTO THE JUNGLE TO SET UP A BASE! YOU'RE ALL IN GREAT DANGER!
ROBOTNIK WILL NEVER FIND OUR CAMP, HEDGEHOG! BESIDES, THE WALRUS TOLD US THAT HE'S AN INVENTOR AND A COOK!
WE NEED HIM TO PREPARE OUR MEALS AND TO BUILD NEW WEAPONS FOR US!
HURRY UP WITH THAT MOBIAN STEW, WALRUS!
HEY! IF IT'S HARD-WARE YOU NEED...
...THERE'S A TON OF WEAPONS HIDDEN NEARBY IF YOU KNOW WHERE TO LOOK! I'LL BRING YOU BACK SOME, IN EXCHANGE FOR OUR FREEDOM!
AGREED! BUT FIRST BRING US THE WEAPONS!
AND DON'T TRY TO ESCAPE OR YOUR FRIEND WILL SUFFER THE CONSEQUENCES!
I'LL BE RIGHT BACK!
THE APES DON'T KNOW HOW FAST I AM, SO I'LL TROT OUT OF SIGHT...

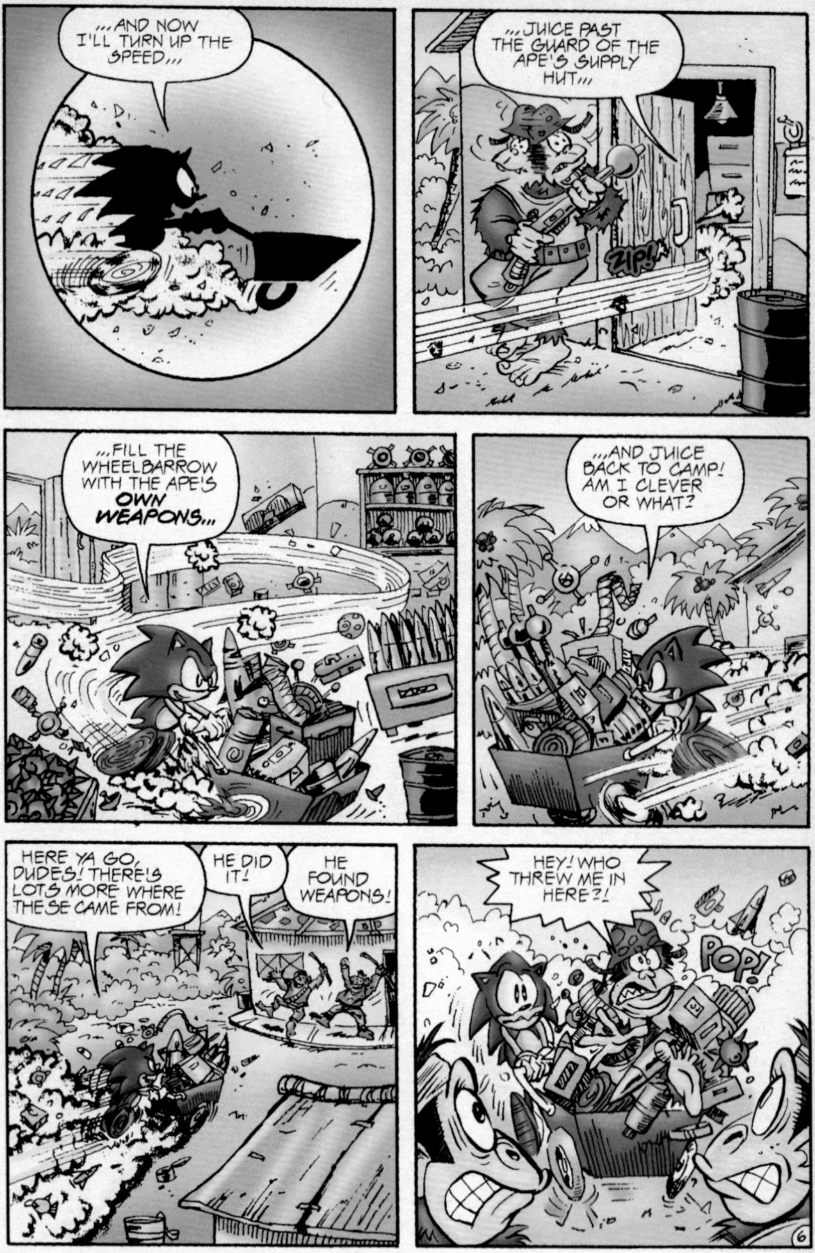
...AND NOW I'LL TURN UP THE SPEED...
...JUICE PAST THE GUARD OF THE APE'S SUPPLY HUT...
ZIP!
...FILL THE WHEELBARROW WITH THE APE'S OWN WEAPONS...
...AND JUICE BACK TO CAMP! AM I CLEVER OR WHAT?
HERE YA GO, DUDES! THERE'S LOTS MORE WHERE THESE CAME FROM!
HE DID IT!
HE FOUND WEAPONS!
HEY! WHO THREW ME IN HERE?!
POP!

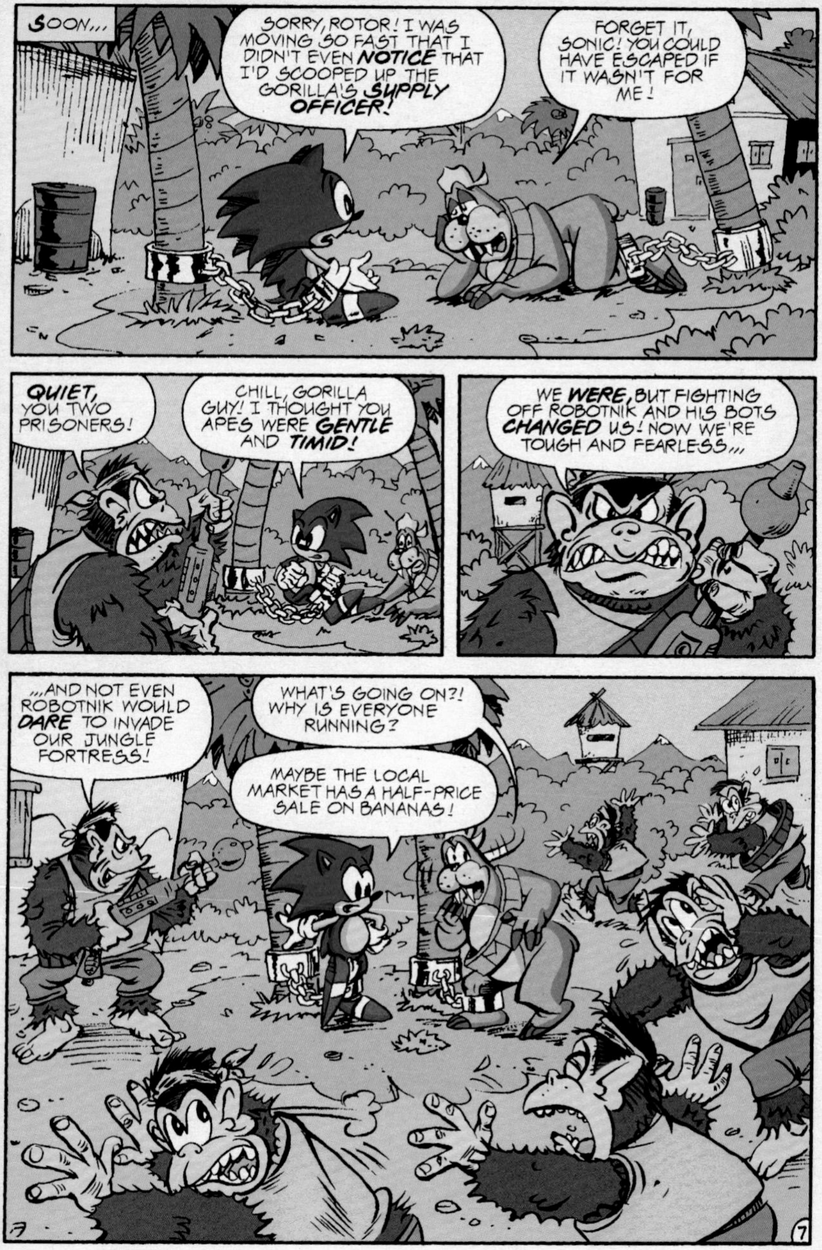
SOON...
SORRY, ROTOR! I WAS MOVING SO FAST THAT I DIDN'T EVEN NOTICE THAT I'D SCOOPED UP THE GORILLA'S SUPPLY OFFICER!
FORGET IT, SONIC! YOU COULD HAVE ESCAPED IF IT WASN'T FOR ME!
QUIET, YOU TWO PRISONERS!
CHILL, GORILLA GUY! I THOUGHT YOU APES WERE GENTLE AND TIMID!
WE WERE, BUT FIGHTING OFF ROBOTNIK AND HIS BOTS CHANGED US! NOW WE'RE TOUGH AND FEARLESS...
...AND NOT EVEN ROBOTNIK WOULD DARE TO INVADE OUR JUNGLE FORTRESS!
WHAT'S GOING ON?! WHY IS EVERYONE RUNNING?
MAYBE THE LOCAL MARKET HAS A HALF-PRICE SALE ON BANANAS!

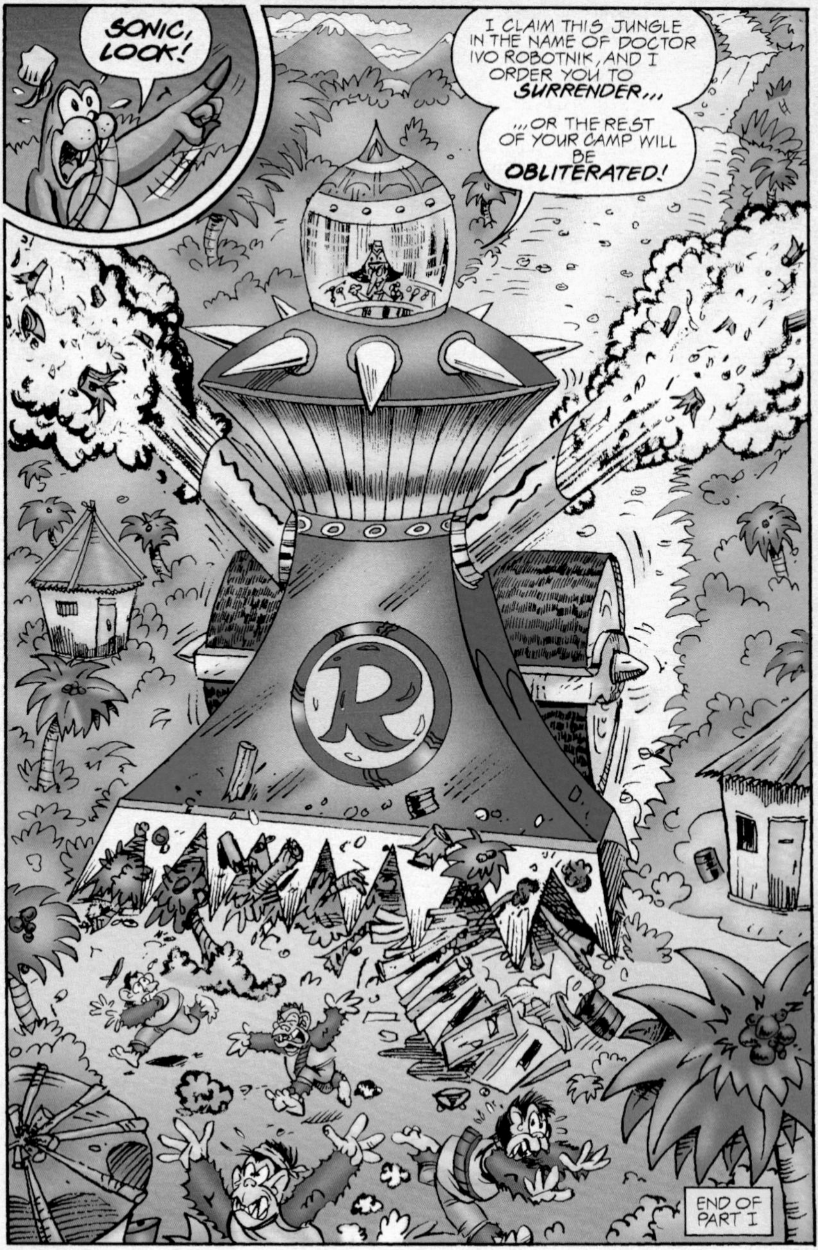
SONIC, LOOK!
I CLAIM THIS JUNGLE IN THE NAME OF DOCTOR IVO ROBOTNIK, AND I ORDER YOU TO SURRENDER...
...OR THE REST OF YOUR CAMP WILL BE OBLITERATED!
END OF PART I

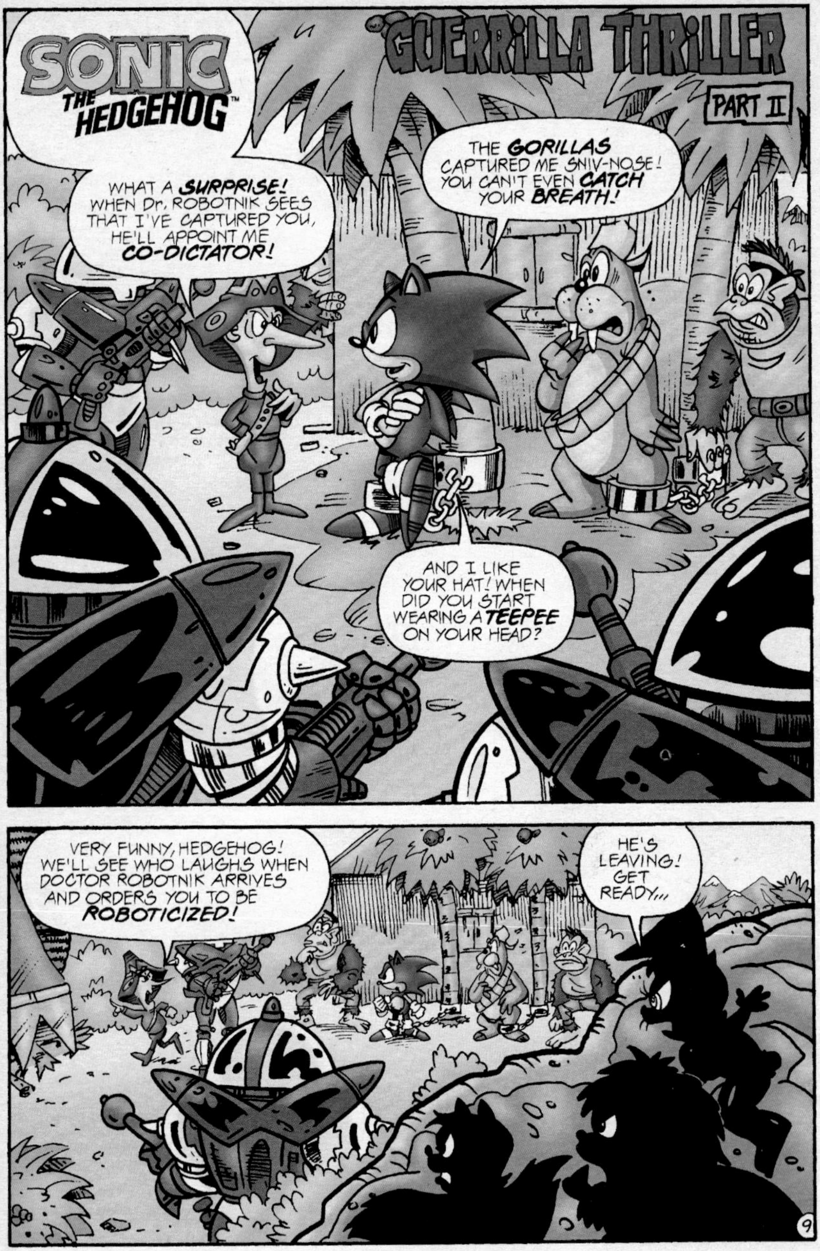
SONIC THE HEDGEHOG™
GUERRILLA THRILLER
PART II
WHAT A SURPRISE! WHEN Dr. ROBOTNIK SEES THAT I'VE CAPTURED YOU, HE'LL APPOINT ME CO-DICTATOR!
THE GORILLAS CAPTURED ME SNIV-NOSE! YOU CAN'T EVEN CATCH YOUR BREATH!
AND I LIKE YOUR HAT! WHEN DID YOU START WEARING A TEEPEE ON YOUR HEAD?
VERY FUNNY, HEDGEHOG! WE'LL SEE WHO LAUGHS WHEN DOCTOR ROBOTNIK ARRIVES AND ORDERS YOU TO BE ROBOTICIZED!
HE'S LEAVING! GET READY...
9

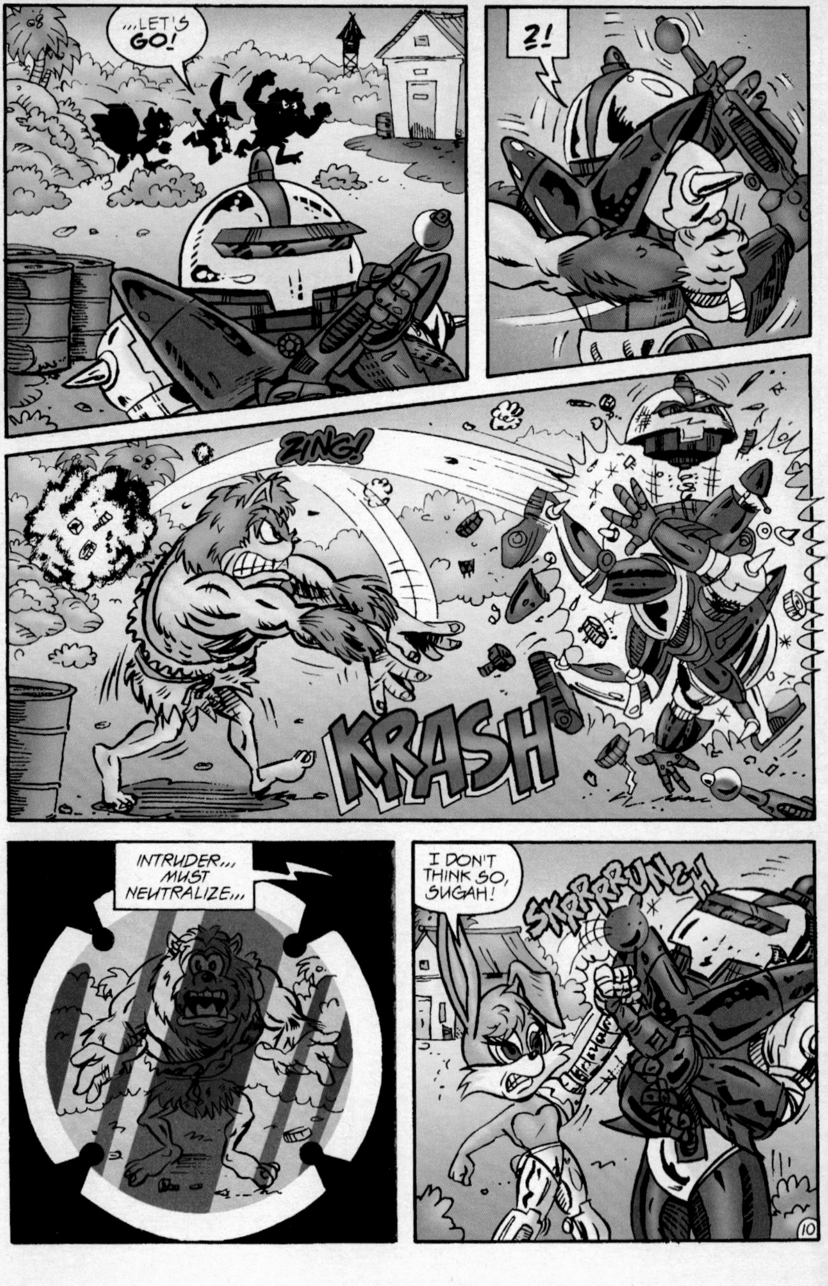
...LET'S GO!
Z!
ZING!
KRASH
INTRUDER... MUST NEUTRALIZE...
I DON'T THINK SO, SUGAH!
SKRRRUNCH

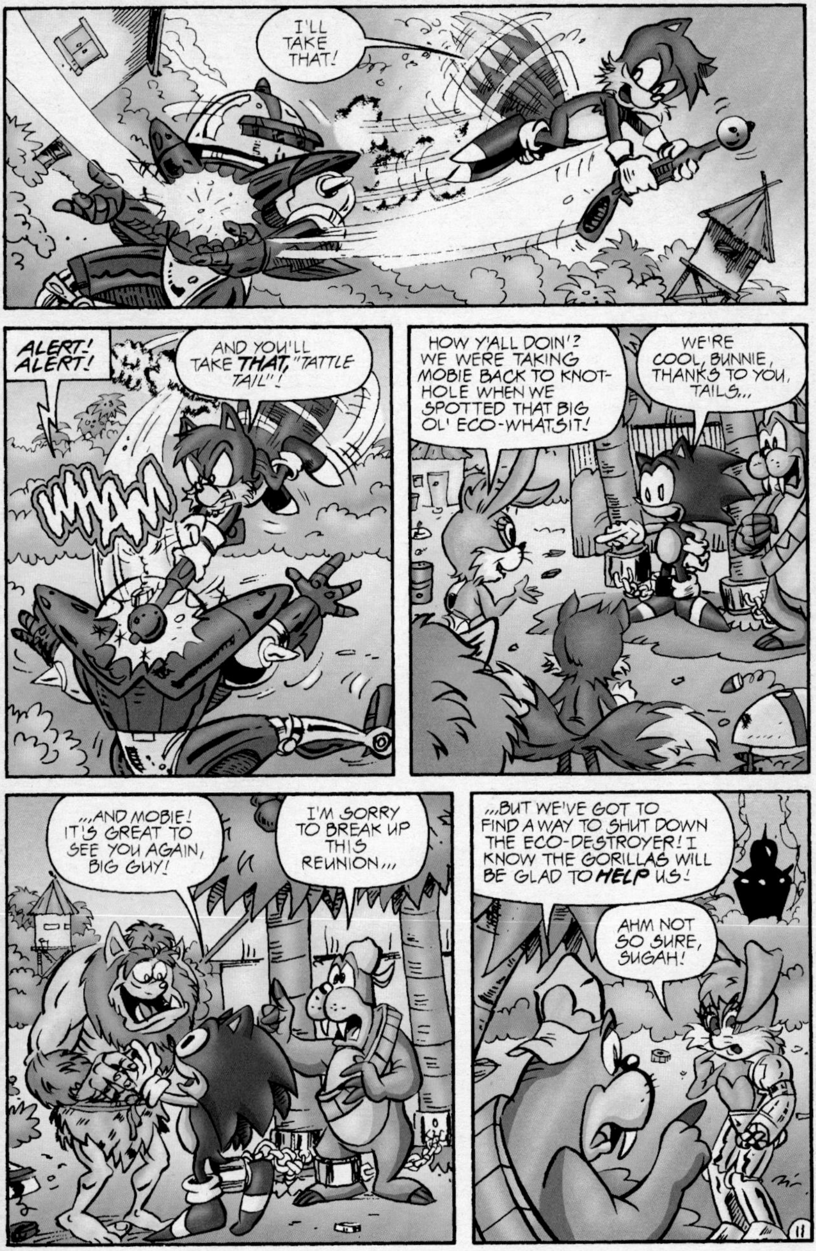
I'LL TAKE THAT!
ALERT! ALERT!
AND YOU'LL TAKE **THAT,** "TATTLE TAIL"!
WHAM
HOW Y'ALL DOIN'? WE WERE TAKING MOBIE BACK TO KNOT-HOLE WHEN WE SPOTTED THAT BIG OL' ECO-WHATSIT!
WE'RE COOL, BUNNIE, THANKS TO YOU, TAILS...
...AND MOBIE! IT'S GREAT TO SEE YOU AGAIN, BIG GUY!
I'M SORRY TO BREAK UP THIS REUNION...
...BUT WE'VE GOT TO FIND A WAY TO SHUT DOWN THE ECO-DESTROYER! I KNOW THE GORILLAS WILL BE GLAD TO **HELP** US!
AHM NOT SO SURE, SUGAH!
11

YOU'LL BE DISTURBING THEIR BEAUTY *REST!*

YEAH, AND THEY *NEED* IT!

Z

THEY'RE ALL *ASLEEP!* HOW'D *THAT* HAPPEN?!

Z

Z

Z

ZZZ

Z

Z

I'M AFRAID *I* CAUSED IT, SONIC!

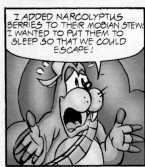

I ADDED NARCOLYPTUS BERRIES TO THEIR MOBIAN STEW! I WANTED TO PUT THEM TO SLEEP SO THAT WE COULD ESCAPE!

SNAP!

THANKS, MOBIE! NOW THAT I'M *FREE* WE WON'T *NEED* ANY HELP!

SOMEDAY, YOU GOTTA TEACH ME HOW TO DO *THAT!*

S00N....

IF I CAN GET INSIDE THIS OVER-SIZED VACUUM CLEANER FOR *HALF A MINUTE,* I CAN DO A *LOT* OF *SERIOUS DAMAGE!*

BUT, SONIC, IF SNIVELY TURNS IT ON, YOU'LL BE *DESTROYED!*

12

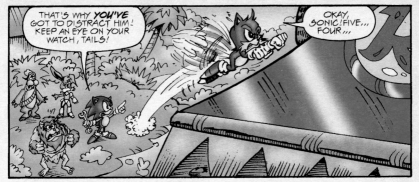

THAT'S WHY **YOU'VE** GOT TO DISTRACT HIM! KEEP AN EYE ON YOUR WATCH, TAILS!

OKAY, SONIC! FIVE... FOUR...

THAT'S RIGHT, SIR! THE MOBIAN JUNGLE IS READY FOR **CONQUEST!**

THREE... TWO... ONE... **NOW!**

HERE I GO... T-MINUS THIRTY SECONDS AND COUNTING!

I'VE ALSO GOT A **SURPRISE PRISONER** FOR YOU, SIR! *Heh-Heh-Heh!*

NEVER MIND THAT... I'M **STILL** NOT CONVINCED THAT I CAN BE **COMFORTABLE** IN THE JUNGLE!

I WANT YOU TO CONTINUE CLEARING AWAY AS MUCH FOLIAGE AS POSSIBLE BEFORE MY PLANE ARRIVES! UNDERSTOOD, SNIVELY?

13

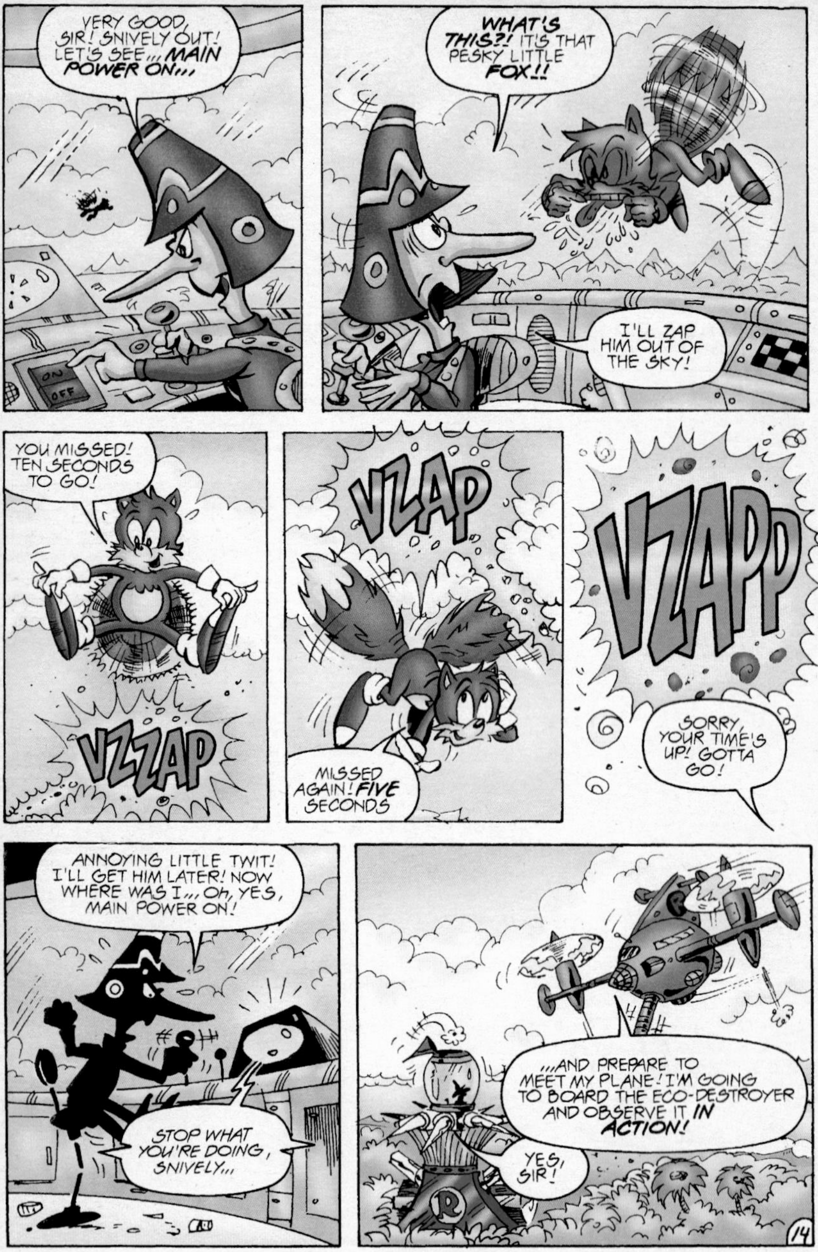
VERY GOOD, SIR! SNIVELY OUT! LET'S SEE... MAIN POWER ON...
ON
OFF
WHAT'S THIS?! IT'S THAT PESKY LITTLE FOX!!
I'LL ZAP HIM OUT OF THE SKY!
YOU MISSED! TEN SECONDS TO GO!
VZZAP
VZAP
MISSED AGAIN! FIVE SECONDS
VZAPP
SORRY, YOUR TIME'S UP! GOTTA GO!
ANNOYING LITTLE TWIT! I'LL GET HIM LATER! NOW WHERE WAS I... Oh, YES, MAIN POWER ON!
STOP WHAT YOU'RE DOING, SNIVELY...
...AND PREPARE TO MEET MY PLANE! I'M GOING TO BOARD THE ECO-DESTROYER AND OBSERVE IT IN ACTION!
YES, SIR!
14

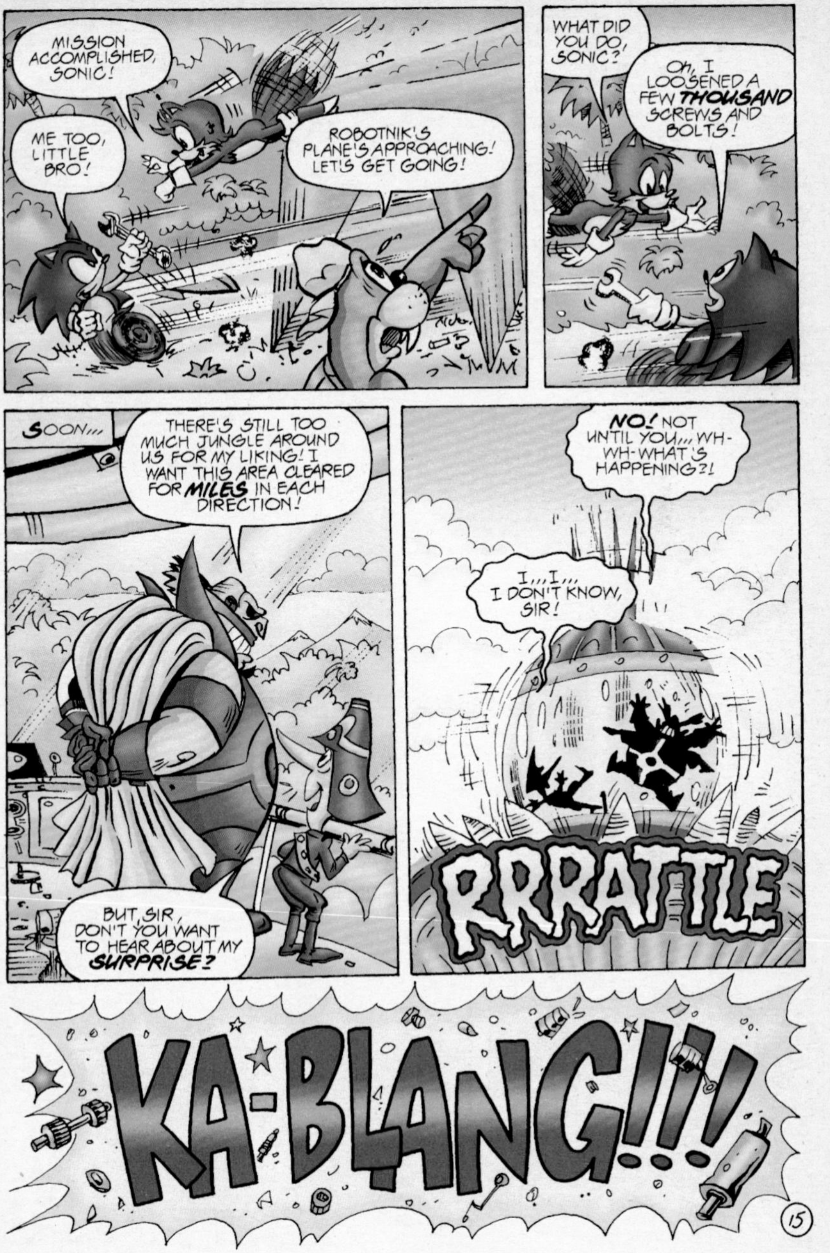
MISSION ACCOMPLISHED, SONIC!
ME TOO, LITTLE BRO!
ROBOTNIK'S PLANE'S APPROACHING! LET'S GET GOING!
WHAT DID YOU DO, SONIC?
OH, I LOOSENED A FEW THOUSAND SCREWS AND BOLTS!
SOON...
THERE'S STILL TOO MUCH JUNGLE AROUND US FOR MY LIKING! I WANT THIS AREA CLEARED FOR MILES IN EACH DIRECTION!
BUT, SIR, DON'T YOU WANT TO HEAR ABOUT MY SURPRISE?
NO! NOT UNTIL YOU... WH-WH-WHAT'S HAPPENING?!
I... I... I DON'T KNOW, SIR!
RRRATTLE
KA-BLANG!!!

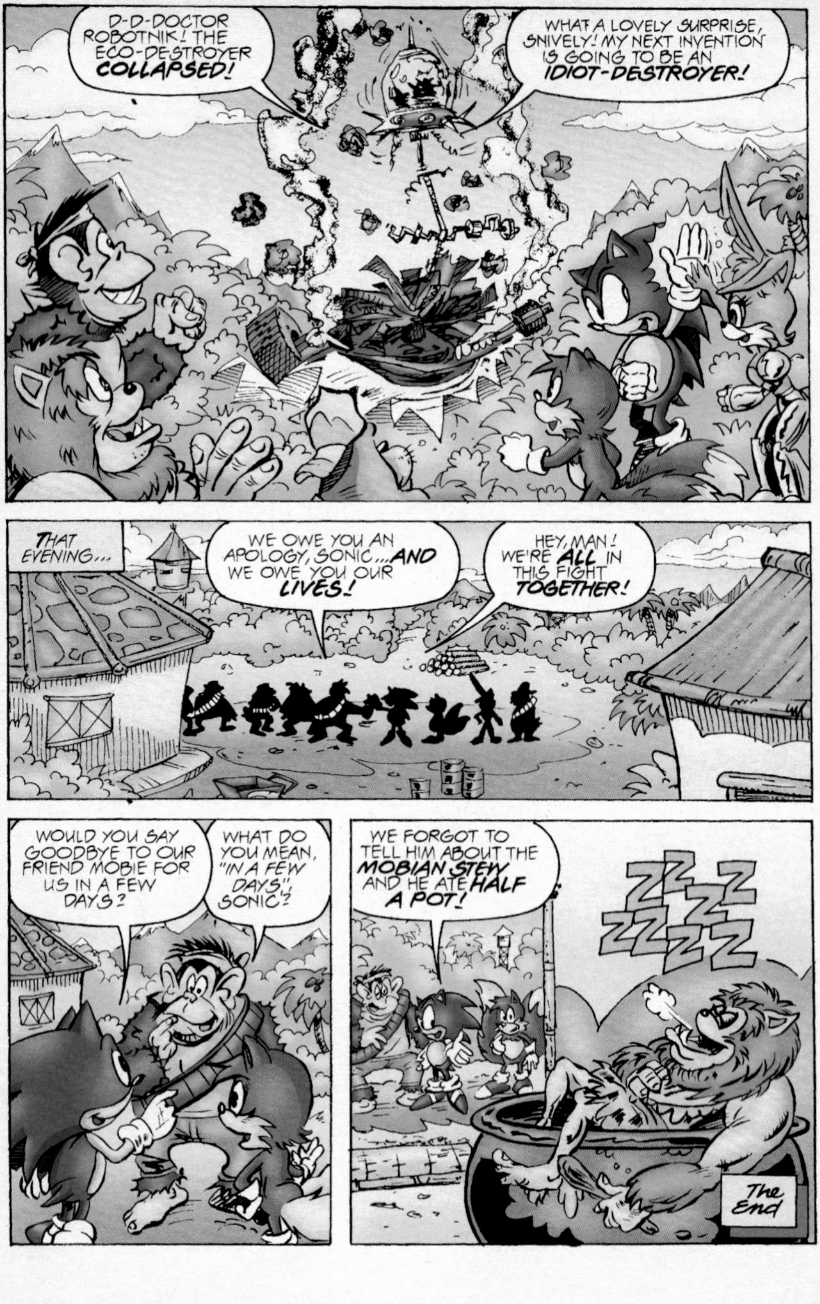
D-D-DOCTOR ROBOTNIK! THE ECO-DESTROYER COLLAPSED!
WHAT A LOVELY SURPRISE, SNIVELY! MY NEXT INVENTION IS GOING TO BE AN IDIOT-DESTROYER!
THAT EVENING...
WE OWE YOU AN APOLOGY, SONIC... AND WE OWE YOU OUR LIVES!
HEY, MAN! WE'RE ALL IN THIS FIGHT TOGETHER!
WOULD YOU SAY GOODBYE TO OUR FRIEND MOBIE FOR US IN A FEW DAYS?
WHAT DO YOU MEAN, "IN A FEW DAYS", SONIC?
WE FORGOT TO TELL HIM ABOUT THE MOBIAN STEW AND HE ATE HALF A POT!
ZZZZZZZZ
The End

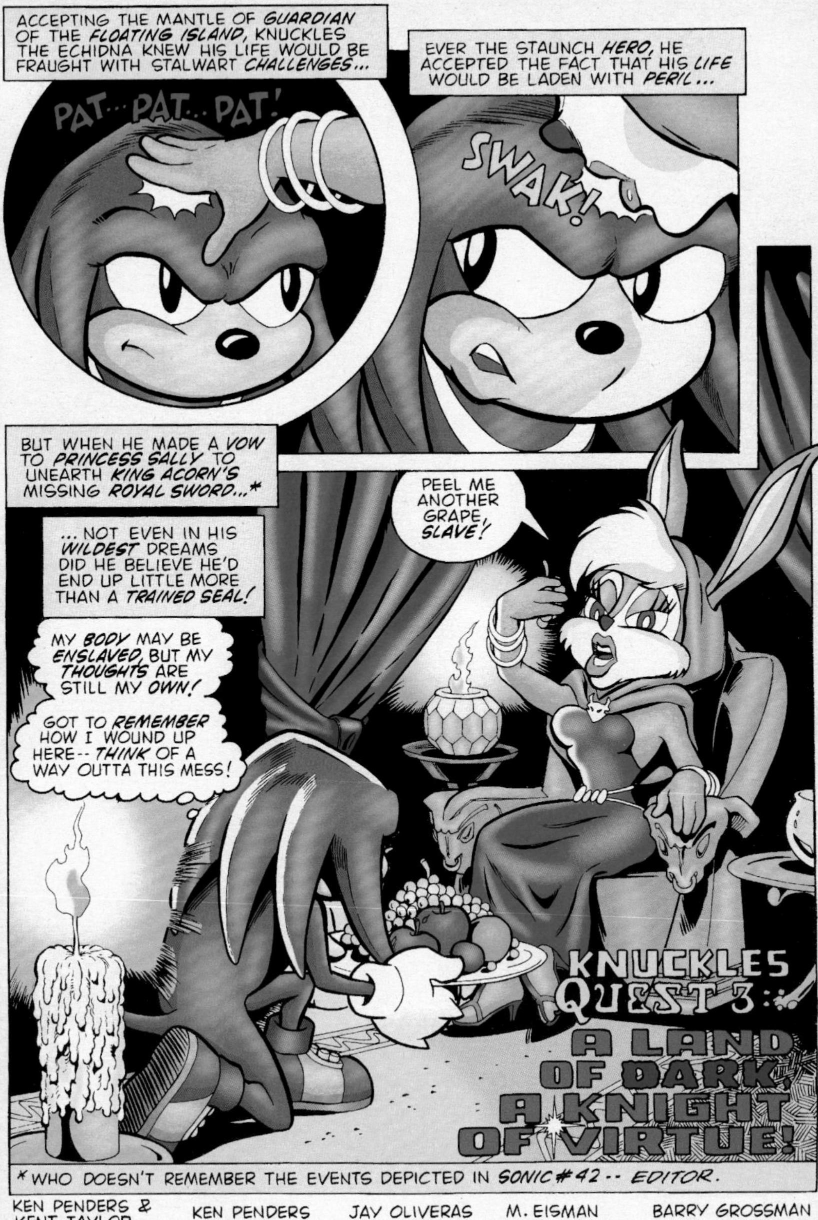
ACCEPTING THE MANTLE OF GUARDIAN OF THE FLOATING ISLAND, KNUCKLES THE ECHIDNA KNEW HIS LIFE WOULD BE FRAUGHT WITH STALWART CHALLENGES...
PAT...PAT...PAT!
EVER THE STAUNCH HERO, HE ACCEPTED THE FACT THAT HIS LIFE WOULD BE LADEN WITH PERIL...
SWAK!
BUT WHEN HE MADE A VOW TO PRINCESS SALLY TO UNEARTH KING ACORN'S MISSING ROYAL SWORD...*
PEEL ME ANOTHER GRAPE, SLAVE!
...NOT EVEN IN HIS WILDEST DREAMS DID HE BELIEVE HE'D END UP LITTLE MORE THAN A TRAINED SEAL!
MY BODY MAY BE ENSLAVED, BUT MY THOUGHTS ARE STILL MY OWN!
GOT TO REMEMBER HOW I WOUND UP HERE-- THINK OF A WAY OUTTA THIS MESS!
KNUCKLES QUEST 3:
A LAND OF DARK, A KNIGHT OF VIRTUE!
* WHO DOESN'T REMEMBER THE EVENTS DEPICTED IN SONIC #42 -- EDITOR.

KEN PENDERS & KENT TAYLOR *WRITERS* · KEN PENDERS *ARTIST* · JAY OLIVERAS *INK ASSIST* · M. EISMAN *LETTERER* · BARRY GROSSMAN *COLORIST*

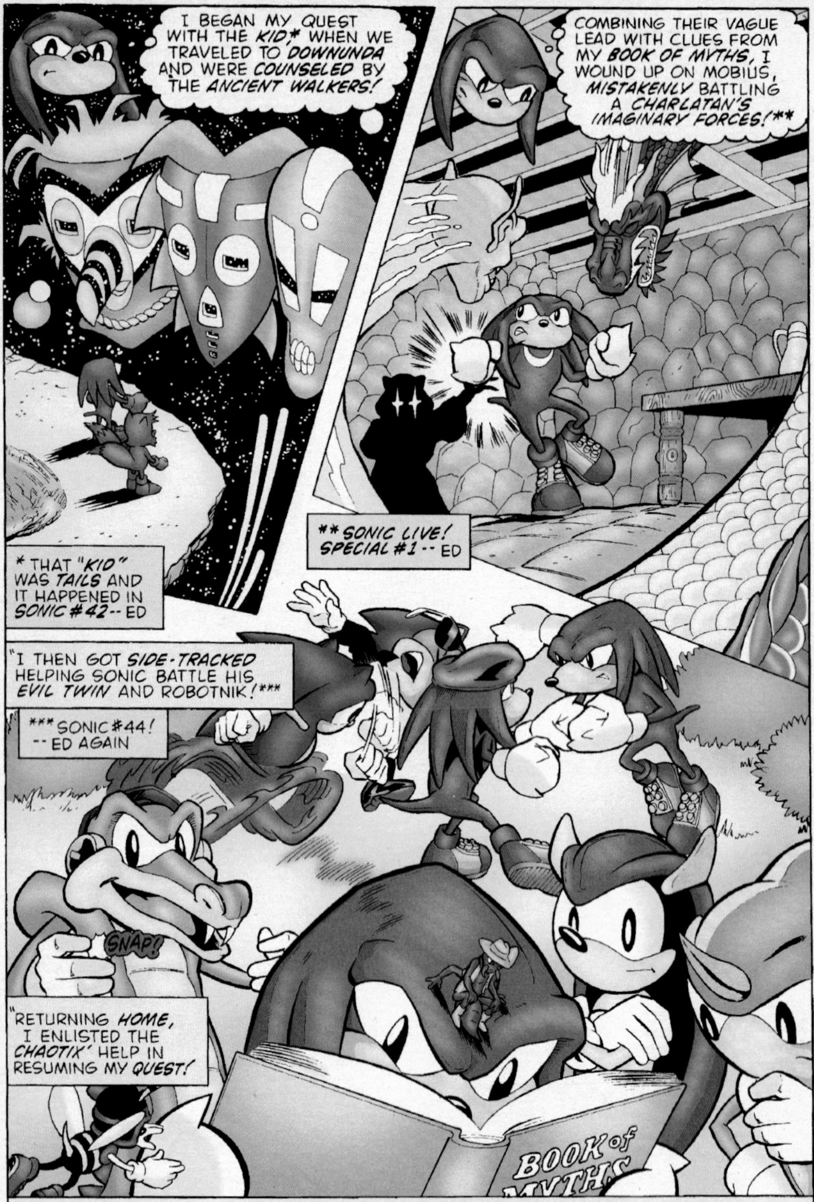
I BEGAN MY QUEST WITH THE KID,* WHEN WE TRAVELED TO DOWNUNDA AND WERE COUNSELED BY THE ANCIENT WALKERS!
* THAT "KID" WAS TAILS AND IT HAPPENED IN SONIC #42 -- ED
COMBINING THEIR VAGUE LEAD WITH CLUES FROM MY BOOK OF MYTHS, I WOUND UP ON MOBIUS, MISTAKENLY BATTLING A CHARLATAN'S IMAGINARY FORCES!**
** SONIC LIVE! SPECIAL #1 -- ED
"I THEN GOT SIDE-TRACKED HELPING SONIC BATTLE HIS EVIL TWIN AND ROBOTNIK!***
*** SONIC #44! -- ED AGAIN
SNAP!
"RETURNING HOME, I ENLISTED THE CHAOTIX' HELP IN RESUMING MY QUEST!
BOOK of MYTHS
" BELIEVING THE CHARLATAN'S CLUE OF THE LAND OF DARK TO BE AN OLD NAME FOR THE OUTSKIRTS OF THE ISLAND'S FORBIDDEN ZONE, I VENTURED FORTH...

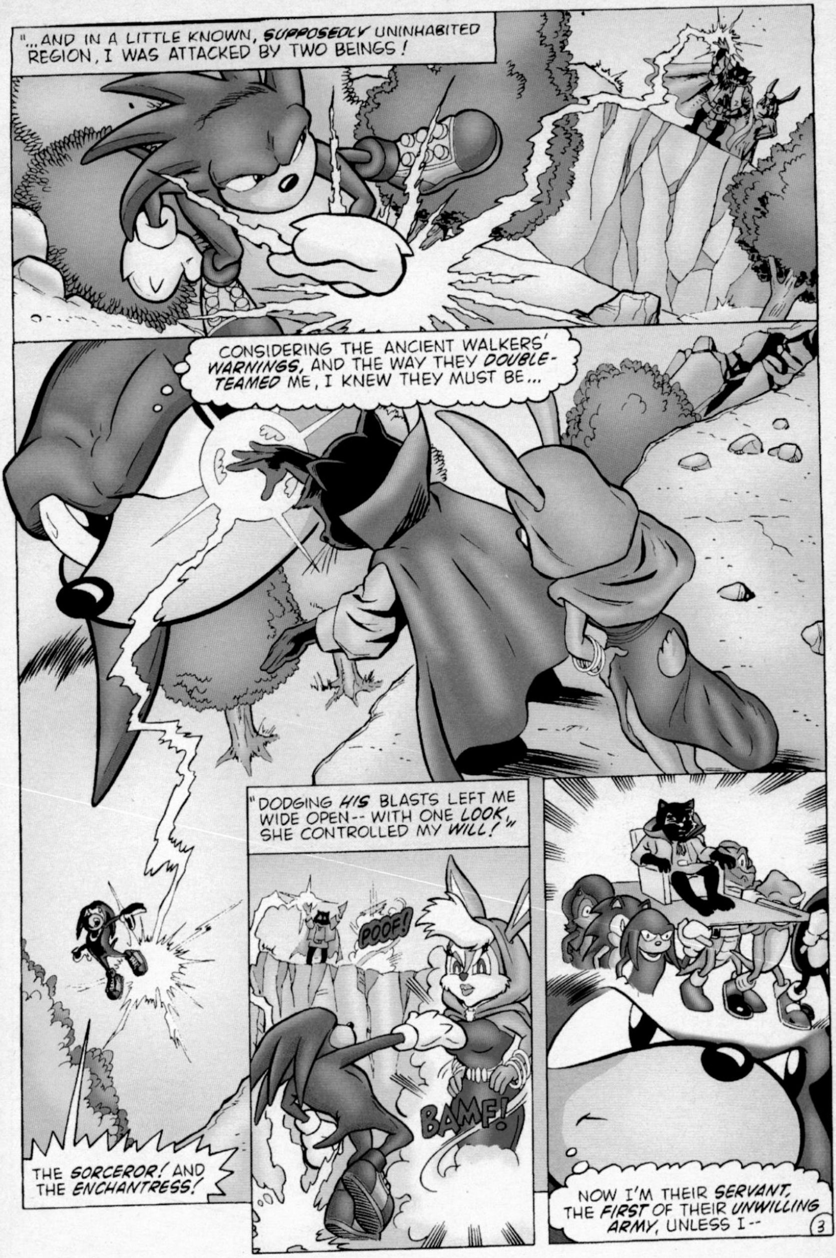
"...AND IN A LITTLE KNOWN, SUPPOSEDLY UNINHABITED REGION, I WAS ATTACKED BY TWO BEINGS!
CONSIDERING THE ANCIENT WALKERS' WARNINGS, AND THE WAY THEY DOUBLE-TEAMED ME, I KNEW THEY MUST BE...
THE SORCEROR! AND THE ENCHANTRESS!
"DODGING HIS BLASTS LEFT ME WIDE OPEN-- WITH ONE LOOK, SHE CONTROLLED MY WILL!"
POOF!
BAMF!
NOW I'M THEIR SERVANT, THE FIRST OF THEIR UNWILLING ARMY, UNLESS I--

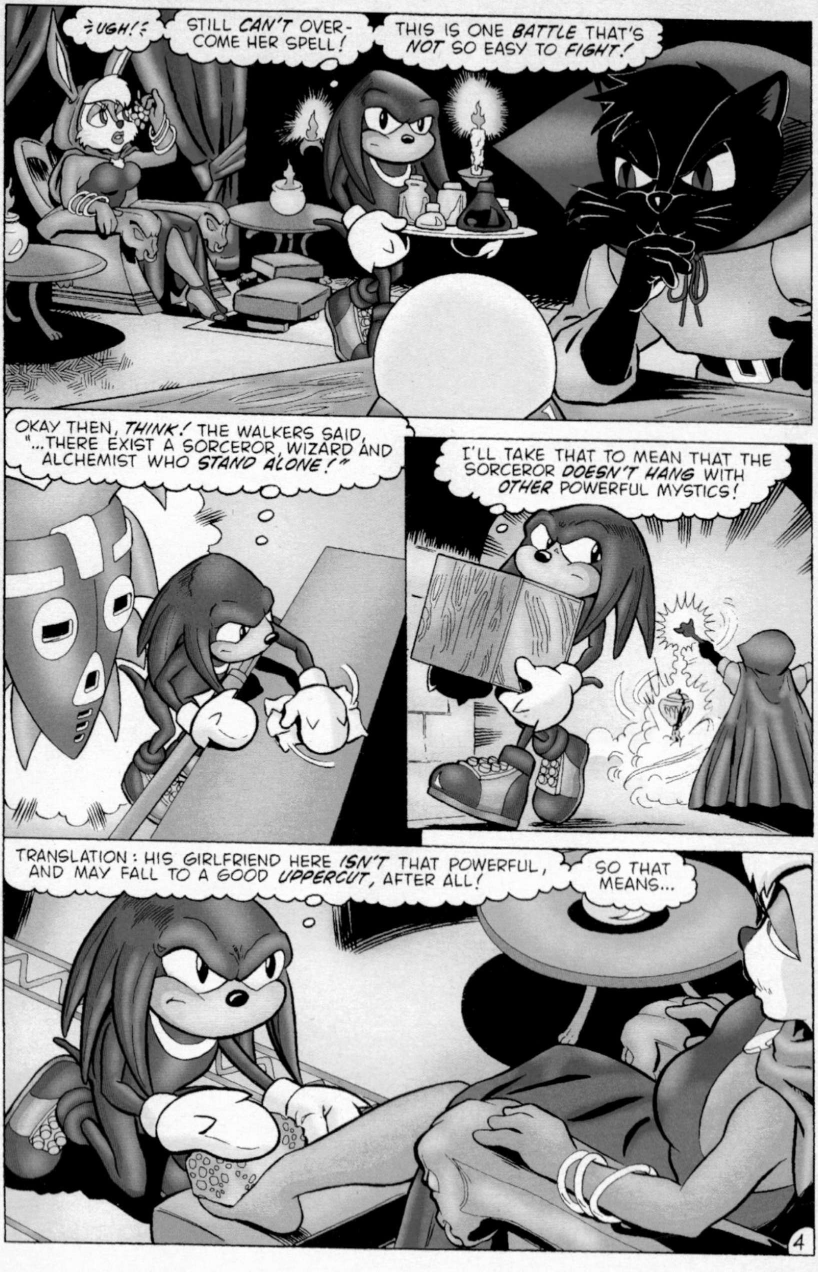

UGH!
STILL CAN'T OVER-COME HER SPELL!
THIS IS ONE BATTLE THAT'S NOT SO EASY TO FIGHT!
OKAY THEN, THINK! THE WALKERS SAID, "...THERE EXIST A SORCEROR, WIZARD AND ALCHEMIST WHO STAND ALONE!"
I'LL TAKE THAT TO MEAN THAT THE SORCEROR DOESN'T HANG WITH OTHER POWERFUL MYSTICS!
TRANSLATION: HIS GIRLFRIEND HERE ISN'T THAT POWERFUL, AND MAY FALL TO A GOOD UPPERCUT, AFTER ALL!
SO THAT MEANS...

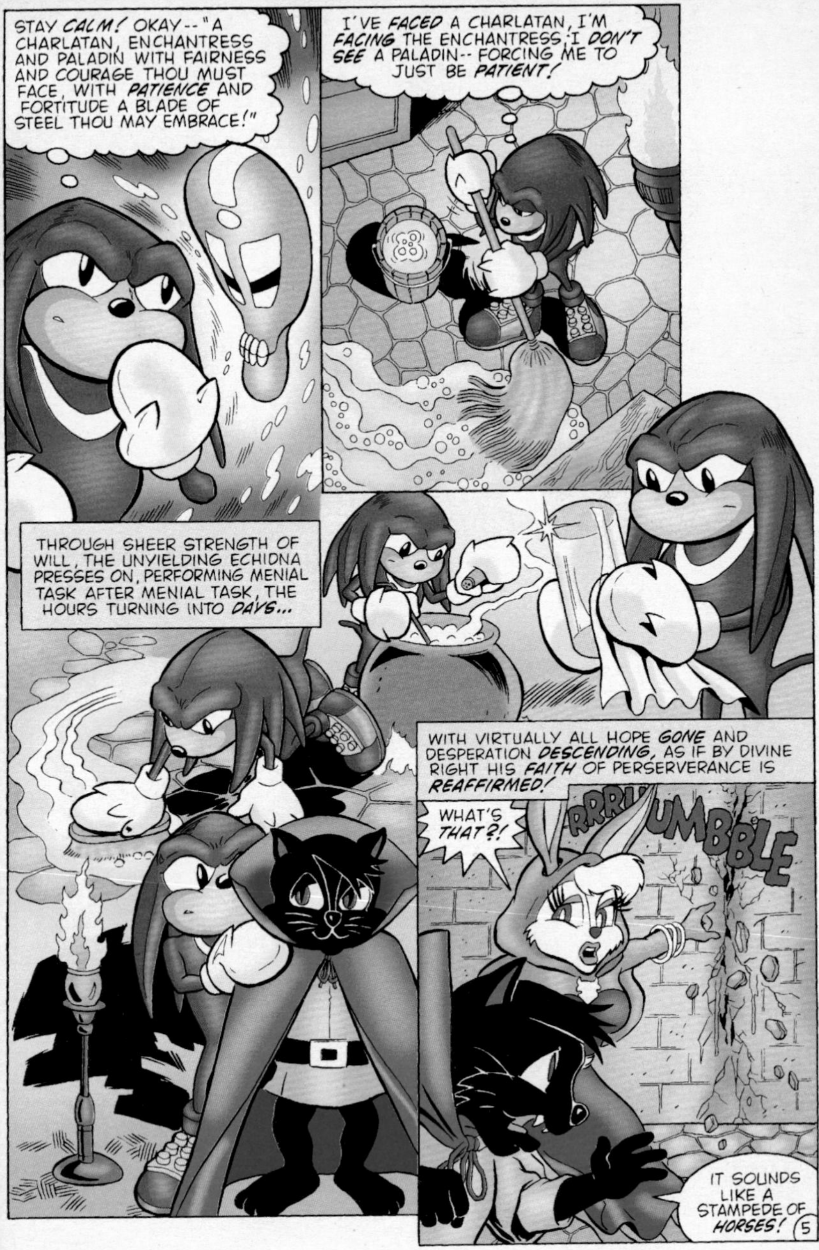
STAY CALM! OKAY--"A CHARLATAN, ENCHANTRESS AND PALADIN WITH FAIRNESS AND COURAGE THOU MUST FACE, WITH PATIENCE AND FORTITUDE A BLADE OF STEEL THOU MAY EMBRACE!"
I'VE FACED A CHARLATAN, I'M FACING THE ENCHANTRESS, I DON'T SEE A PALADIN-- FORCING ME TO JUST BE PATIENT!
THROUGH SHEER STRENGTH OF WILL, THE UNYIELDING ECHIDNA PRESSES ON, PERFORMING MENIAL TASK AFTER MENIAL TASK, THE HOURS TURNING INTO DAYS...
WITH VIRTUALLY ALL HOPE GONE AND DESPERATION DESCENDING, AS IF BY DIVINE RIGHT HIS FAITH OF PERSERVERANCE IS REAFFIRMED!
WHAT'S THAT?!
RRRUUMBBLE
IT SOUNDS LIKE A STAMPEDE OF HORSES!

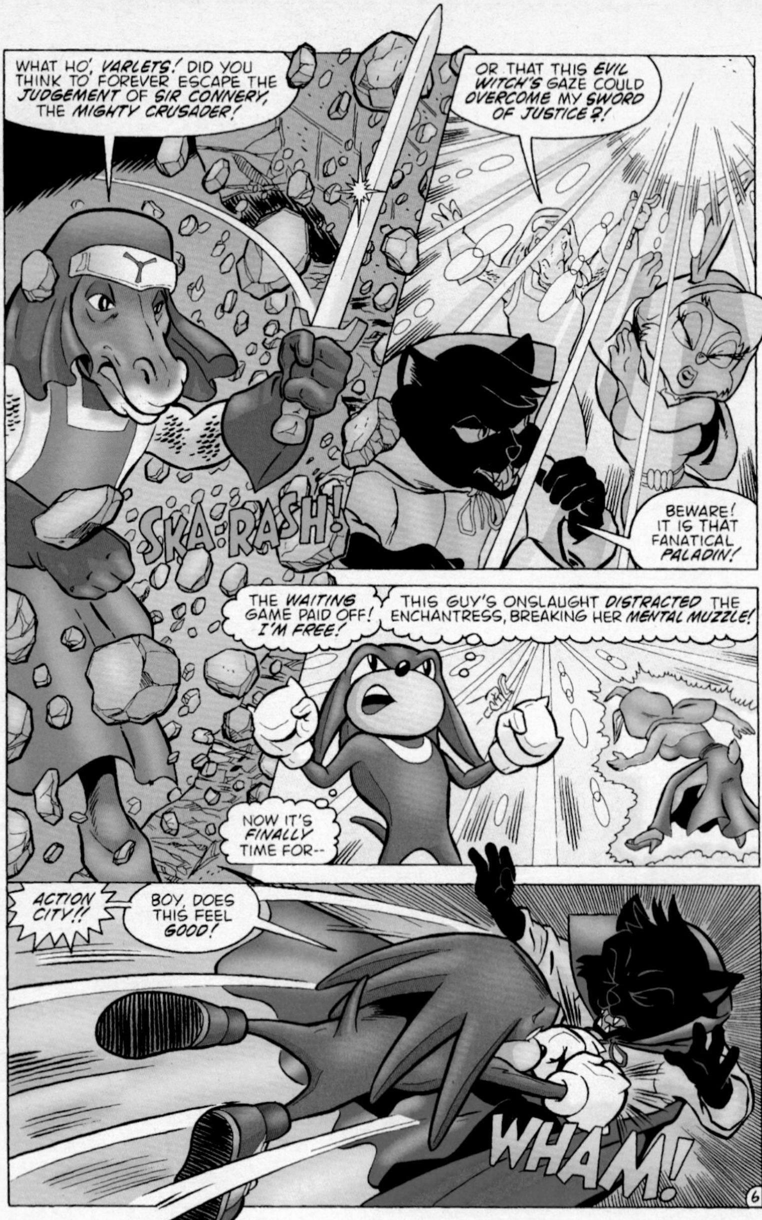
WHAT HO', VARLETS! DID YOU THINK TO FOREVER ESCAPE THE JUDGEMENT OF SIR CONNERY, THE MIGHTY CRUSADER!
OR THAT THIS EVIL WITCH'S GAZE COULD OVERCOME MY SWORD OF JUSTICE?!
SKA-RASH!
BEWARE! IT IS THAT FANATICAL PALADIN!
THE WAITING GAME PAID OFF! I'M FREE!
THIS GUY'S ONSLAUGHT DISTRACTED THE ENCHANTRESS, BREAKING HER MENTAL MUZZLE!
NOW IT'S FINALLY TIME FOR--
ACTION CITY!!
BOY, DOES THIS FEEL GOOD!
WHAM!

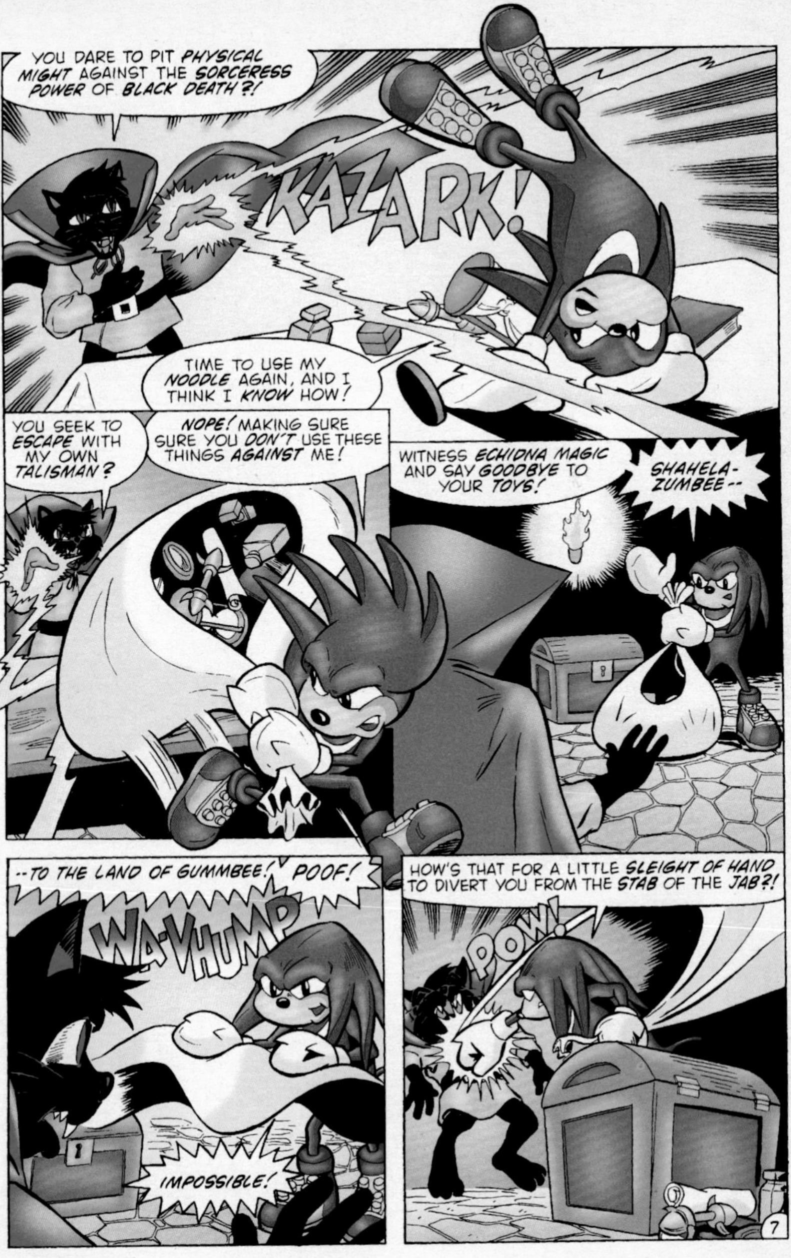
YOU DARE TO PIT PHYSICAL MIGHT AGAINST THE SORCERESS POWER OF BLACK DEATH?!
KAZARK!
TIME TO USE MY NOODLE AGAIN, AND I THINK I KNOW HOW!
YOU SEEK TO ESCAPE WITH MY OWN TALISMAN?
NOPE! MAKING SURE SURE YOU DON'T USE THESE THINGS AGAINST ME!
WITNESS ECHIDNA MAGIC AND SAY GOODBYE TO YOUR TOYS!
SHAHELA-ZUMBEE--
--TO THE LAND OF GUMMBEE!
POOF!
WA-VHUMP
IMPOSSIBLE!
HOW'S THAT FOR A LITTLE SLEIGHT OF HAND TO DIVERT YOU FROM THE STAB OF THE JAB?!
POW!

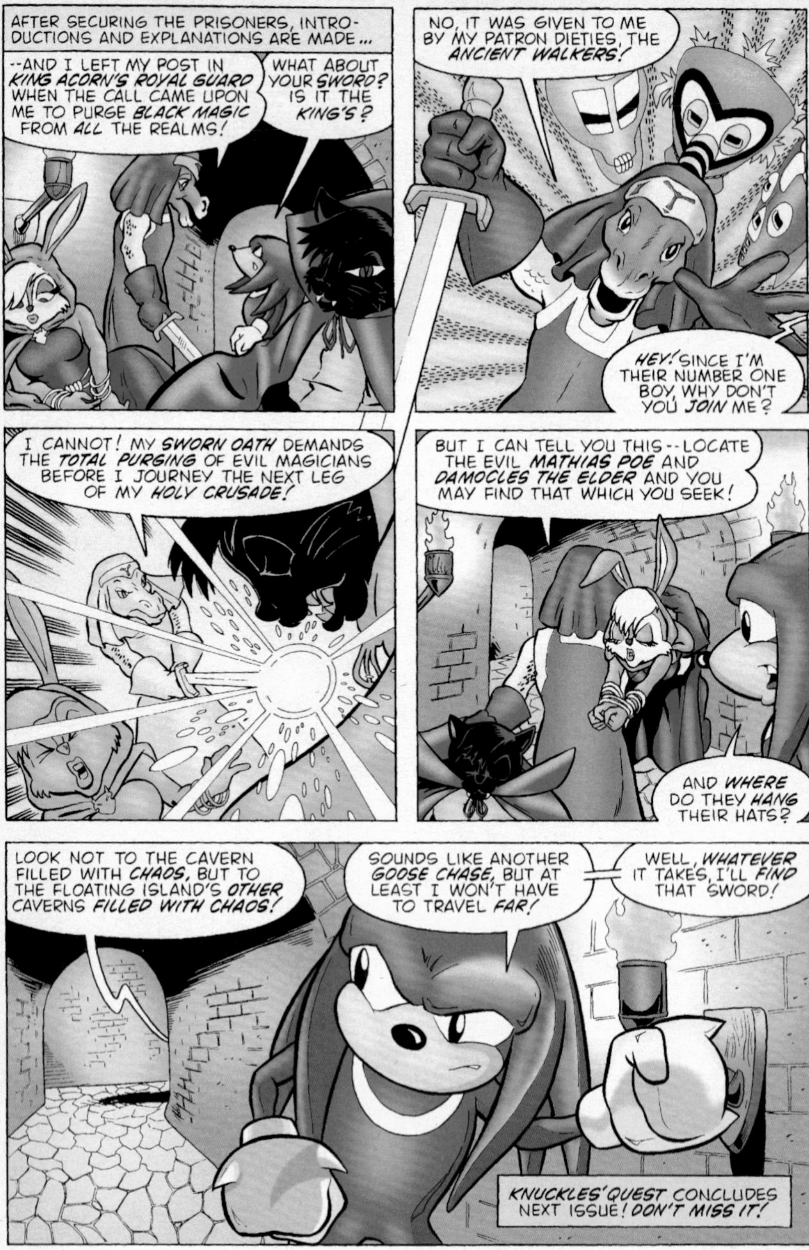
AFTER SECURING THE PRISONERS, INTRODUCTIONS AND EXPLANATIONS ARE MADE...
--AND I LEFT MY POST IN KING ACORN'S ROYAL GUARD WHEN THE CALL CAME UPON ME TO PURGE BLACK MAGIC FROM ALL THE REALMS!
WHAT ABOUT YOUR SWORD? IS IT THE KING'S?
NO, IT WAS GIVEN TO ME BY MY PATRON DIETIES, THE ANCIENT WALKERS!
HEY! SINCE I'M THEIR NUMBER ONE BOY, WHY DON'T YOU JOIN ME?
I CANNOT! MY SWORN OATH DEMANDS THE TOTAL PURGING OF EVIL MAGICIANS BEFORE I JOURNEY THE NEXT LEG OF MY HOLY CRUSADE!
BUT I CAN TELL YOU THIS--LOCATE THE EVIL MATHIAS POE AND DAMOCLES THE ELDER AND YOU MAY FIND THAT WHICH YOU SEEK!
AND WHERE DO THEY HANG THEIR HATS?
LOOK NOT TO THE CAVERN FILLED WITH CHAOS, BUT TO THE FLOATING ISLAND'S OTHER CAVERNS FILLED WITH CHAOS!
SOUNDS LIKE ANOTHER GOOSE CHASE, BUT AT LEAST I WON'T HAVE TO TRAVEL FAR!
WELL, WHATEVER IT TAKES, I'LL FIND THAT SWORD!
KNUCKLES' QUEST CONCLUDES NEXT ISSUE! DON'T MISS IT!

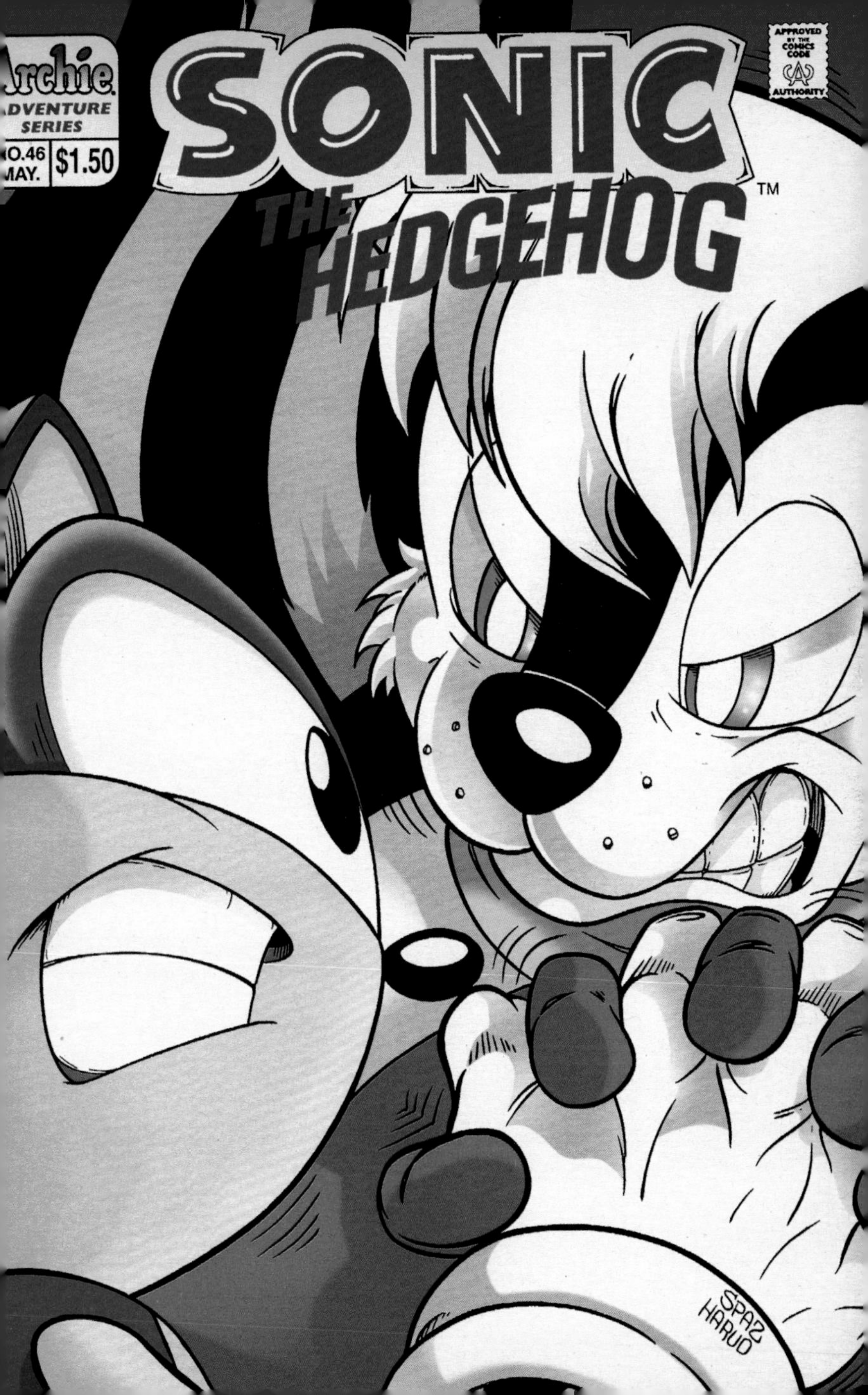
Archie
DVENTURE SERIES
O.46
MAY.
$1.50
SONIC THE HEDGEHOG™
APPROVED BY THE COMICS CODE AUTHORITY
SPAZ

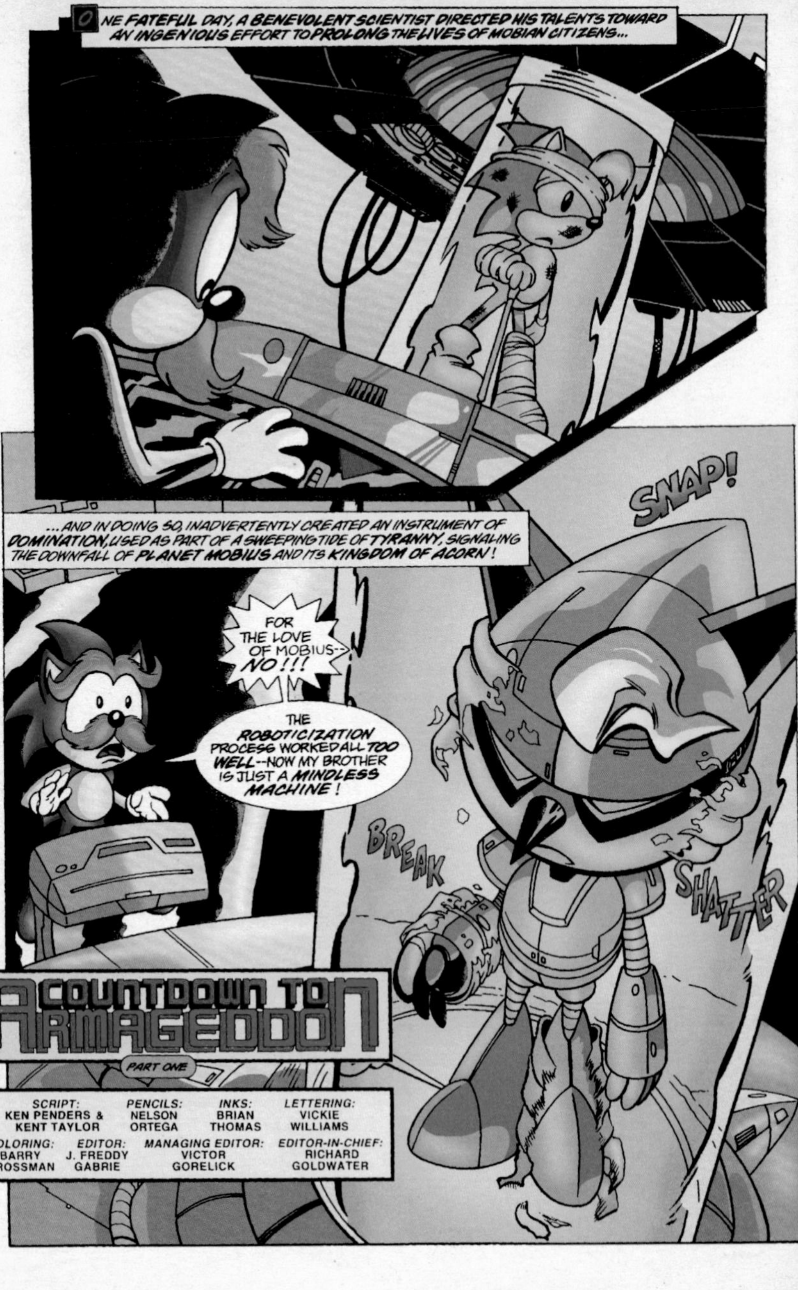

ONE FATEFUL DAY, A BENEVOLENT SCIENTIST DIRECTED HIS TALENTS TOWARD AN INGENIOUS EFFORT TO PROLONG THE LIVES OF MOBIAN CITIZENS...
SNAP!
...AND IN DOING SO, INADVERTENTLY CREATED AN INSTRUMENT OF DOMINATION, USED AS PART OF A SWEEPING TIDE OF TYRANNY, SIGNALING THE DOWNFALL OF PLANET MOBIUS AND ITS KINGDOM OF ACORN!
FOR THE LOVE OF MOBIUS--NO!!!
THE ROBOTICIZATION PROCESS WORKED ALL TOO WELL--NOW MY BROTHER IS JUST A MINDLESS MACHINE!
BREAK
SHATTER
A COUNTDOWN TO ARMAGEDDON
PART ONE
SCRIPT: KEN PENDERS & KENT TAYLOR
PENCILS: NELSON ORTEGA
INKS: BRIAN THOMAS
LETTERING: VICKIE WILLIAMS
COLORING: BARRY GROSSMAN
EDITOR: J. FREDDY GABRIE
MANAGING EDITOR: VICTOR GORELICK
EDITOR-IN-CHIEF: RICHARD GOLDWATER

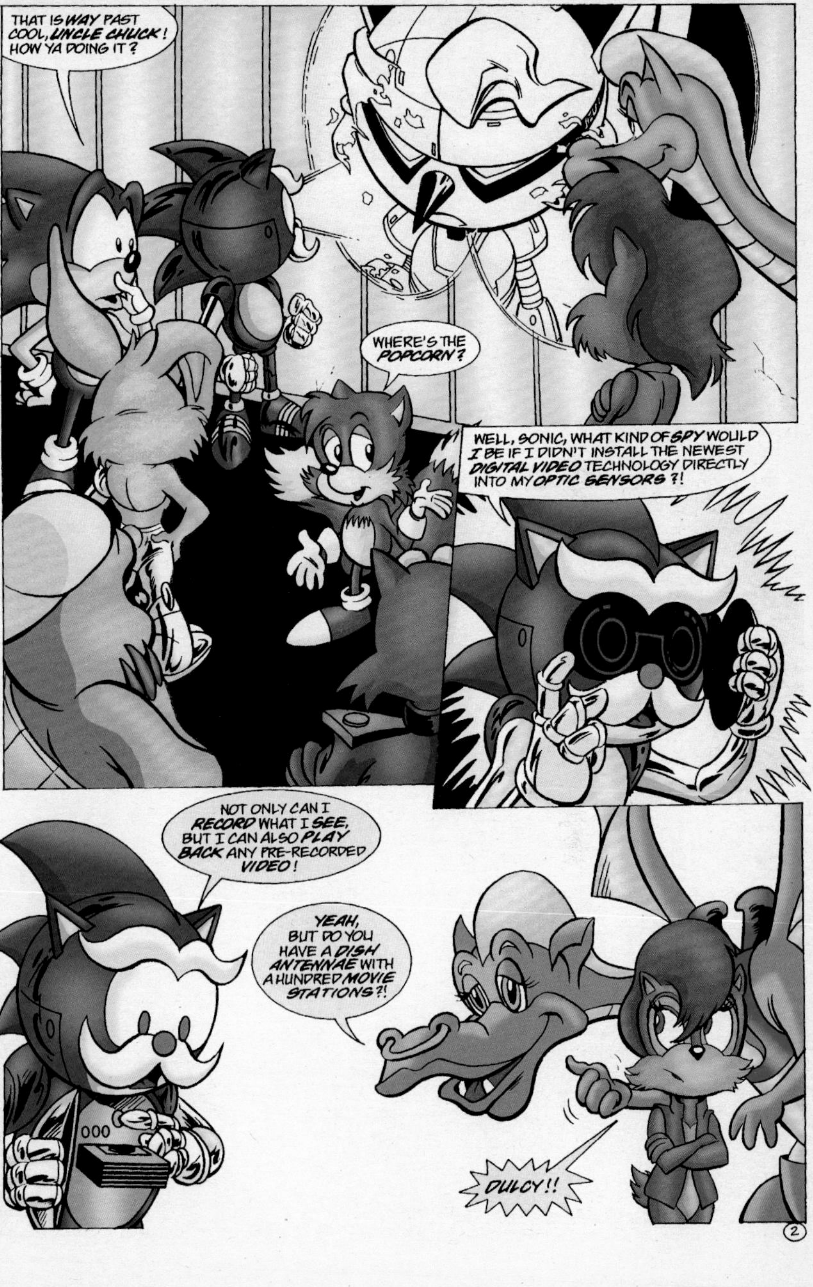
THAT IS WAY PAST COOL, UNCLE CHUCK! HOW YA DOING IT?
WHERE'S THE POPCORN?
WELL, SONIC, WHAT KIND OF SPY WOULD I BE IF I DIDN'T INSTALL THE NEWEST DIGITAL VIDEO TECHNOLOGY DIRECTLY INTO MY OPTIC SENSORS?!
NOT ONLY CAN I RECORD WHAT I SEE, BUT I CAN ALSO PLAY BACK ANY PRE-RECORDED VIDEO!
YEAH, BUT DO YOU HAVE A DISH ANTENNAE WITH A HUNDRED MOVIE STATIONS?!
DULCY!!

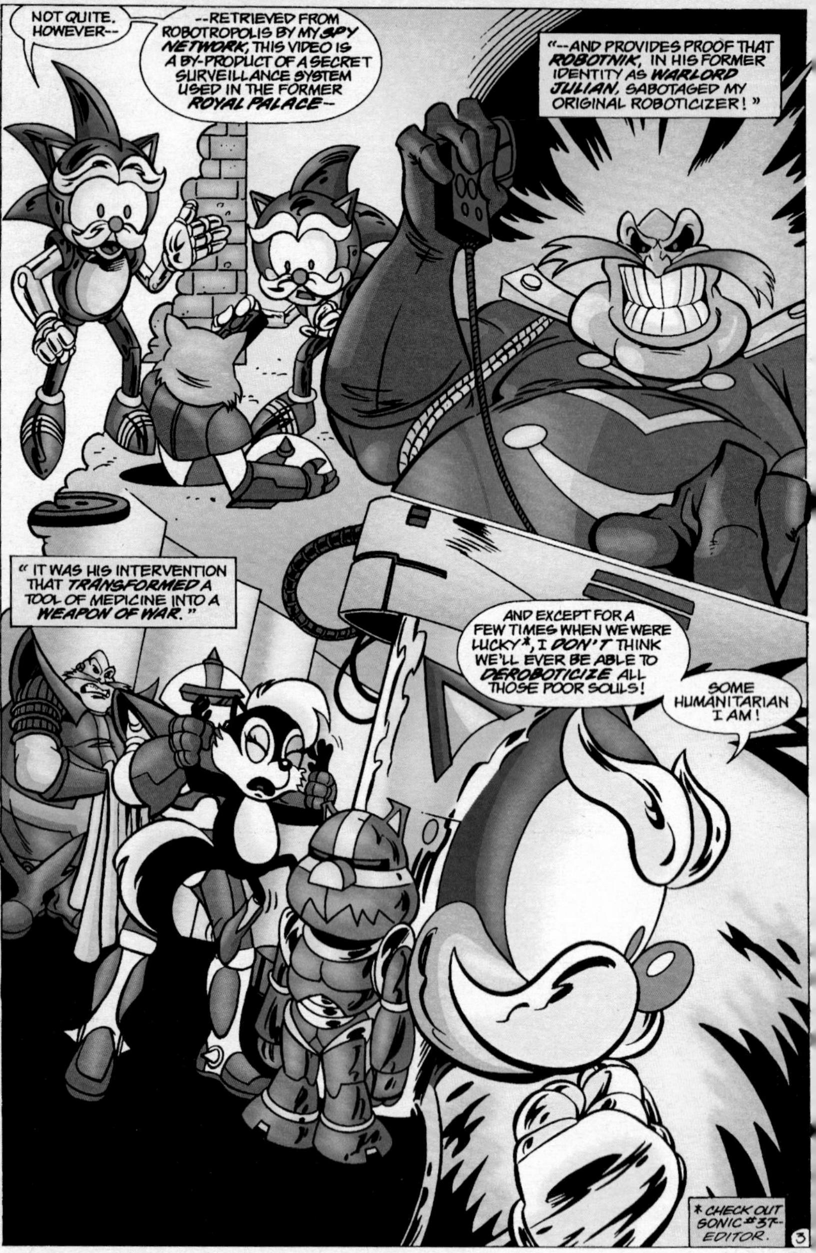
NOT QUITE. HOWEVER--
--RETRIEVED FROM ROBOTROPOLIS BY MY SPY NETWORK, THIS VIDEO IS A BY-PRODUCT OF A SECRET SURVEILLANCE SYSTEM USED IN THE FORMER ROYAL PALACE--
"--AND PROVIDES PROOF THAT ROBOTNIK, IN HIS FORMER IDENTITY AS WARLORD JULIAN, SABOTAGED MY ORIGINAL ROBOTICIZER!"
"IT WAS HIS INTERVENTION THAT TRANSFORMED A TOOL OF MEDICINE INTO A WEAPON OF WAR."
AND EXCEPT FOR A FEW TIMES WHEN WE WERE LUCKY*, I DON'T THINK WE'LL EVER BE ABLE TO DEROBOTICIZE ALL THOSE POOR SOULS!
SOME HUMANITARIAN I AM!
*CHECK OUT SONIC #37-- EDITOR.
3

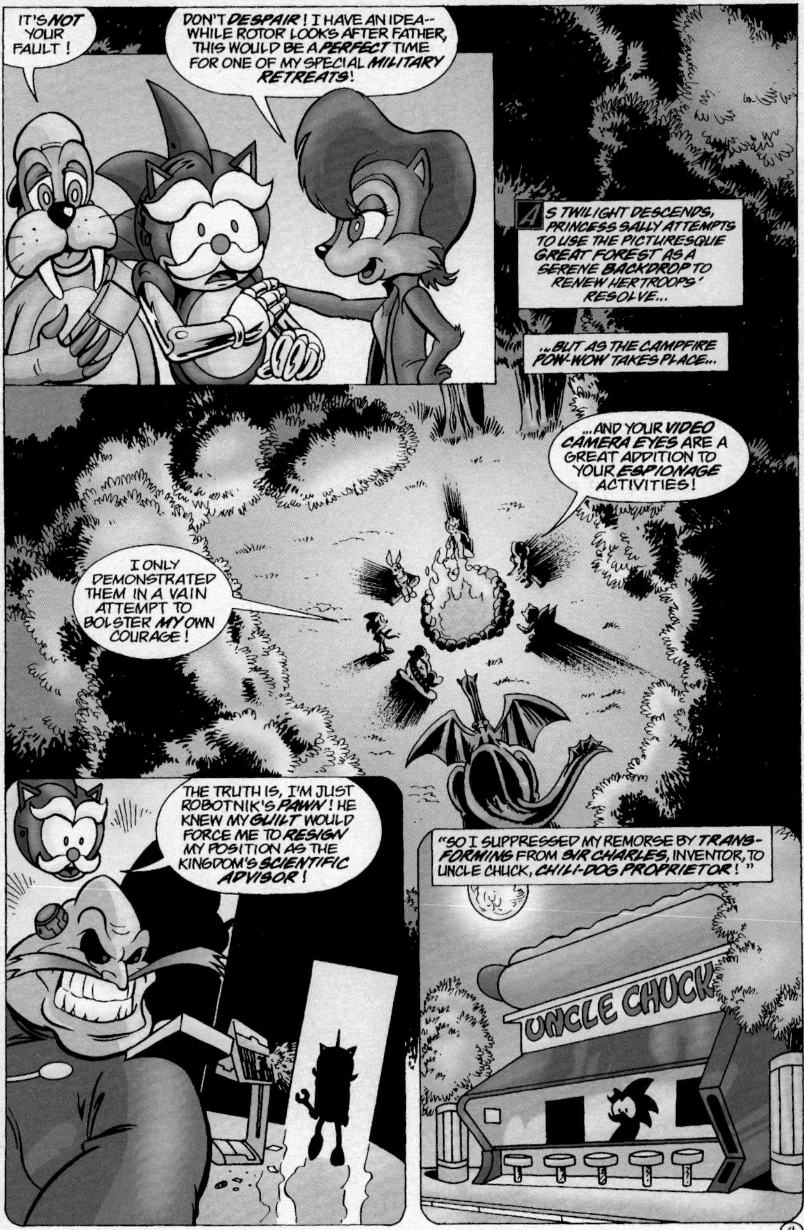
IT'S NOT YOUR FAULT!
DON'T DESPAIR! I HAVE AN IDEA-- WHILE ROTOR LOOKS AFTER FATHER, THIS WOULD BE A PERFECT TIME FOR ONE OF MY SPECIAL MILITARY RETREATS!
AS TWILIGHT DESCENDS, PRINCESS SALLY ATTEMPTS TO USE THE PICTURESQUE GREAT FOREST AS A SERENE BACKDROP TO RENEW HER TROOPS' RESOLVE...
...BUT AS THE CAMPFIRE POW-WOW TAKES PLACE...
...AND YOUR VIDEO CAMERA EYES ARE A GREAT ADDITION TO YOUR ESPIONAGE ACTIVITIES!
I ONLY DEMONSTRATED THEM IN A VAIN ATTEMPT TO BOLSTER MY OWN COURAGE!
THE TRUTH IS, I'M JUST ROBOTNIK'S PAWN! HE KNEW MY GUILT WOULD FORCE ME TO RESIGN MY POSITION AS THE KINGDOM'S SCIENTIFIC ADVISOR!
"SO I SUPPRESSED MY REMORSE BY TRANSFORMING FROM SIR CHARLES, INVENTOR, TO UNCLE CHUCK, CHILI-DOG PROPRIETOR!"
UNCLE CHUCK

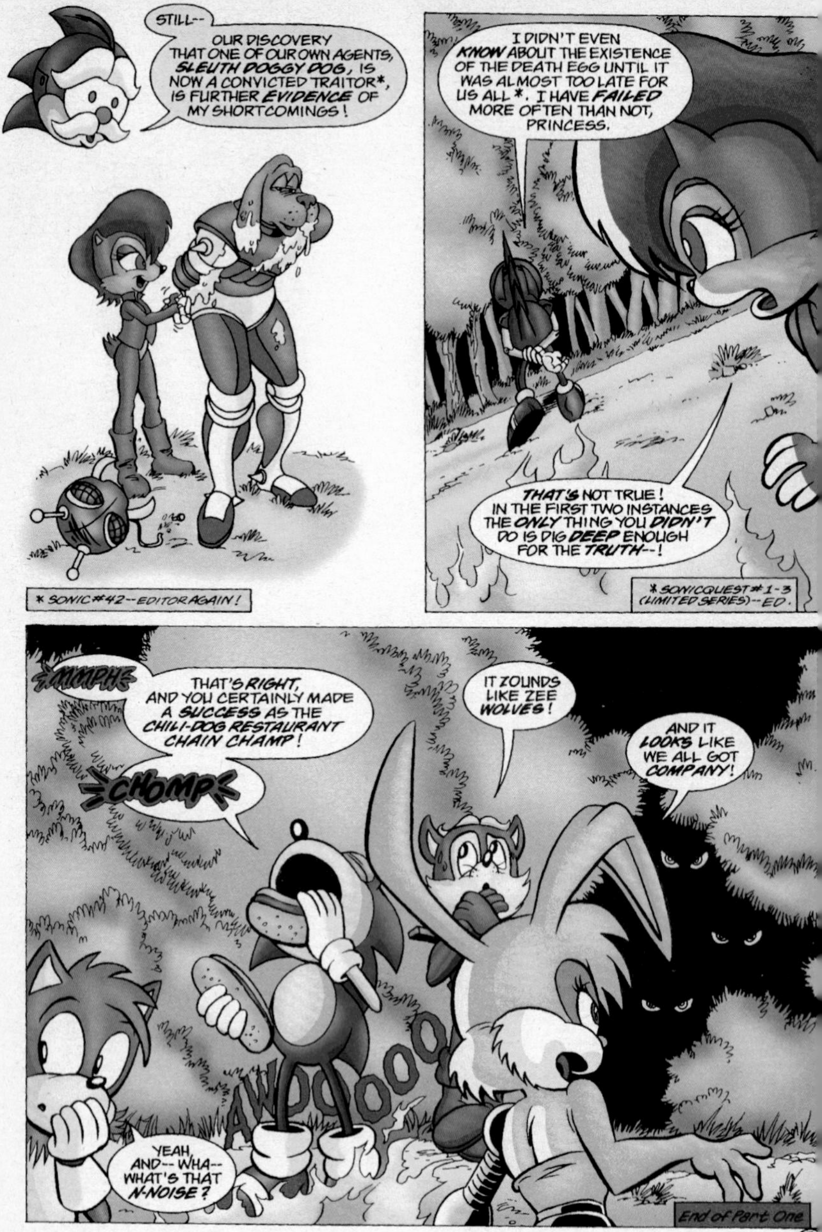
STILL--
OUR DISCOVERY THAT ONE OF OUR OWN AGENTS, SLEUTH DOGGY DOG, IS NOW A CONVICTED TRAITOR*, IS FURTHER EVIDENCE OF MY SHORTCOMINGS!
* SONIC #42--EDITOR AGAIN!
I DIDN'T EVEN KNOW ABOUT THE EXISTENCE OF THE DEATH EGG UNTIL IT WAS ALMOST TOO LATE FOR US ALL *. I HAVE FAILED MORE OFTEN THAN NOT, PRINCESS.
THAT'S NOT TRUE! IN THE FIRST TWO INSTANCES THE ONLY THING YOU DIDN'T DO IS DIG DEEP ENOUGH FOR THE TRUTH--!
* SONICQUEST #1-3 (LIMITED SERIES)--ED.
MMPH
THAT'S RIGHT, AND YOU CERTAINLY MADE A SUCCESS AS THE CHILI-DOG RESTAURANT CHAIN CHAMP!
CHOMP
IT ZOUNDS LIKE ZEE WOLVES!
AND IT LOOKS LIKE WE ALL GOT COMPANY!
AWOOOOOO
YEAH, AND-- WHA-- WHAT'S THAT N-NOISE?
End of Part One

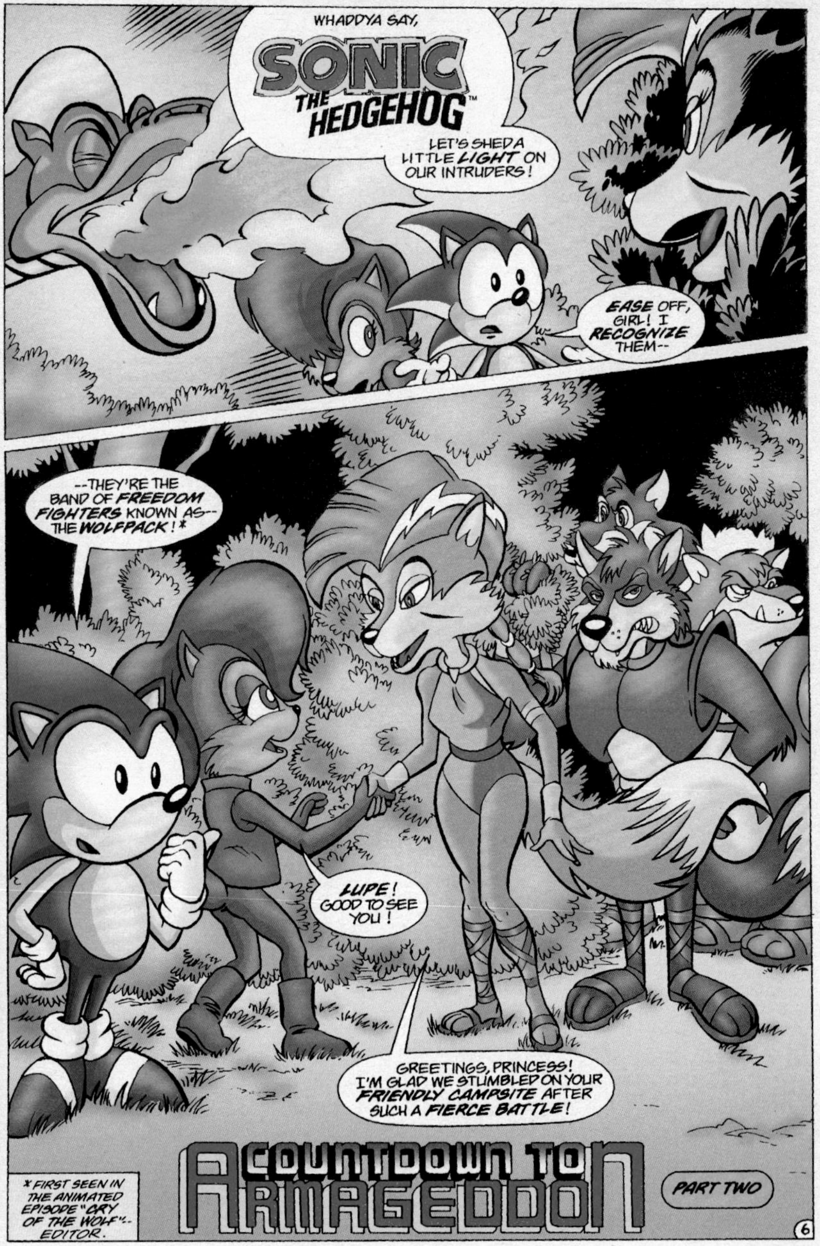

WHADDYA SAY,
SONIC THE HEDGEHOG™
LET'S SHED A LITTLE LIGHT ON OUR INTRUDERS!
EASE OFF, GIRL! I RECOGNIZE THEM--
--THEY'RE THE BAND OF FREEDOM FIGHTERS KNOWN AS-- THE WOLFPACK!*
LUPE! GOOD TO SEE YOU!
GREETINGS, PRINCESS! I'M GLAD WE STUMBLED ON YOUR FRIENDLY CAMPSITE AFTER SUCH A FIERCE BATTLE!
COUNTDOWN TO ARMAGEDDON
PART TWO
* FIRST SEEN IN THE ANIMATED EPISODE "CRY OF THE WOLF".- EDITOR.
6

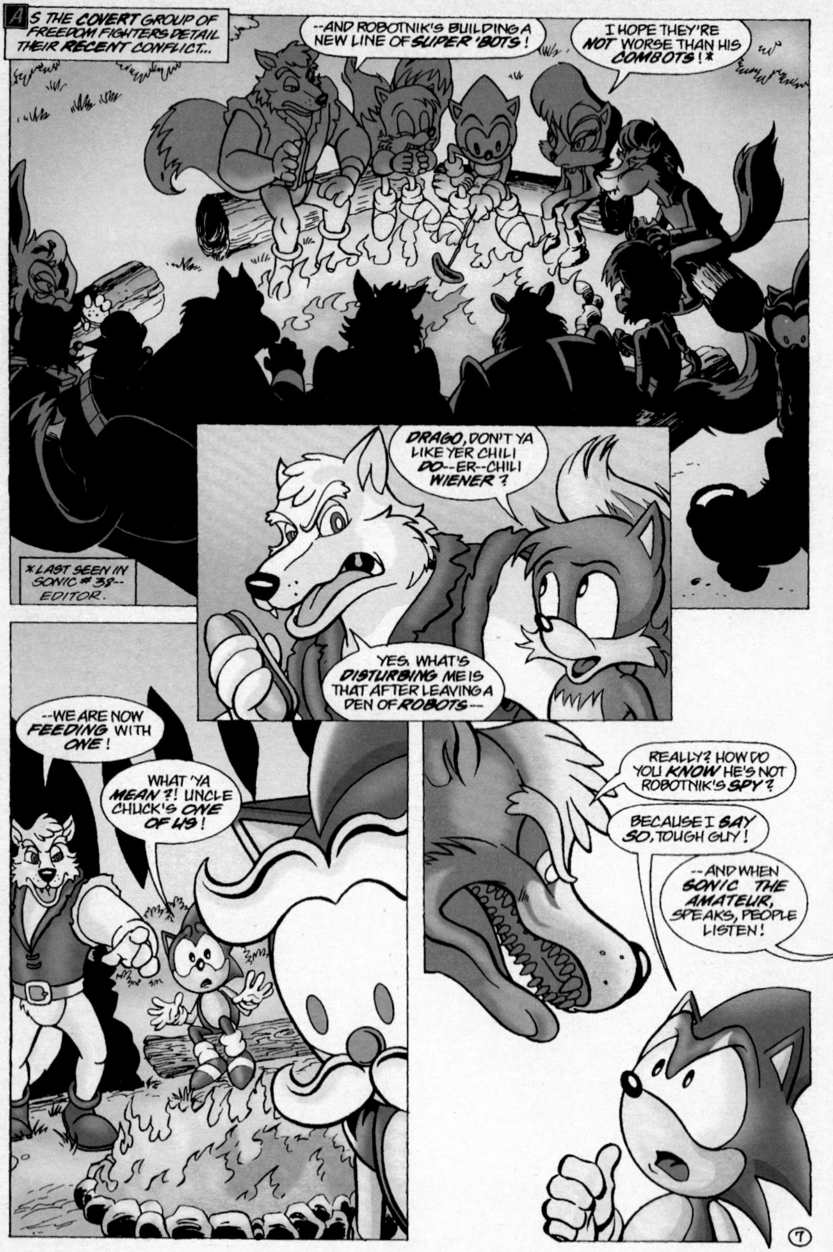
AS THE COVERT GROUP OF FREEDOM FIGHTERS DETAIL THEIR RECENT CONFLICT...
--AND ROBOTNIK'S BUILDING A NEW LINE OF SUPER 'BOTS!
I HOPE THEY'RE NOT WORSE THAN HIS COMBOTS!*
*LAST SEEN IN SONIC #38-- EDITOR.
DRAGO, DON'T YA LIKE YER CHILI DO--ER--CHILI WIENER?
YES. WHAT'S DISTURBING ME IS THAT AFTER LEAVING A DEN OF ROBOTS--
--WE ARE NOW FEEDING WITH ONE!
WHAT 'YA MEAN?! UNCLE CHUCK'S ONE OF US!
REALLY? HOW DO YOU KNOW HE'S NOT ROBOTNIK'S SPY?
BECAUSE I SAY SO, TOUGH GUY!
--AND WHEN SONIC THE AMATEUR, SPEAKS, PEOPLE LISTEN!
7

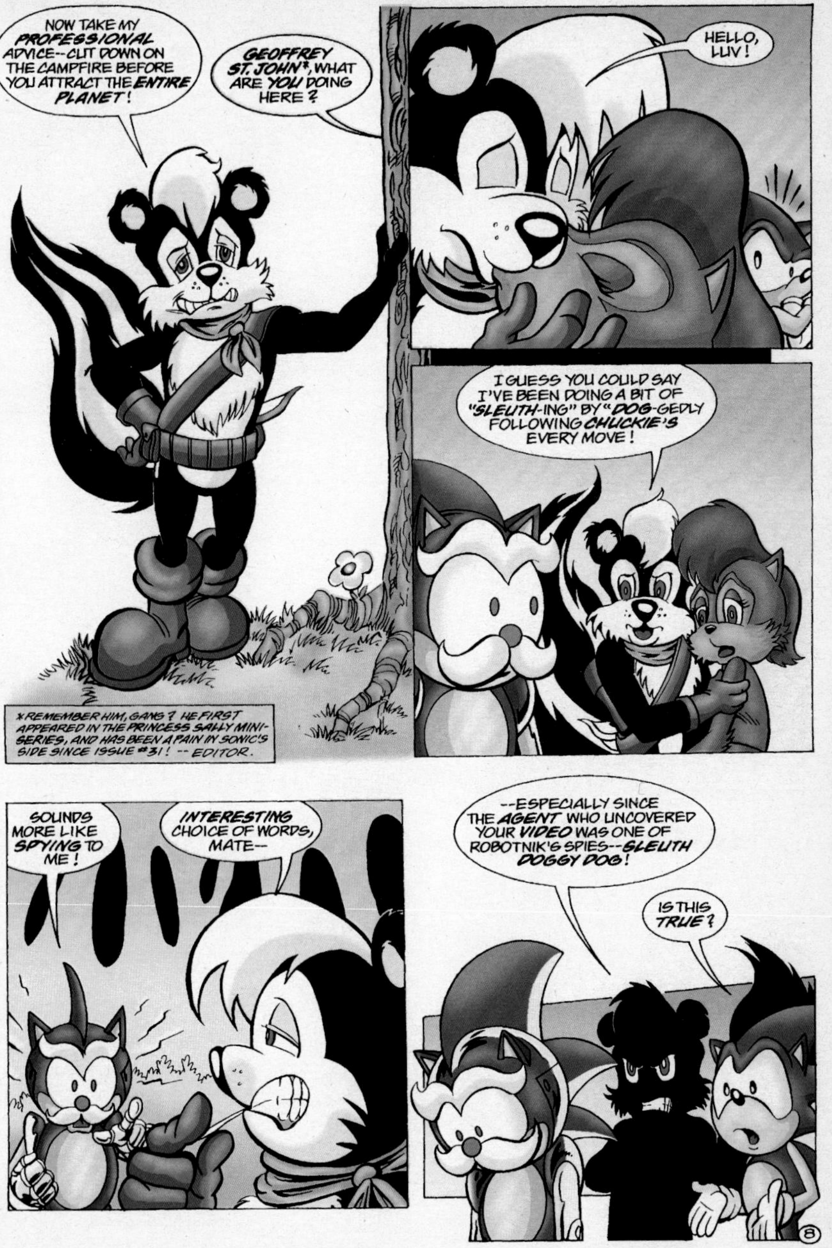

NOW TAKE MY PROFESSIONAL ADVICE--CUT DOWN ON THE CAMPFIRE BEFORE YOU ATTRACT THE ENTIRE PLANET!
GEOFFREY ST. JOHN*, WHAT ARE YOU DOING HERE?
*REMEMBER HIM, GANG? HE FIRST APPEARED IN THE PRINCESS SALLY MINI-SERIES, AND HAS BEEN A PAIN IN SONIC'S SIDE SINCE ISSUE #31! -- EDITOR.
HELLO, LUV!
I GUESS YOU COULD SAY I'VE BEEN DOING A BIT OF "SLEUTH-ING" BY "DOG-GEDLY FOLLOWING CHUCKIE'S EVERY MOVE!
SOUNDS MORE LIKE SPYING TO ME!
INTERESTING CHOICE OF WORDS, MATE--
--ESPECIALLY SINCE THE AGENT WHO UNCOVERED YOUR VIDEO WAS ONE OF ROBOTNIK'S SPIES--SLEUTH DOGGY DOG!
IS THIS TRUE?
8

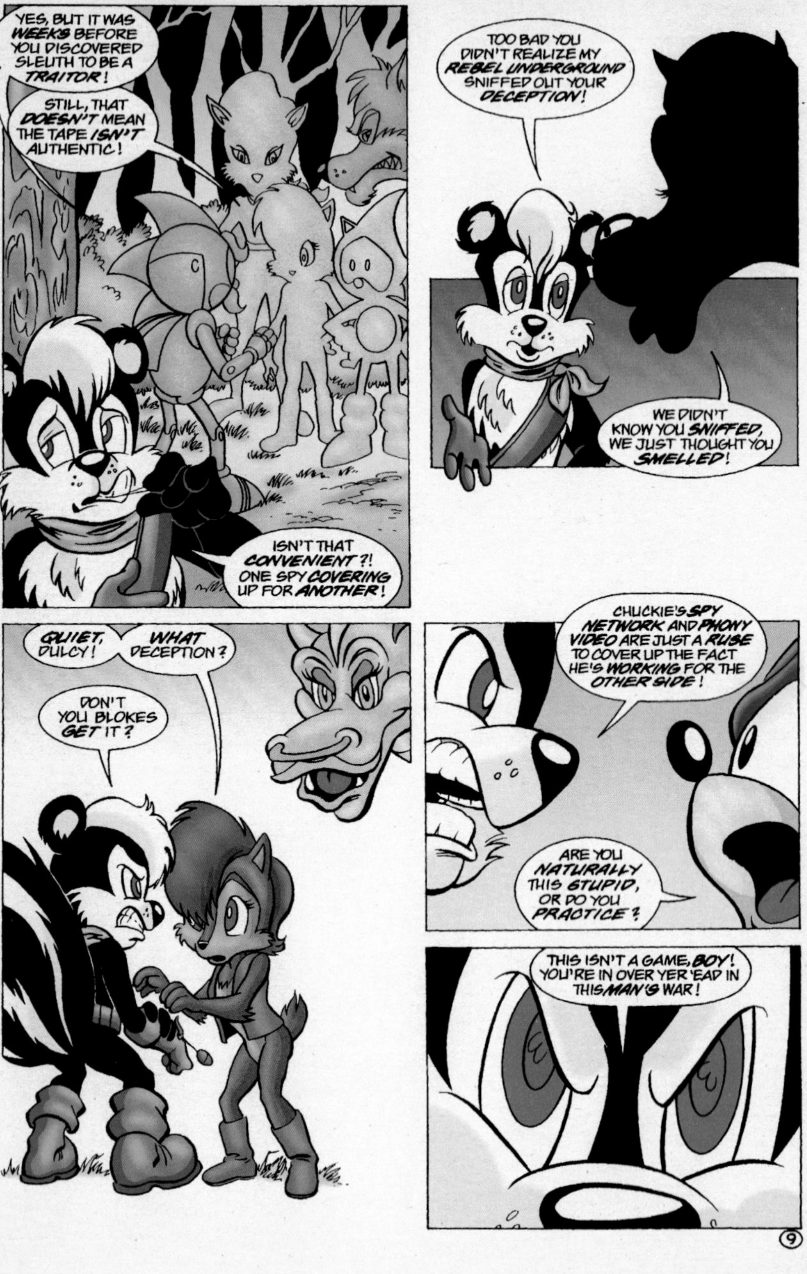
YES, BUT IT WAS WEEKS BEFORE YOU DISCOVERED SLEUTH TO BE A TRAITOR!
STILL, THAT DOESN'T MEAN THE TAPE ISN'T AUTHENTIC!
ISN'T THAT CONVENIENT?! ONE SPY COVERING UP FOR ANOTHER!
TOO BAD YOU DIDN'T REALIZE MY REBEL UNDERGROUND SNIFFED OUT YOUR DECEPTION!
WE DIDN'T KNOW YOU SNIFFED, WE JUST THOUGHT YOU SMELLED!
QUIET, DULCY!
WHAT DECEPTION?
DON'T YOU BLOKES GET IT?
CHUCKIE'S SPY NETWORK AND PHONY VIDEO ARE JUST A RUSE TO COVER UP THE FACT HE'S WORKING FOR THE OTHER SIDE!
ARE YOU NATURALLY THIS STUPID, OR DO YOU PRACTICE?
THIS ISN'T A GAME, BOY! YOU'RE IN OVER YER 'EAD IN THIS MAN'S WAR!

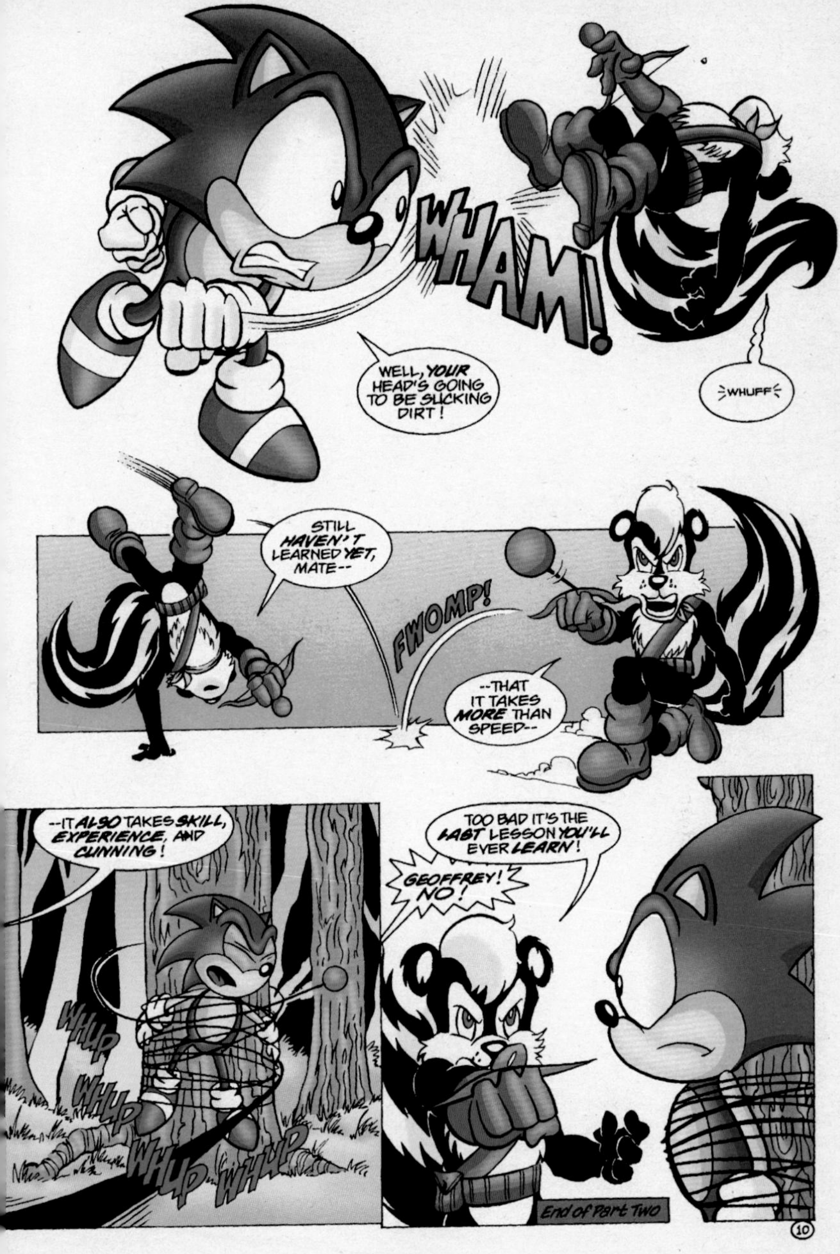
WHAM!
WELL, YOUR HEAD'S GOING TO BE SUCKING DIRT!
WHUFF
STILL HAVEN'T LEARNED YET, MATE--
FWOMP!
--THAT IT TAKES MORE THAN SPEED--
--IT ALSO TAKES SKILL, EXPERIENCE, AND CUNNING!
WHUP
WHUP
WHUP
WHUP
TOO BAD IT'S THE LAST LESSON YOU'LL EVER LEARN!
GEOFFREY! NO!
End of Part Two

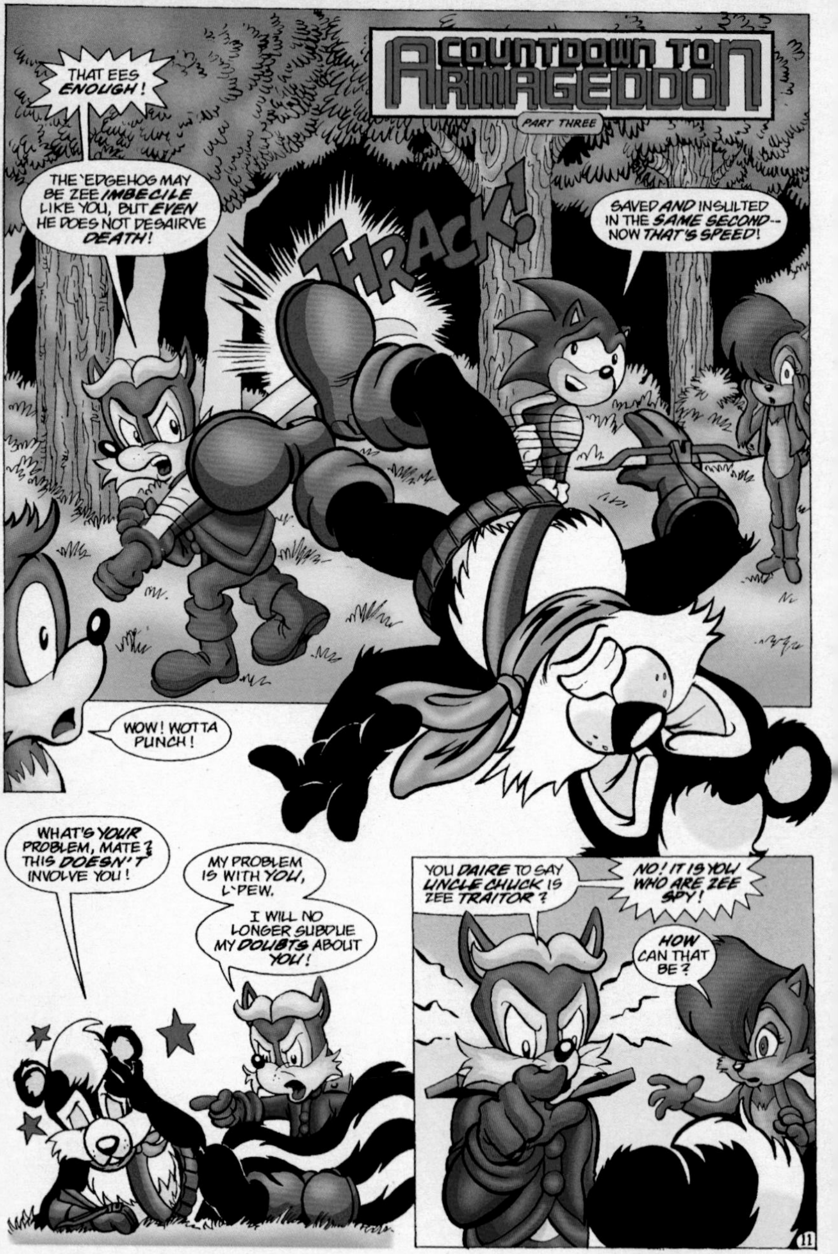

COUNTDOWN TO ARMAGEDDON
PART THREE
THAT EES ENOUGH!
THE 'EDGEHOG MAY BE ZEE IMBECILE LIKE YOU, BUT EVEN HE DOES NOT DESAIRVE DEATH!
THRACK!
SAVED AND INSULTED IN THE SAME SECOND-- NOW THAT'S SPEED!
WOW! WOTTA PUNCH!
WHAT'S YOUR PROBLEM, MATE? THIS DOESN'T INVOLVE YOU!
MY PROBLEM IS WITH YOU, L'PEW.
I WILL NO LONGER SUBDUE MY DOUBTS ABOUT YOU!
YOU DAIRE TO SAY UNCLE CHUCK IS ZEE TRAITOR?
NO! IT IS YOU WHO ARE ZEE SPY!
HOW CAN THAT BE?

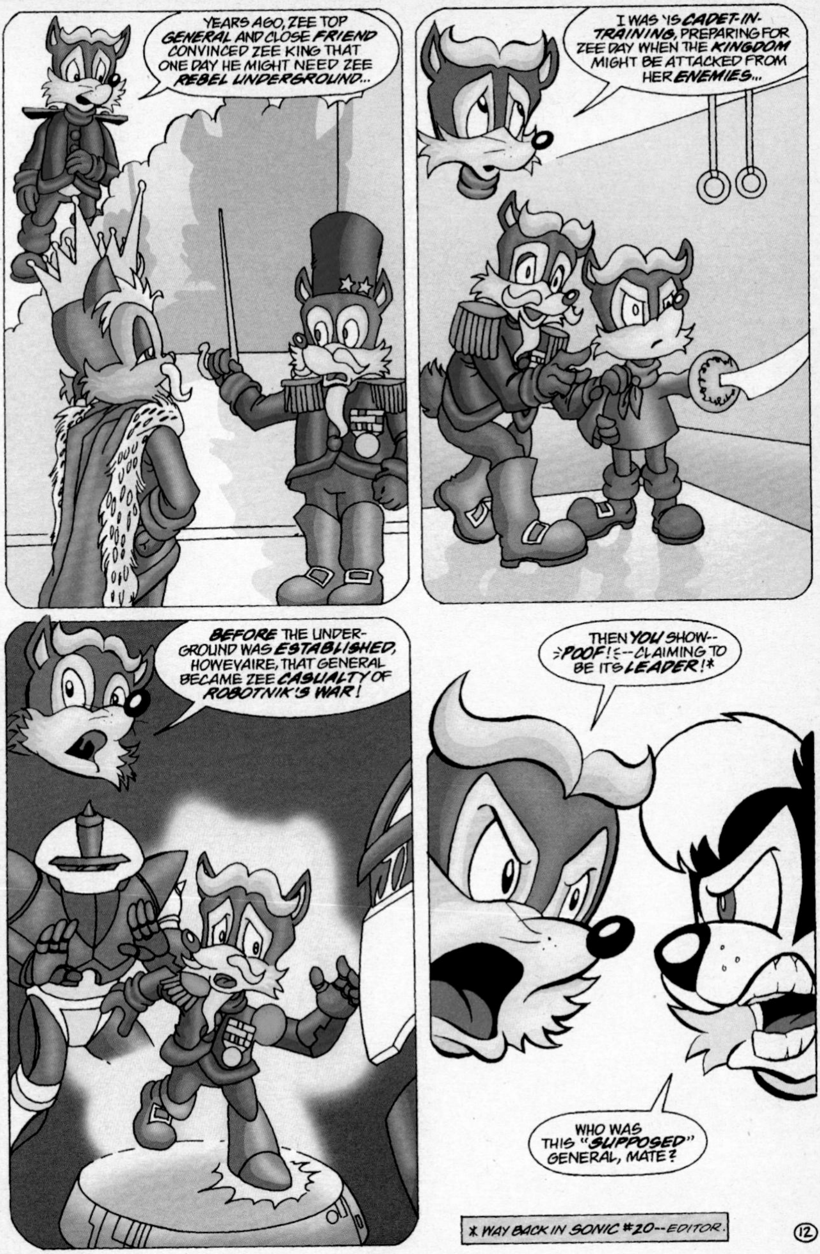
YEARS AGO, ZEE TOP GENERAL AND CLOSE FRIEND CONVINCED ZEE KING THAT ONE DAY HE MIGHT NEED ZEE REBEL UNDERGROUND...
I WAS 'IS CADET-IN-TRAINING, PREPARING FOR ZEE DAY WHEN THE KINGDOM MIGHT BE ATTACKED FROM HER ENEMIES...
BEFORE THE UNDERGROUND WAS ESTABLISHED, HOWEVAIRE, THAT GENERAL BECAME ZEE CASUALTY OF ROBOTNIK'S WAR!
THEN YOU SHOW-- POOF!--CLAIMING TO BE ITS LEADER!*
WHO WAS THIS "SUPPOSED" GENERAL, MATE?
* WAY BACK IN SONIC #20--EDITOR.

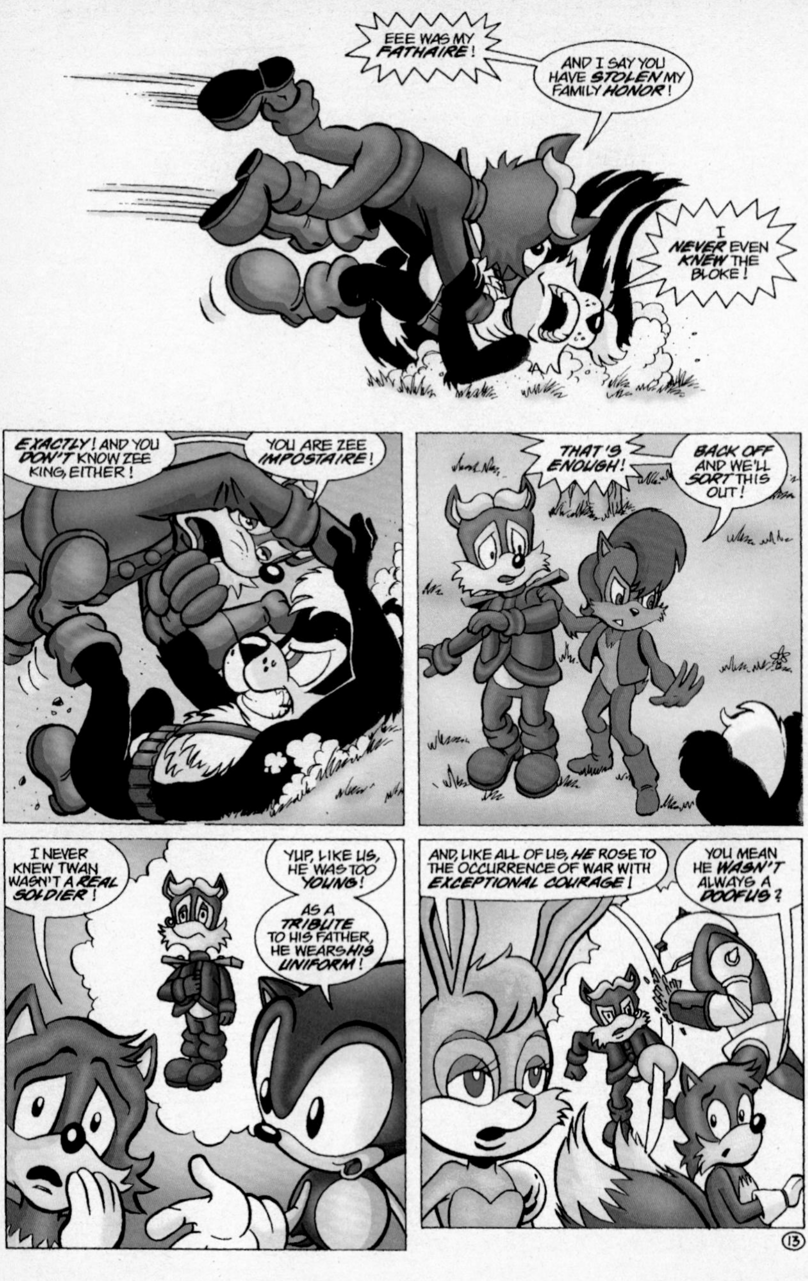
EEE WAS MY FATHAIRE!
AND I SAY YOU HAVE STOLEN MY FAMILY HONOR!
I NEVER EVEN KNEW THE BLOKE!
EXACTLY! AND YOU DON'T KNOW ZEE KING, EITHER!
YOU ARE ZEE IMPOSTAIRE!
THAT'S ENOUGH!
BACK OFF AND WE'LL SORT THIS OUT!
I NEVER KNEW TWAN WASN'T A REAL SOLDIER!
YUP, LIKE US, HE WAS TOO YOUNG!
AS A TRIBUTE TO HIS FATHER, HE WEARS HIS UNIFORM!
AND, LIKE ALL OF US, HE ROSE TO THE OCCURRENCE OF WAR WITH EXCEPTIONAL COURAGE!
YOU MEAN HE WASN'T ALWAYS A DOOFUS?

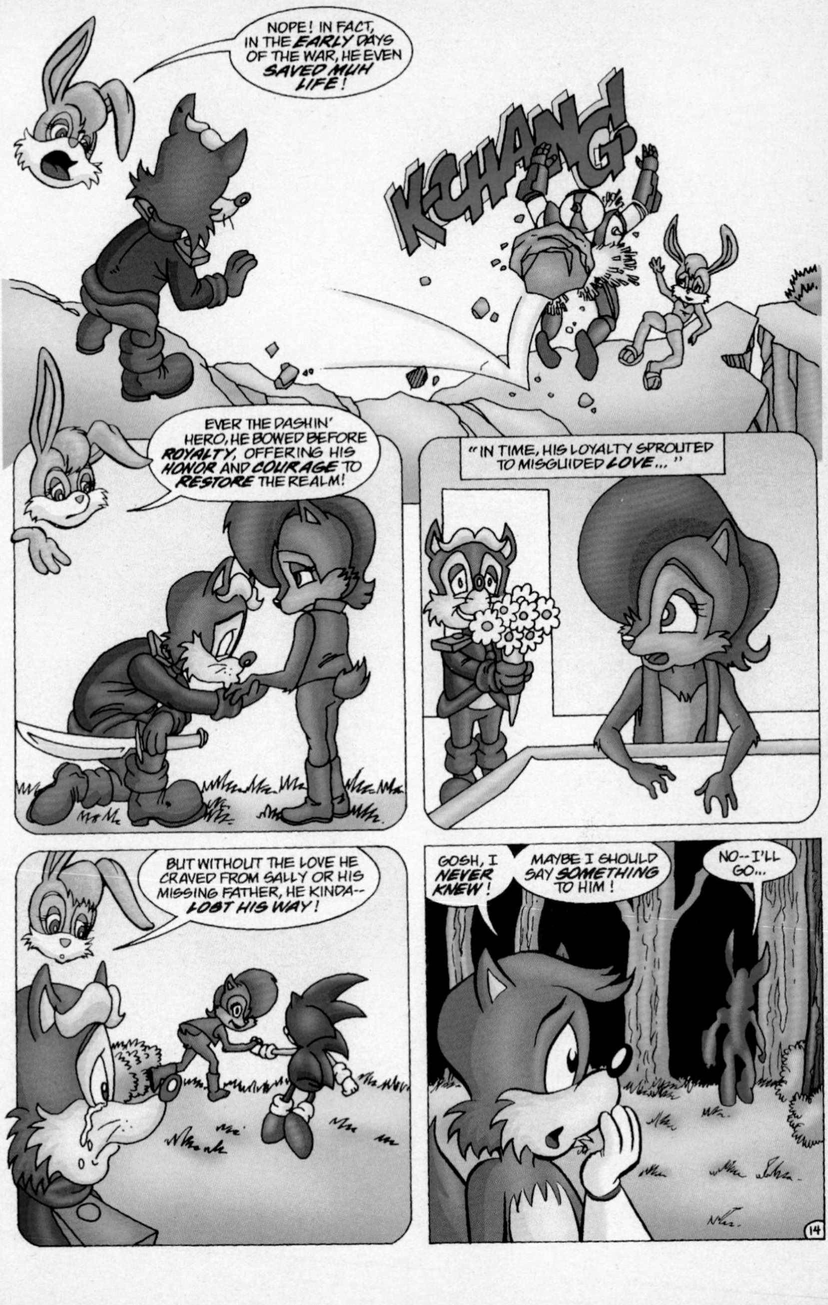
NOPE! IN FACT, IN THE EARLY DAYS OF THE WAR, HE EVEN SAVED MUH LIFE!
K-CHANG!
EVER THE DASHIN' HERO, HE BOWED BEFORE ROYALTY, OFFERING HIS HONOR AND COURAGE TO RESTORE THE REALM!
"IN TIME, HIS LOYALTY SPROUTED TO MISGUIDED LOVE..."
BUT WITHOUT THE LOVE HE CRAVED FROM SALLY OR HIS MISSING FATHER, HE KINDA-- LOST HIS WAY!
GOSH, I NEVER KNEW!
MAYBE I SHOULD SAY SOMETHING TO HIM!
NO--I'LL GO...
14

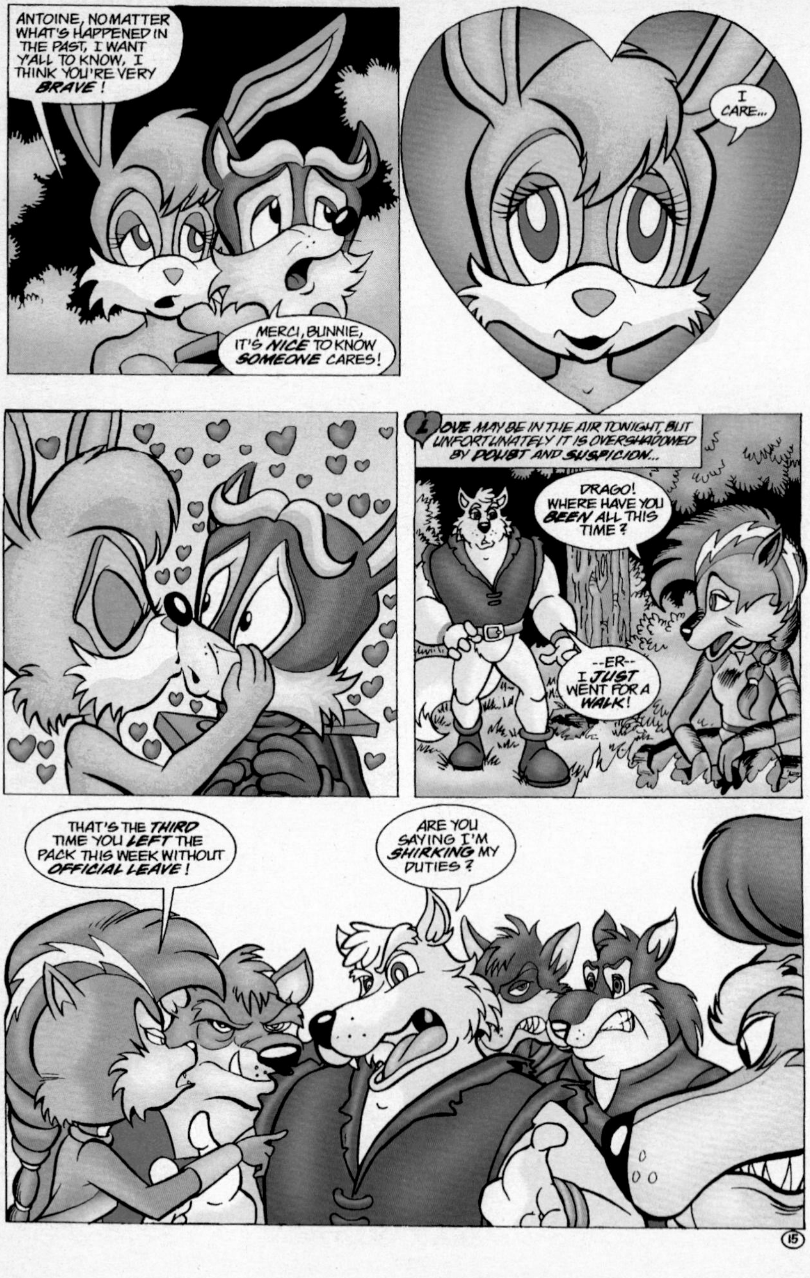
ANTOINE, NO MATTER WHAT'S HAPPENED IN THE PAST, I WANT Y'ALL TO KNOW, I THINK YOU'RE VERY BRAVE!
MERCI, BUNNIE, IT'S NICE TO KNOW SOMEONE CARES!
I CARE...
LOVE MAY BE IN THE AIR TONIGHT, BUT UNFORTUNATELY IT IS OVERSHADOWED BY DOUBT AND SUSPICION...
DRAGO! WHERE HAVE YOU BEEN ALL THIS TIME?
--ER-- I JUST WENT FOR A WALK!
THAT'S THE THIRD TIME YOU LEFT THE PACK THIS WEEK WITHOUT OFFICIAL LEAVE!
ARE YOU SAYING I'M SHIRKING MY DUTIES?

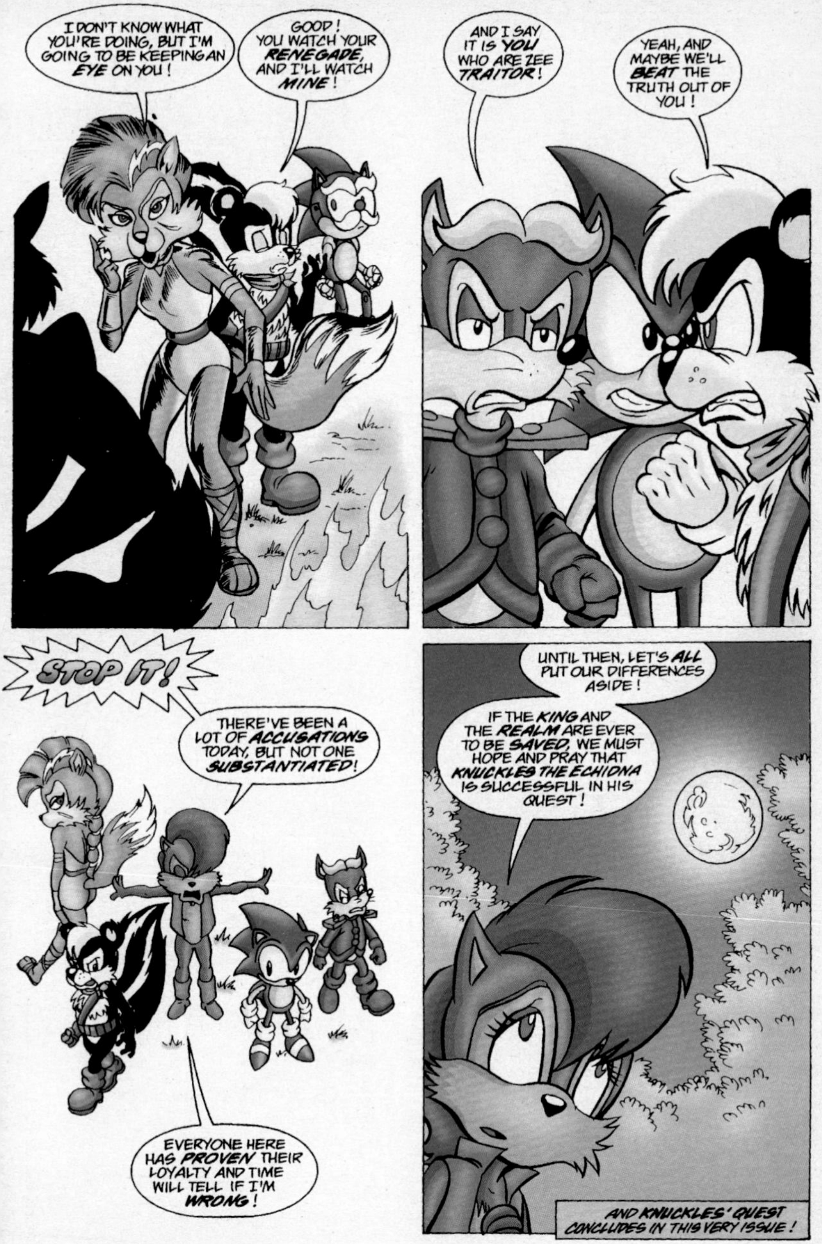
I DON'T KNOW WHAT YOU'RE DOING, BUT I'M GOING TO BE KEEPING AN EYE ON YOU!
GOOD! YOU WATCH YOUR RENEGADE, AND I'LL WATCH MINE!
AND I SAY IT IS YOU WHO ARE ZEE TRAITOR!
YEAH, AND MAYBE WE'LL BEAT THE TRUTH OUT OF YOU!
STOP IT!
THERE'VE BEEN A LOT OF ACCUSATIONS TODAY, BUT NOT ONE SUBSTANTIATED!
EVERYONE HERE HAS PROVEN THEIR LOYALTY AND TIME WILL TELL IF I'M WRONG!
UNTIL THEN, LET'S ALL PUT OUR DIFFERENCES ASIDE!
IF THE KING AND THE REALM ARE EVER TO BE SAVED, WE MUST HOPE AND PRAY THAT KNUCKLES THE ECHIDNA IS SUCCESSFUL IN HIS QUEST!
AND KNUCKLES' QUEST CONCLUDES IN THIS VERY ISSUE!

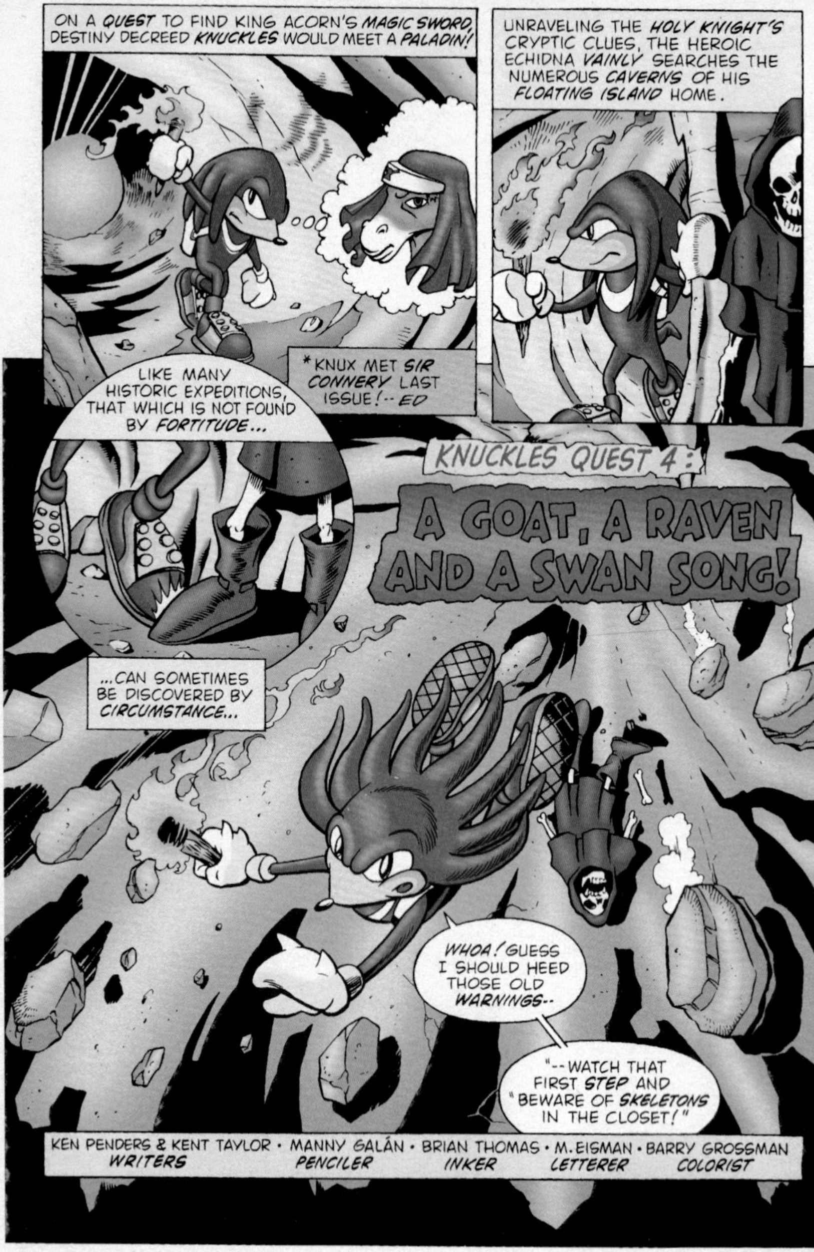

ON A QUEST TO FIND KING ACORN'S MAGIC SWORD, DESTINY DECREED KNUCKLES WOULD MEET A PALADIN!
*KNUX MET SIR CONNERY LAST ISSUE! --ED
UNRAVELING THE HOLY KNIGHT'S CRYPTIC CLUES, THE HEROIC ECHIDNA VAINLY SEARCHES THE NUMEROUS CAVERNS OF HIS FLOATING ISLAND HOME.
LIKE MANY HISTORIC EXPEDITIONS, THAT WHICH IS NOT FOUND BY FORTITUDE...
KNUCKLES QUEST 4:
A GOAT, A RAVEN AND A SWAN SONG!
...CAN SOMETIMES BE DISCOVERED BY CIRCUMSTANCE...
WHOA! GUESS I SHOULD HEED THOSE OLD WARNINGS--
"--WATCH THAT FIRST STEP AND "BEWARE OF SKELETONS IN THE CLOSET!"
KEN PENDERS & KENT TAYLOR · MANNY GALÁN · BRIAN THOMAS · M. EISMAN · BARRY GROSSMAN
WRITERS PENCILER INKER LETTERER COLORIST

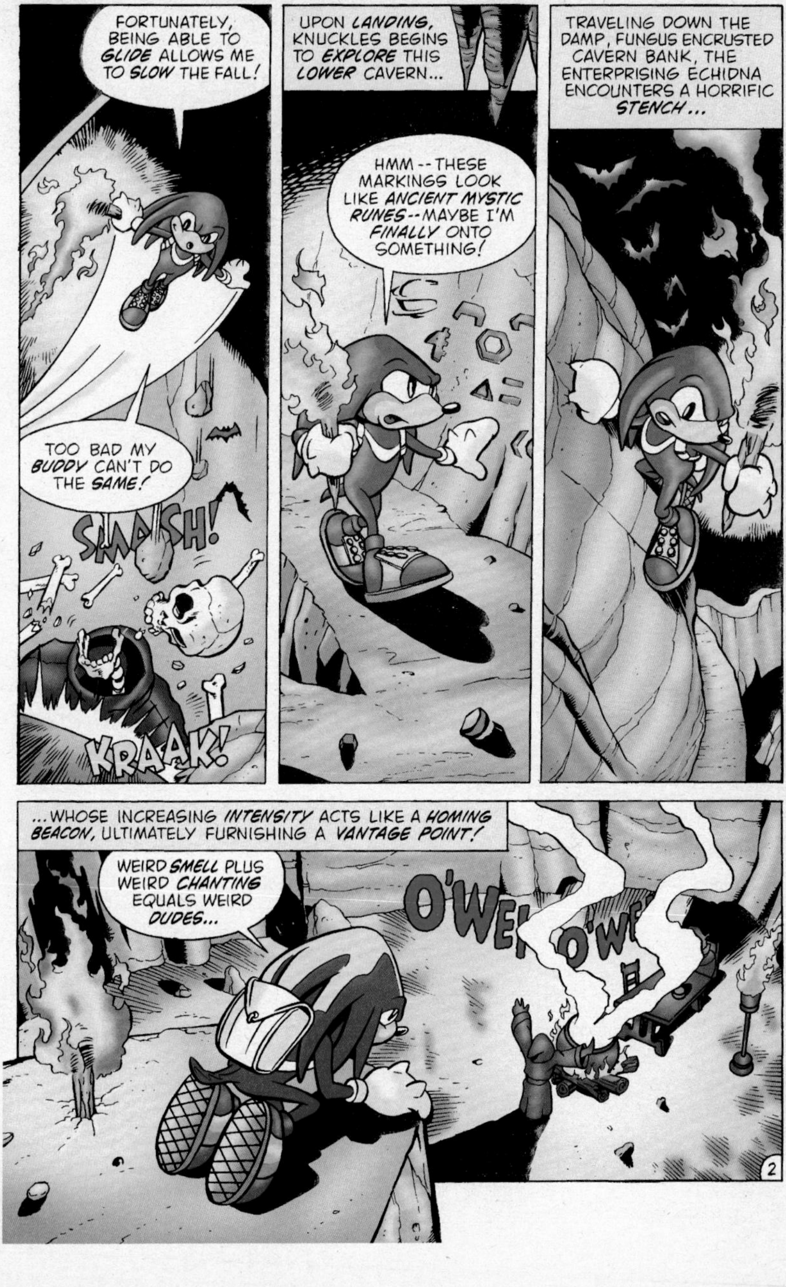
FORTUNATELY, BEING ABLE TO GLIDE ALLOWS ME TO SLOW THE FALL!
TOO BAD MY BUDDY CAN'T DO THE SAME!
SMASH!
KRAAK!
UPON LANDING, KNUCKLES BEGINS TO EXPLORE THIS LOWER CAVERN...
HMM--THESE MARKINGS LOOK LIKE ANCIENT MYSTIC RUNES--MAYBE I'M FINALLY ONTO SOMETHING!
TRAVELING DOWN THE DAMP, FUNGUS ENCRUSTED CAVERN BANK, THE ENTERPRISING ECHIDNA ENCOUNTERS A HORRIFIC STENCH...
...WHOSE INCREASING INTENSITY ACTS LIKE A HOMING BEACON, ULTIMATELY FURNISHING A VANTAGE POINT!
WEIRD SMELL PLUS WEIRD CHANTING EQUALS WEIRD DUDES...
O'WE
O'WE

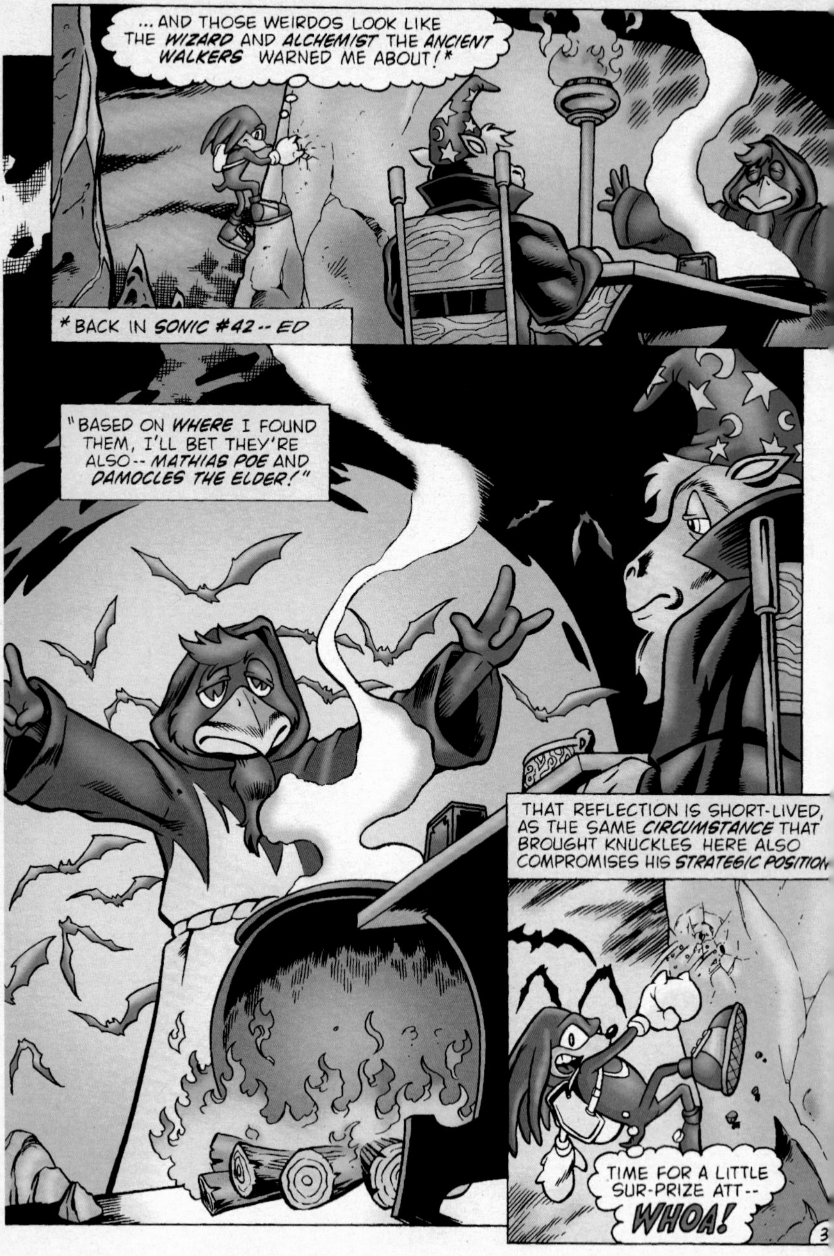
...AND THOSE WEIRDOS LOOK LIKE THE WIZARD AND ALCHEMIST THE ANCIENT WALKERS WARNED ME ABOUT!*
*BACK IN SONIC #42 -- ED
"BASED ON WHERE I FOUND THEM, I'LL BET THEY'RE ALSO -- MATHIAS POE AND DAMOCLES THE ELDER!"
THAT REFLECTION IS SHORT-LIVED, AS THE SAME CIRCUMSTANCE THAT BROUGHT KNUCKLES HERE ALSO COMPROMISES HIS STRATEGIC POSITION
TIME FOR A LITTLE SUR-PRIZE ATT --
WHOA!

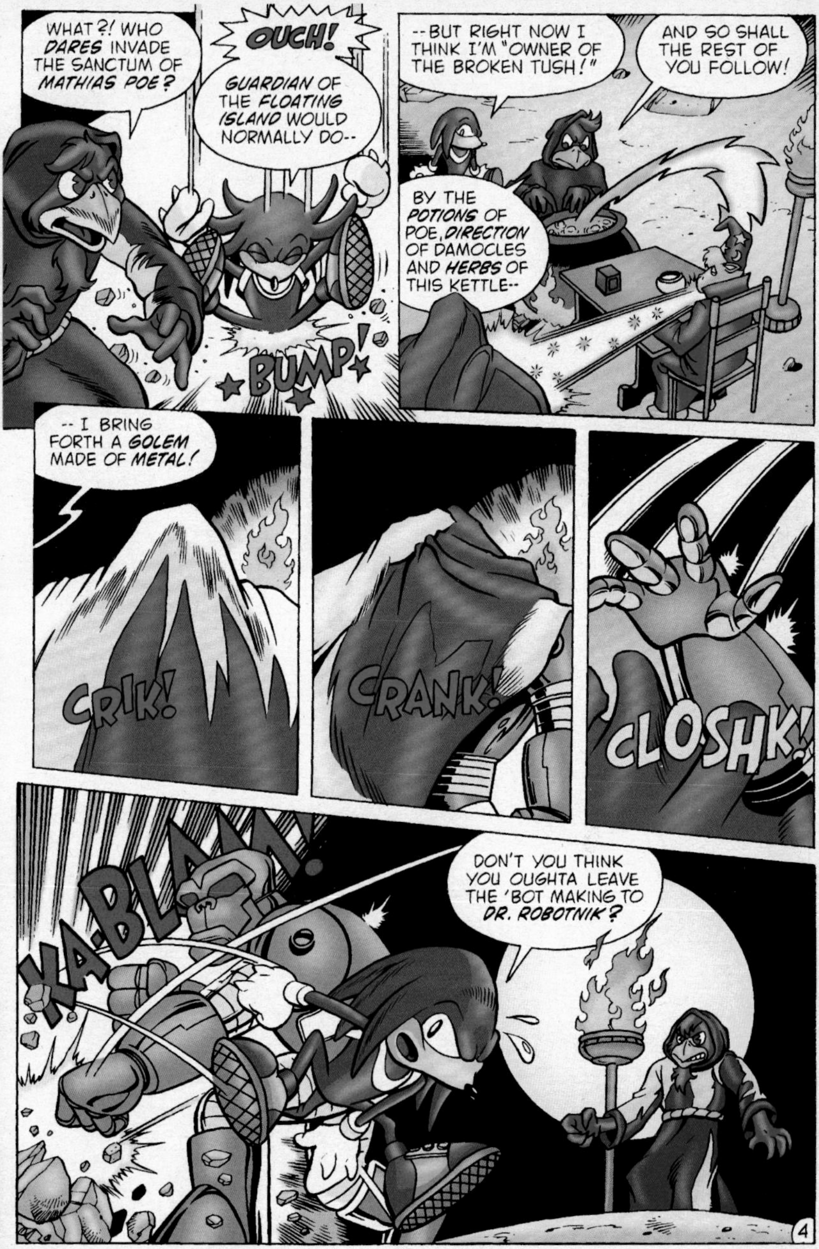
WHAT?! WHO DARES INVADE THE SANCTUM OF MATHIAS POE?
OUCH!
GUARDIAN OF THE FLOATING ISLAND WOULD NORMALLY DO--
BUMP!
--BUT RIGHT NOW I THINK I'M "OWNER OF THE BROKEN TUSH!"
AND SO SHALL THE REST OF YOU FOLLOW!
BY THE POTIONS OF POE, DIRECTION OF DAMOCLES AND HERBS OF THIS KETTLE--
-- I BRING FORTH A GOLEM MADE OF METAL!
CRIK!
CRANK!
CLOSHK!
KA-BLAM!
DON'T YOU THINK YOU OUGHTA LEAVE THE 'BOT MAKING TO DR. ROBOTNIK?

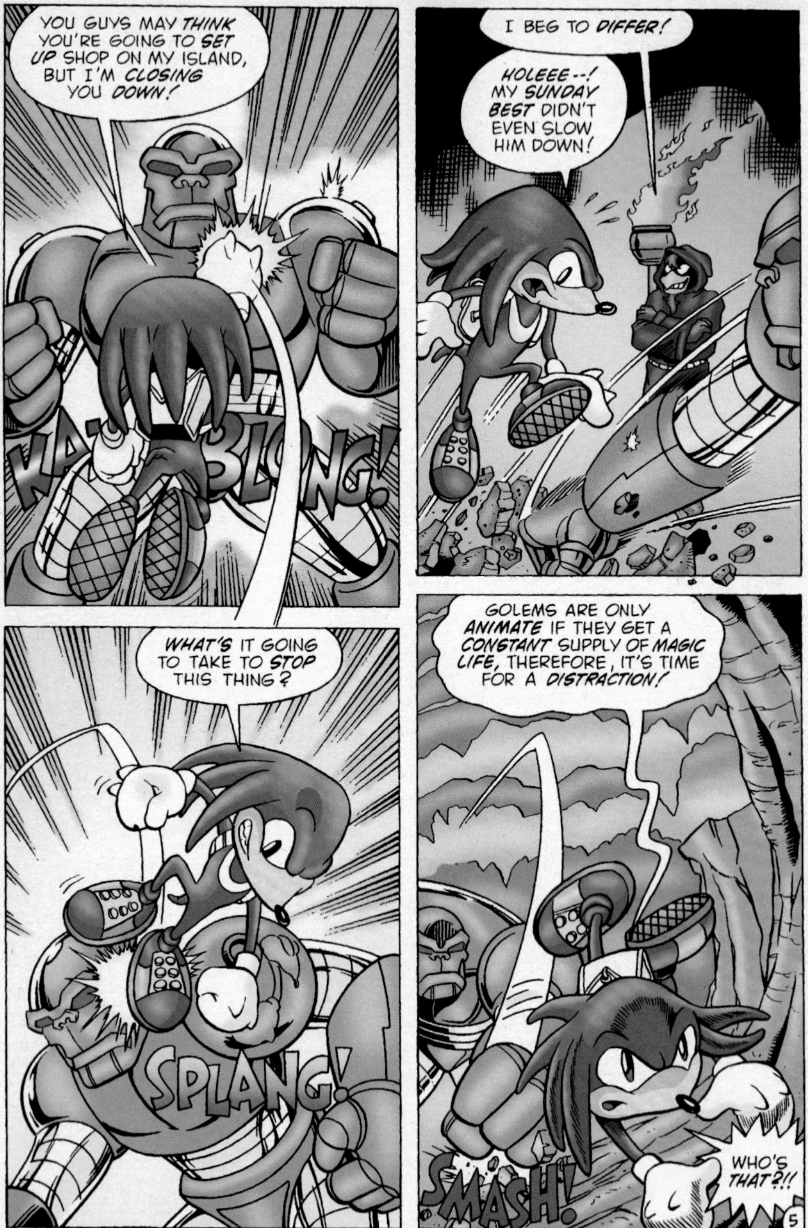
YOU GUYS MAY THINK YOU'RE GOING TO SET UP SHOP ON MY ISLAND, BUT I'M CLOSING YOU DOWN!
KA-BLONG!
I BEG TO DIFFER!
HOLEEE--! MY SUNDAY BEST DIDN'T EVEN SLOW HIM DOWN!
WHAT'S IT GOING TO TAKE TO STOP THIS THING?
SPLANG!
GOLEMS ARE ONLY ANIMATE IF THEY GET A CONSTANT SUPPLY OF MAGIC LIFE, THEREFORE, IT'S TIME FOR A DISTRACTION!
SMASH!
WHO'S THAT?!!

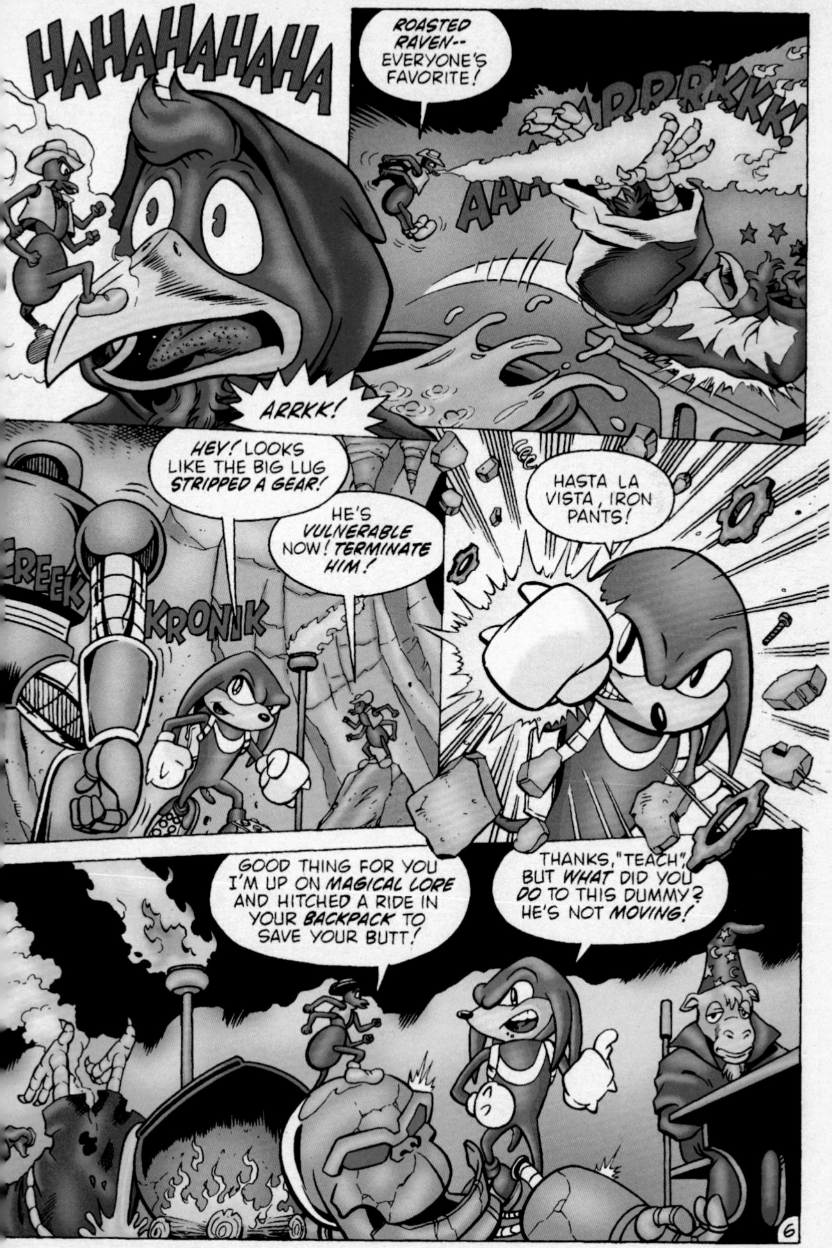
HAHAHAHAHAHA
ROASTED RAVEN-- EVERYONE'S FAVORITE!
RRRKKK!
AAH
ARRKK!
HEY! LOOKS LIKE THE BIG LUG STRIPPED A GEAR!
HE'S VULNERABLE NOW! TERMINATE HIM!
CREEEK
KRONIK
HASTA LA VISTA, IRON PANTS!
GOOD THING FOR YOU I'M UP ON MAGICAL LORE AND HITCHED A RIDE IN YOUR BACKPACK TO SAVE YOUR BUTT!
THANKS, "TEACH", BUT WHAT DID YOU DO TO THIS DUMMY? HE'S NOT MOVING!

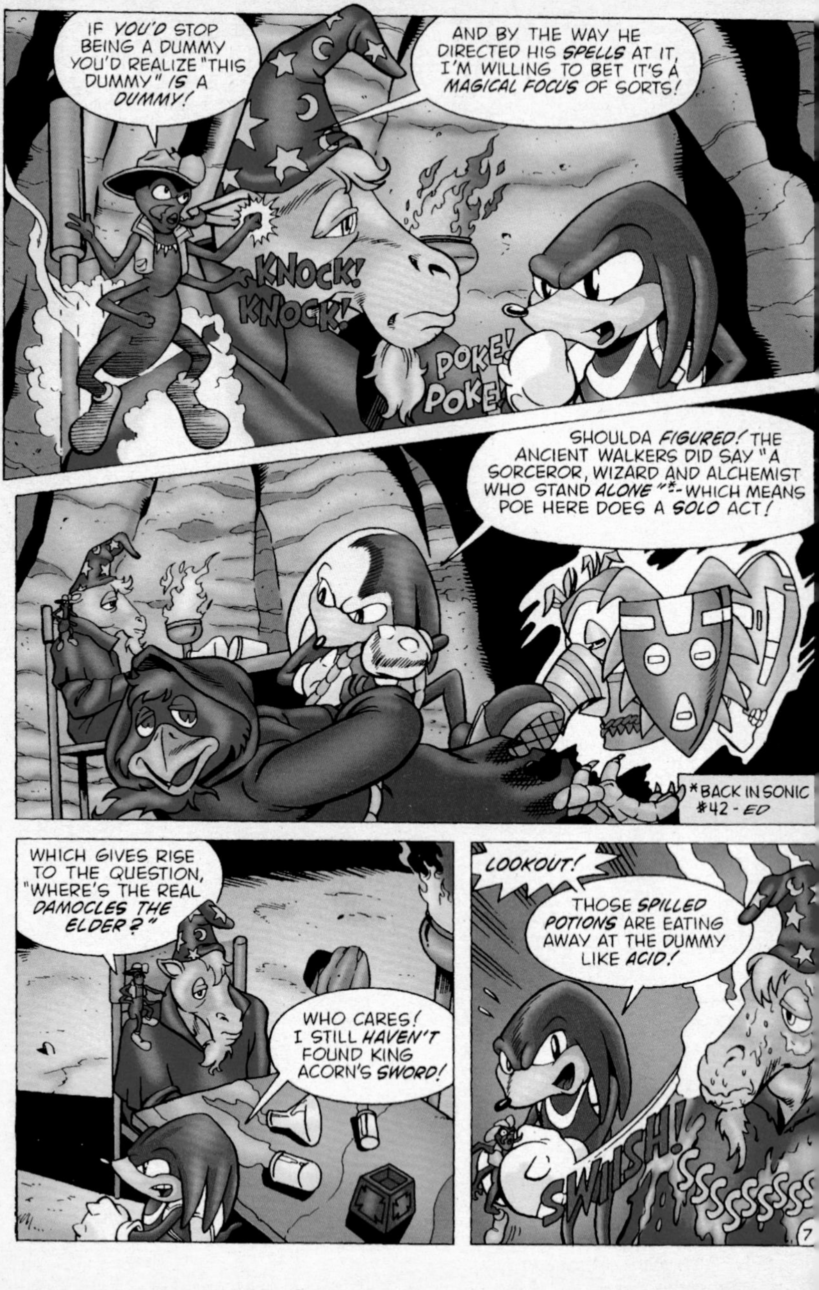
IF YOU'D STOP BEING A DUMMY YOU'D REALIZE "THIS DUMMY" IS A DUMMY!
AND BY THE WAY HE DIRECTED HIS SPELLS AT IT, I'M WILLING TO BET IT'S A MAGICAL FOCUS OF SORTS!
KNOCK! KNOCK!
POKE! POKE!
SHOULDA FIGURED! THE ANCIENT WALKERS DID SAY "A SORCEROR, WIZARD AND ALCHEMIST WHO STAND ALONE"*- WHICH MEANS POE HERE DOES A SOLO ACT!
*BACK IN SONIC #42 - ED
WHICH GIVES RISE TO THE QUESTION, "WHERE'S THE REAL DAMOCLES THE ELDER?"
WHO CARES! I STILL HAVEN'T FOUND KING ACORN'S SWORD!
LOOKOUT!
THOSE SPILLED POTIONS ARE EATING AWAY AT THE DUMMY LIKE ACID!
SWIIISH!
SSSSSSSS

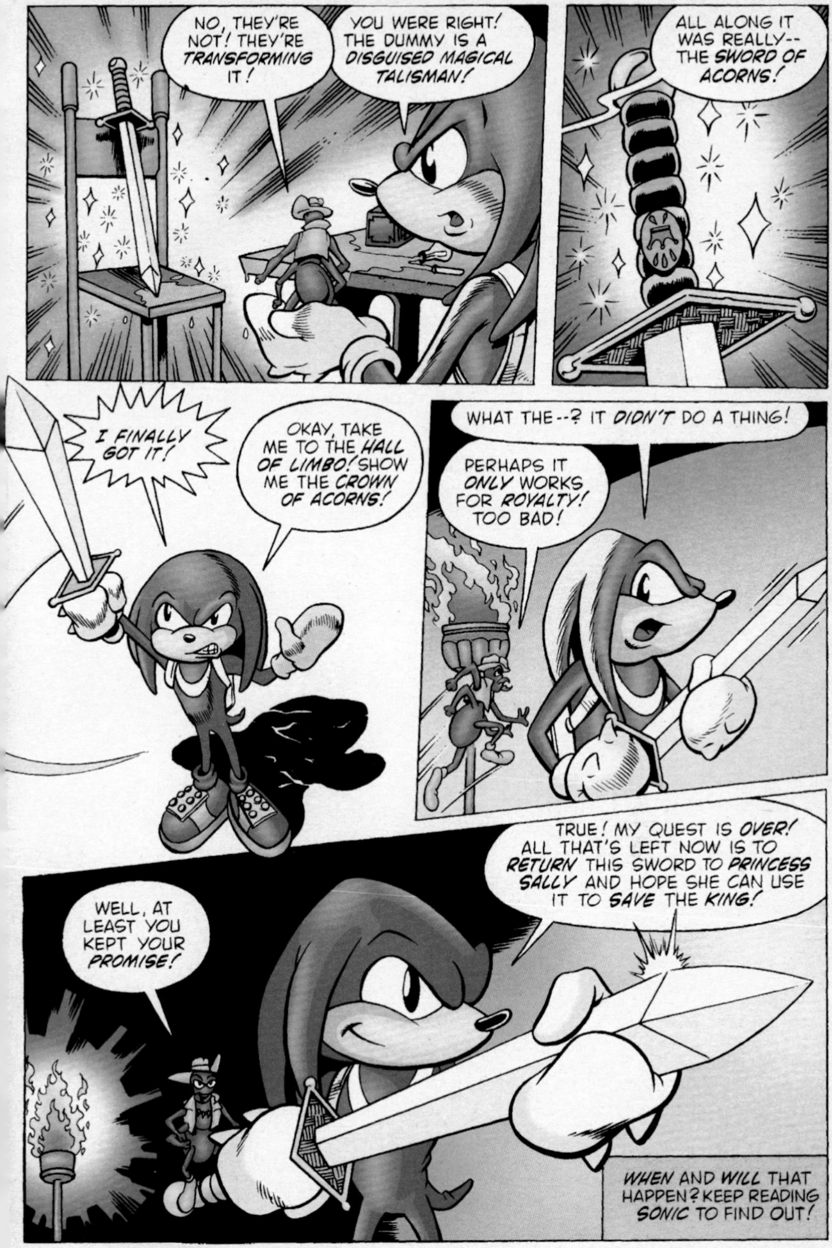
NO, THEY'RE NOT! THEY'RE TRANSFORMING IT!
YOU WERE RIGHT! THE DUMMY IS A DISGUISED MAGICAL TALISMAN!
ALL ALONG IT WAS REALLY-- THE SWORD OF ACORNS!
I FINALLY GOT IT!
OKAY, TAKE ME TO THE HALL OF LIMBO! SHOW ME THE CROWN OF ACORNS!
WHAT THE--? IT DIDN'T DO A THING!
PERHAPS IT ONLY WORKS FOR ROYALTY! TOO BAD!
TRUE! MY QUEST IS OVER! ALL THAT'S LEFT NOW IS TO RETURN THIS SWORD TO PRINCESS SALLY AND HOPE SHE CAN USE IT TO SAVE THE KING!
WELL, AT LEAST YOU KEPT YOUR PROMISE!
WHEN AND WILL THAT HAPPEN? KEEP READING SONIC TO FIND OUT!

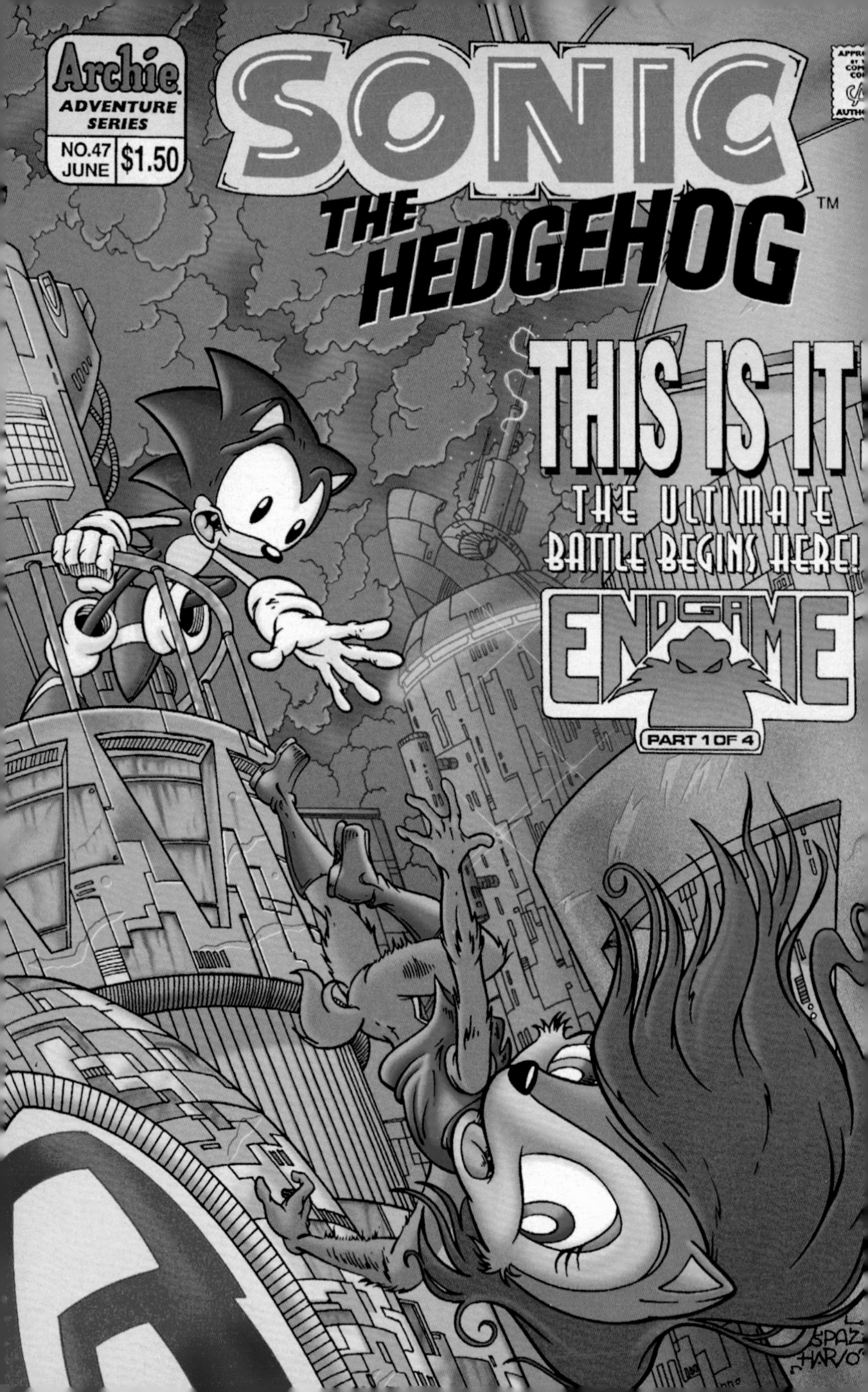
Archie
ADVENTURE SERIES
NO.47 JUNE
$1.50
SONIC THE HEDGEHOG™
THIS IS IT!
THE ULTIMATE BATTLE BEGINS HERE!
ENDGAME
PART 1 OF 4

It is the year 3235 on the planet Mobius and the war being fought upon its surface lands has entered its eleventh year. A war that began as another had just concluded. A war that had its origins from the seeds of betrayal within.

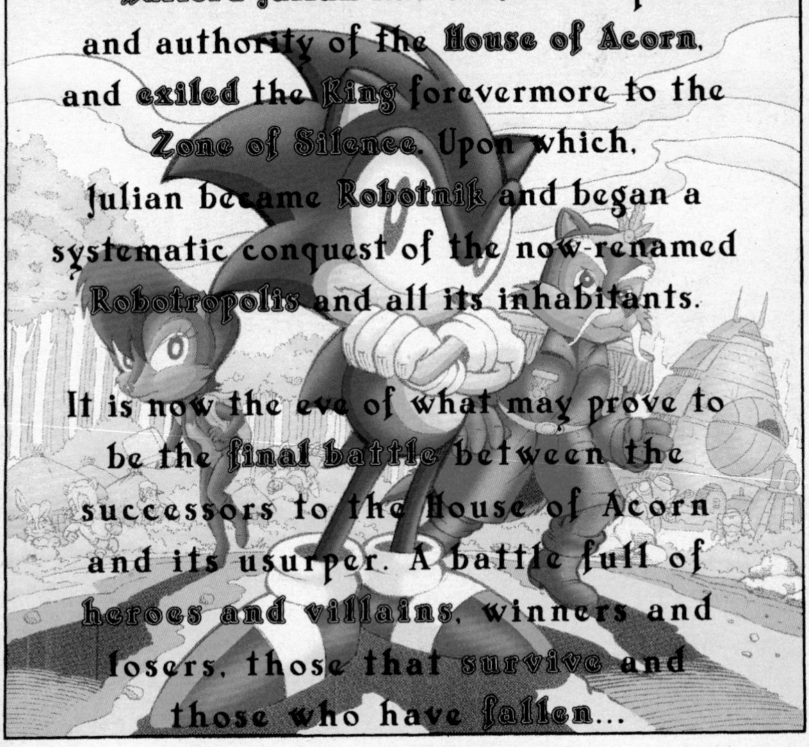

Warlord Julian had seized the power and authority of the House of Acorn, and exiled the King forevermore to the Zone of Silence. Upon which, Julian became Robotnik and began a systematic conquest of the now-renamed Robotropolis and all its inhabitants.

It is now the eve of what may prove to be the final battle between the successors to the House of Acorn and its usurper. A battle full of heroes and villains, winners and losers, those that survive and those who have fallen...

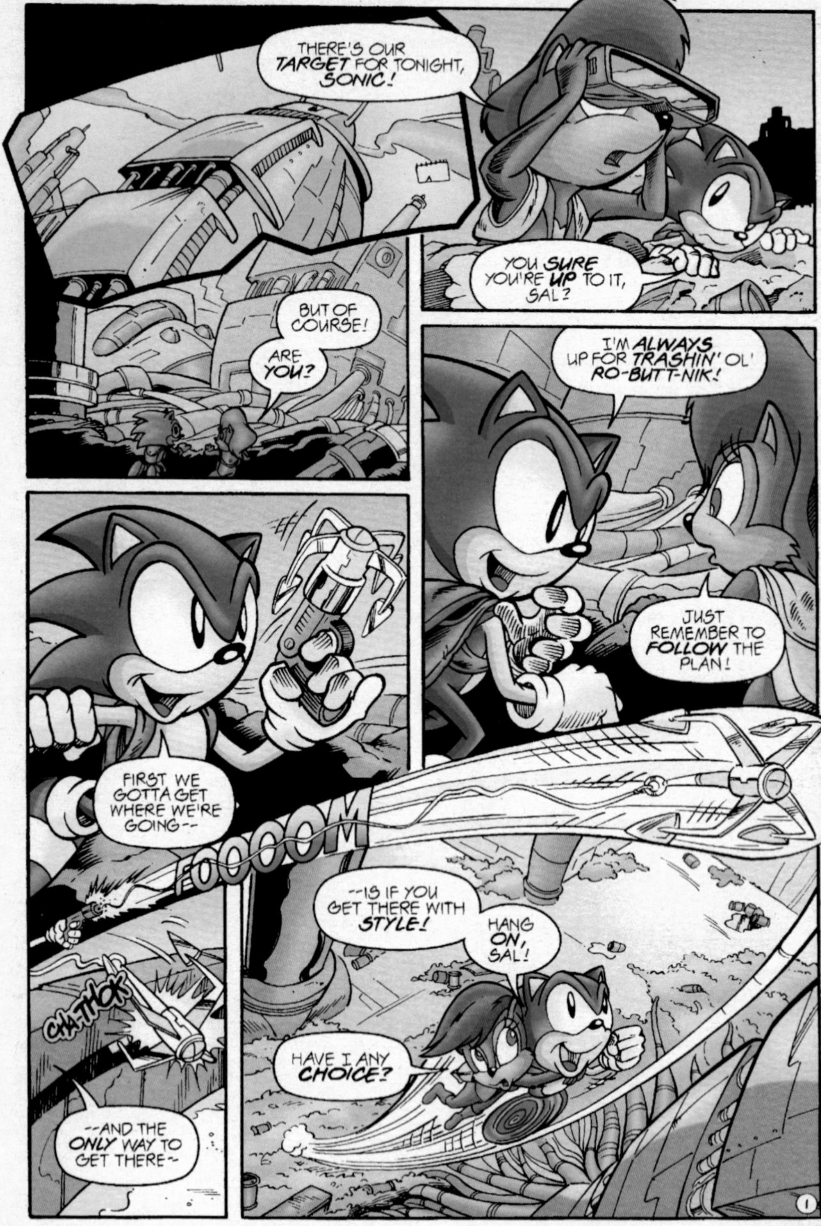
THERE'S OUR TARGET FOR TONIGHT, SONIC!
YOU SURE YOU'RE UP TO IT, SAL?
BUT OF COURSE!
ARE YOU?
I'M ALWAYS UP FOR TRASHIN' OL' RO-BUTT-NIK!
JUST REMEMBER TO FOLLOW THE PLAN!
FIRST WE GOTTA GET WHERE WE'RE GOING--
FOOOOOM
CHA-THOK
--AND THE ONLY WAY TO GET THERE--
--IS IF YOU GET THERE WITH STYLE!
HANG ON, SAL!
HAVE I ANY CHOICE?

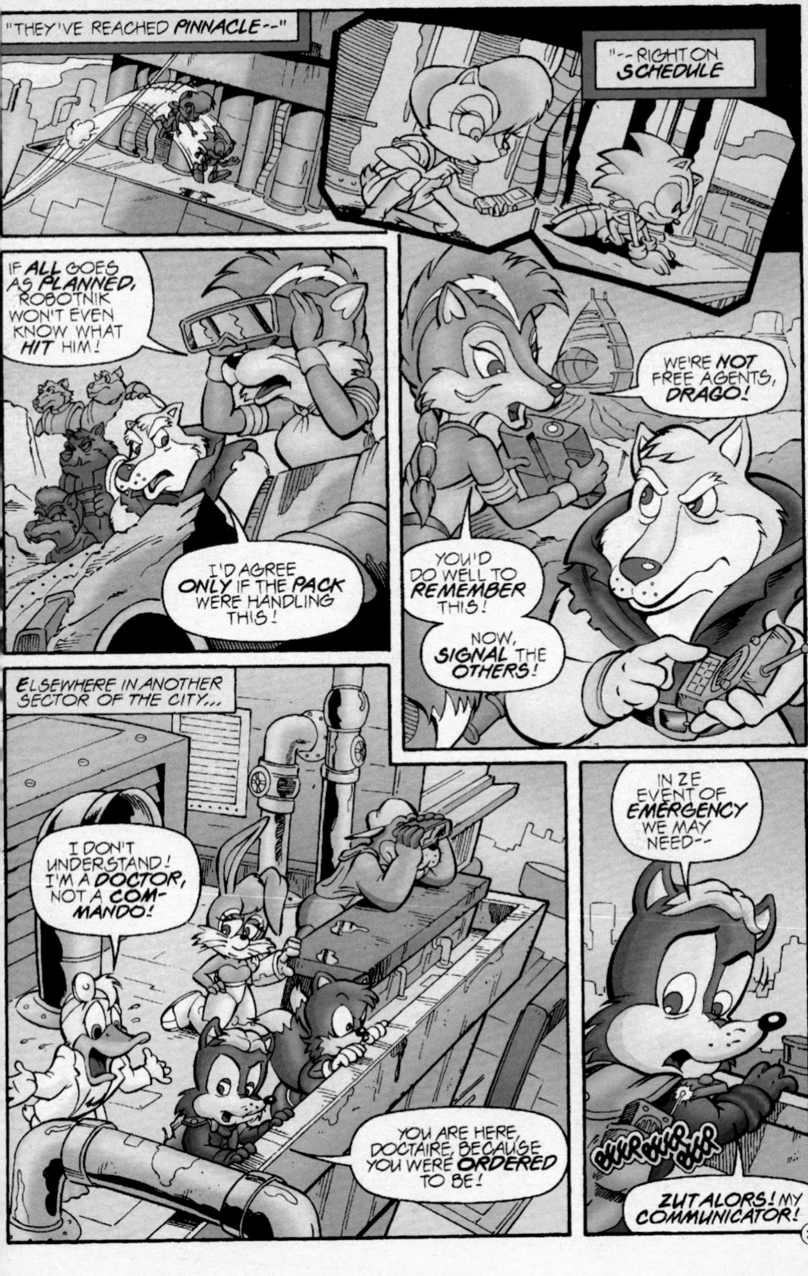
"THEY'VE REACHED PINNACLE--"
"--RIGHT ON SCHEDULE
IF ALL GOES AS PLANNED, ROBOTNIK WON'T EVEN KNOW WHAT HIT HIM!
I'D AGREE ONLY IF THE PACK WERE HANDLING THIS!
WE'RE NOT FREE AGENTS, DRAGO!
YOU'D DO WELL TO REMEMBER THIS!
NOW, SIGNAL THE OTHERS!
ELSEWHERE IN ANOTHER SECTOR OF THE CITY...
I DON'T UNDERSTAND! I'M A DOCTOR, NOT A COMMANDO!
YOU ARE HERE, DOCTAIRE, BECAUSE YOU WERE ORDERED TO BE!
IN ZE EVENT OF EMERGENCY WE MAY NEED--
ZUT ALORS! MY COMMUNICATOR!

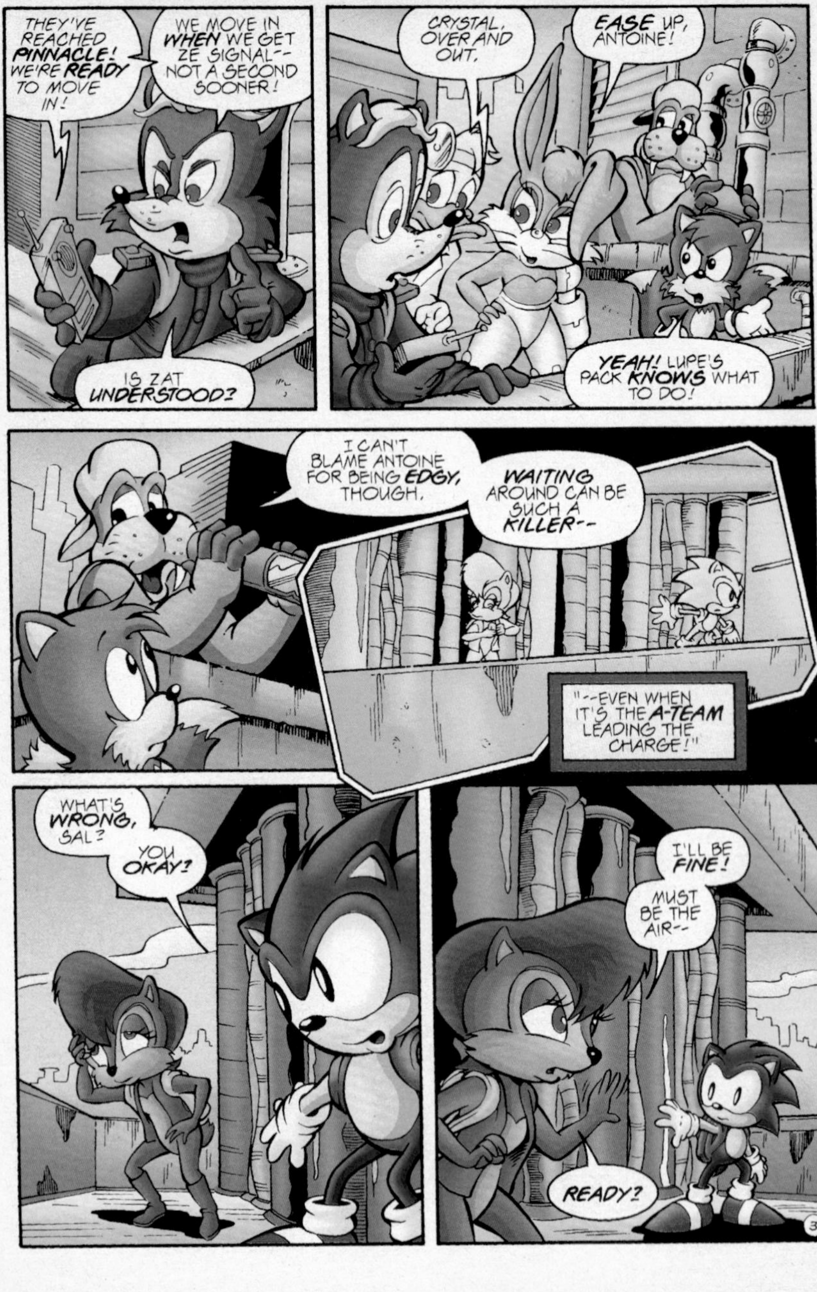
THEY'VE REACHED PINNACLE! WE'RE READY TO MOVE IN!
WE MOVE IN WHEN WE GET ZE SIGNAL--NOT A SECOND SOONER!
IS ZAT UNDERSTOOD?
CRYSTAL, OVER AND OUT.
EASE UP, ANTOINE!
YEAH! LUPE'S PACK KNOWS WHAT TO DO!
I CAN'T BLAME ANTOINE FOR BEING EDGY, THOUGH.
WAITING AROUND CAN BE SUCH A KILLER--
"--EVEN WHEN IT'S THE A-TEAM LEADING THE CHARGE!"
WHAT'S WRONG, SAL?
YOU OKAY?
I'LL BE FINE!
MUST BE THE AIR--
READY?

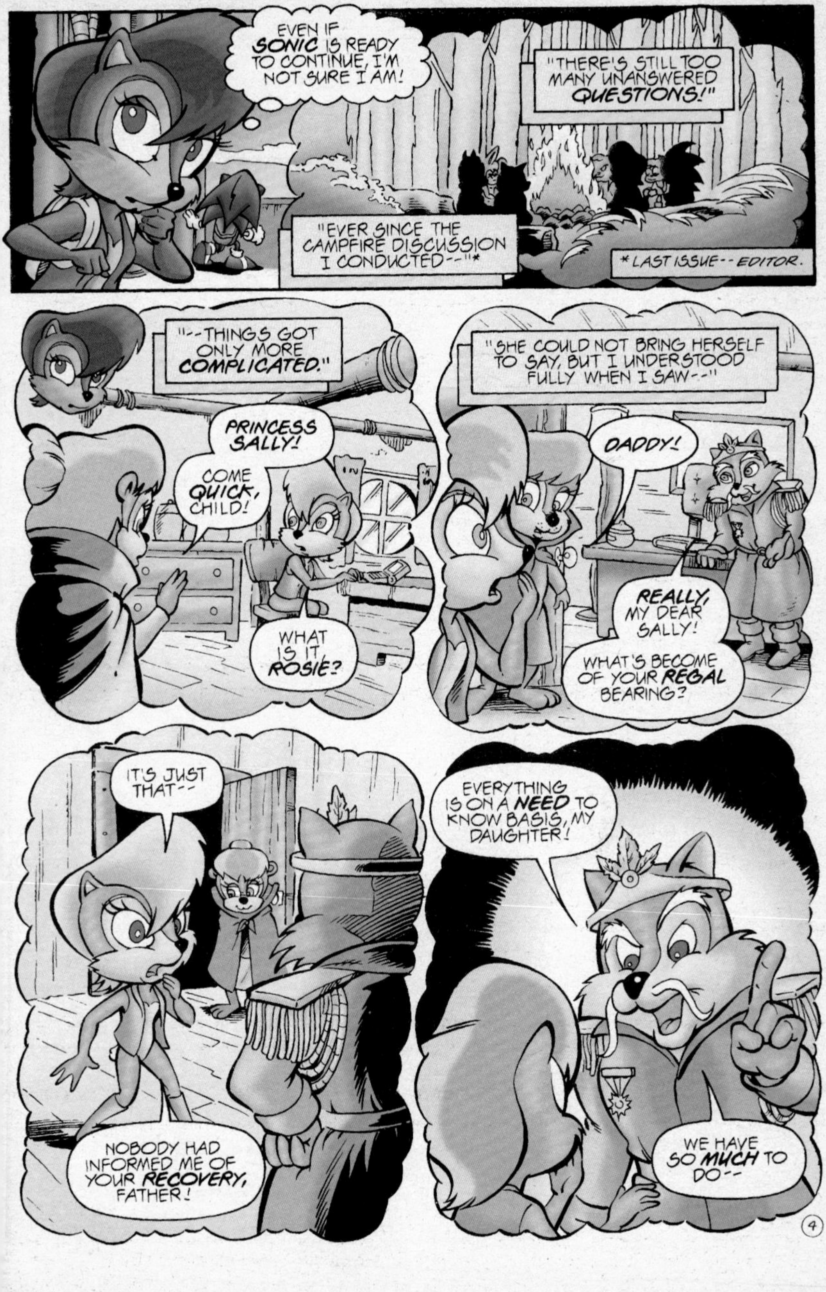
EVEN IF SONIC IS READY TO CONTINUE, I'M NOT SURE I AM!
"THERE'S STILL TOO MANY UNANSWERED QUESTIONS!"
"EVER SINCE THE CAMPFIRE DISCUSSION I CONDUCTED--"*
* LAST ISSUE--EDITOR.
"--THINGS GOT ONLY MORE COMPLICATED."
PRINCESS SALLY!
COME QUICK, CHILD!
WHAT IS IT, ROSIE?
"SHE COULD NOT BRING HERSELF TO SAY, BUT I UNDERSTOOD FULLY WHEN I SAW--"
DADDY!
REALLY, MY DEAR SALLY!
WHAT'S BECOME OF YOUR REGAL BEARING?
IT'S JUST THAT--
NOBODY HAD INFORMED ME OF YOUR RECOVERY, FATHER!
EVERYTHING IS ON A NEED TO KNOW BASIS, MY DAUGHTER!
WE HAVE SO MUCH TO DO--

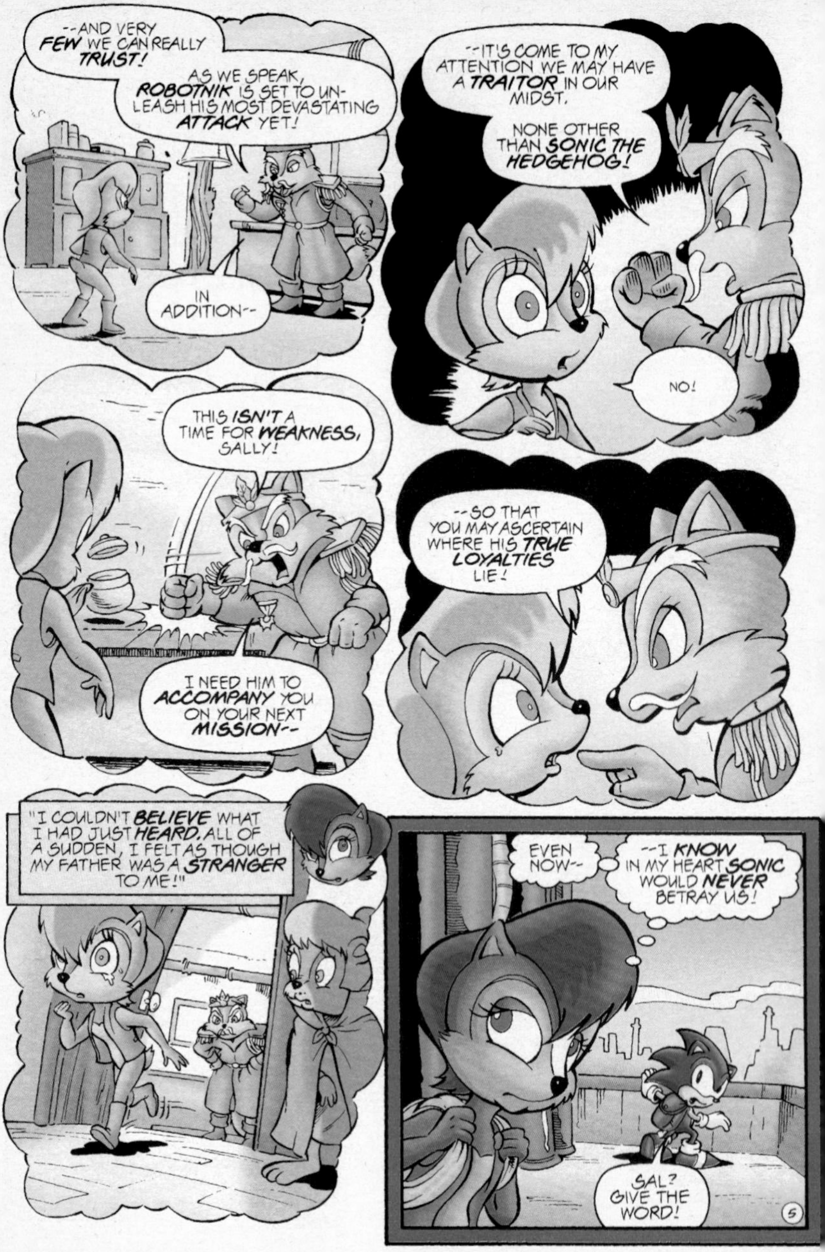
--AND VERY FEW WE CAN REALLY TRUST!
AS WE SPEAK, ROBOTNIK IS SET TO UN-LEASH HIS MOST DEVASTATING ATTACK YET!
IN ADDITION--
--IT'S COME TO MY ATTENTION WE MAY HAVE A TRAITOR IN OUR MIDST.
NONE OTHER THAN SONIC THE HEDGEHOG!
NO!
THIS ISN'T A TIME FOR WEAKNESS, SALLY!
I NEED HIM TO ACCOMPANY YOU ON YOUR NEXT MISSION--
--SO THAT YOU MAY ASCERTAIN WHERE HIS TRUE LOYALTIES LIE!
"I COULDN'T BELIEVE WHAT I HAD JUST HEARD. ALL OF A SUDDEN, I FELT AS THOUGH MY FATHER WAS A STRANGER TO ME!"
EVEN NOW--
--I KNOW IN MY HEART SONIC WOULD NEVER BETRAY US!
SAL? GIVE THE WORD!
5

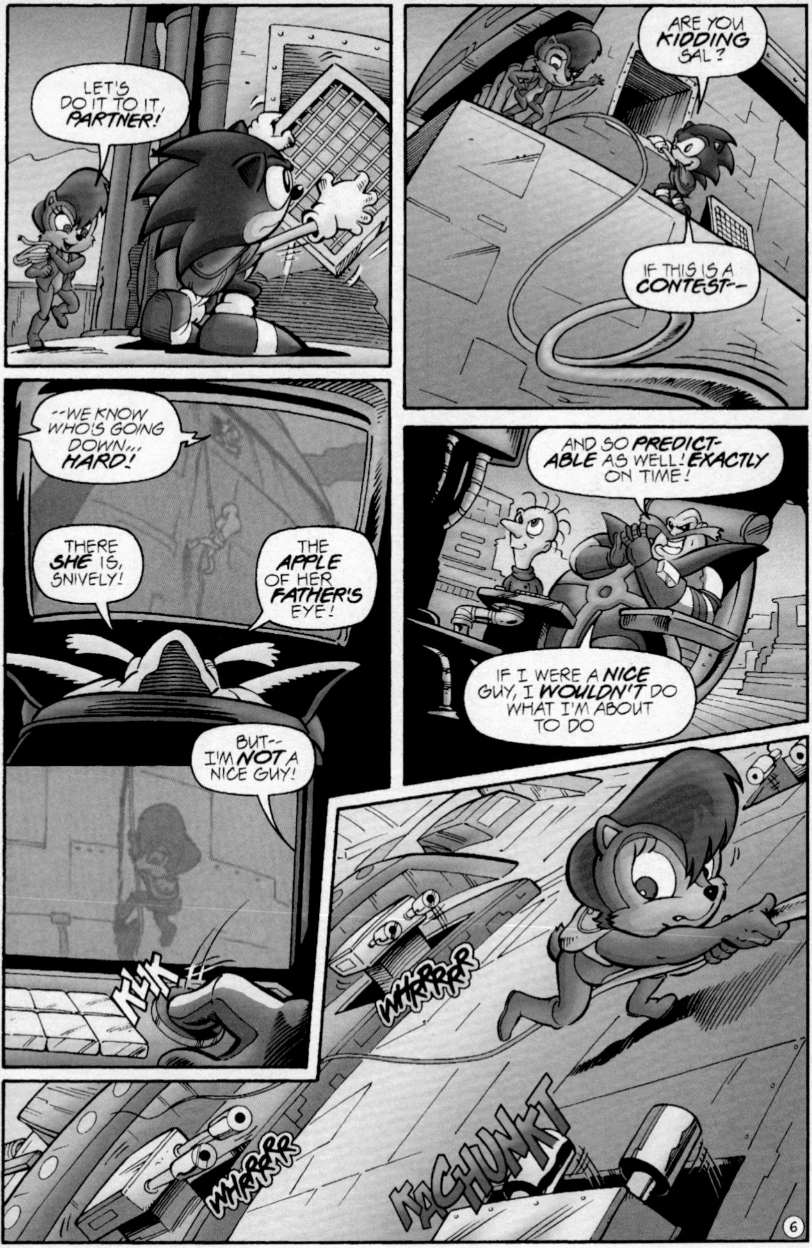
LET'S DO IT TO IT, PARTNER!
ARE YOU KIDDING SAL?
IF THIS IS A CONTEST--
--WE KNOW WHO'S GOING DOWN... HARD!
AND SO PREDICTABLE AS WELL! EXACTLY ON TIME!
THERE SHE IS, SNIVELY!
THE APPLE OF HER FATHER'S EYE!
IF I WERE A NICE GUY, I WOULDN'T DO WHAT I'M ABOUT TO DO
BUT-- I'M NOT A NICE GUY!
KLIK
WHRRRRR
WHRRRR
KACHUNKT

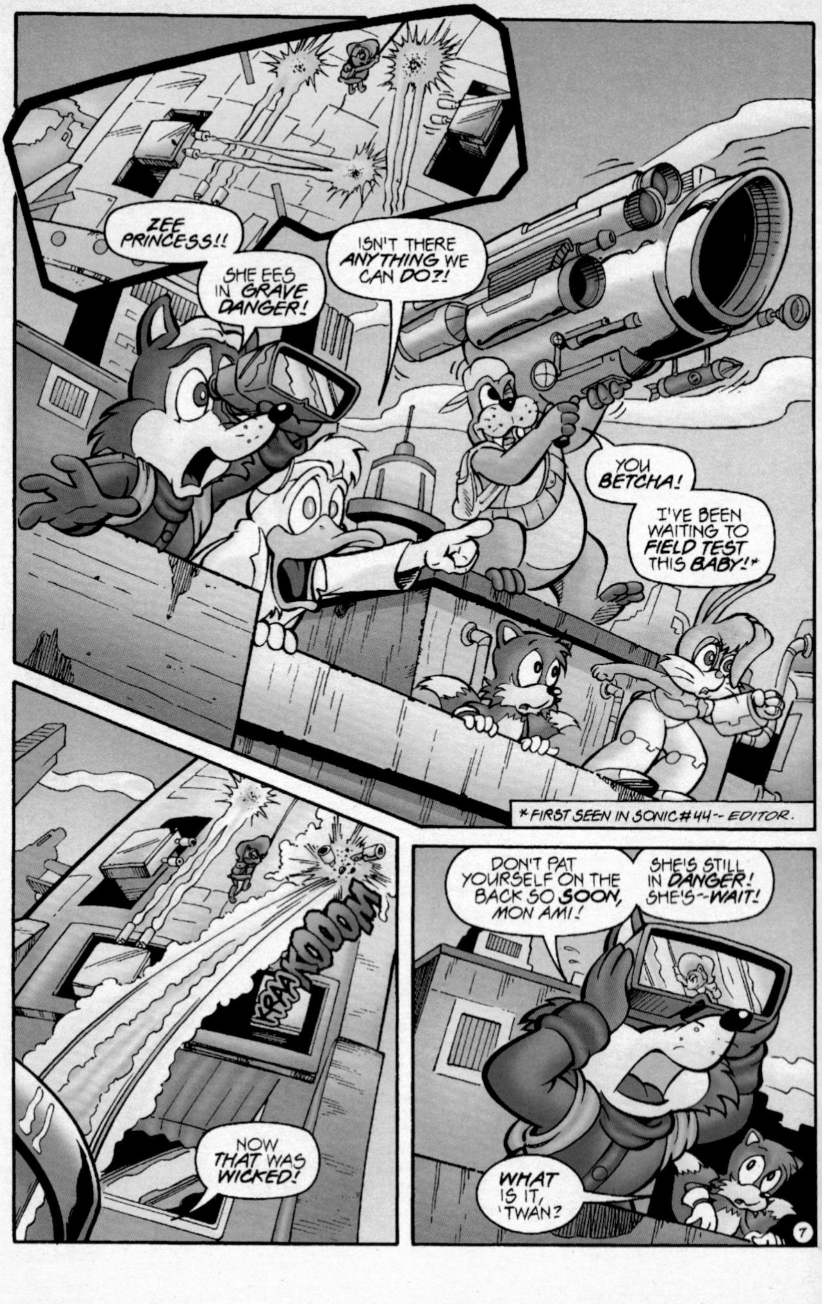
ZEE PRINCESS!!
SHE EES IN GRAVE DANGER!
ISN'T THERE ANYTHING WE CAN DO?!
YOU BETCHA!
I'VE BEEN WAITING TO FIELD TEST THIS BABY!*
*FIRST SEEN IN SONIC #44-- EDITOR.
KRAA-KOOOM
NOW THAT WAS WICKED!
DON'T PAT YOURSELF ON THE BACK SO SOON, MON AMI!
SHE'S STILL IN DANGER! SHE'S--WAIT!
WHAT IS IT, 'TWAN?
7

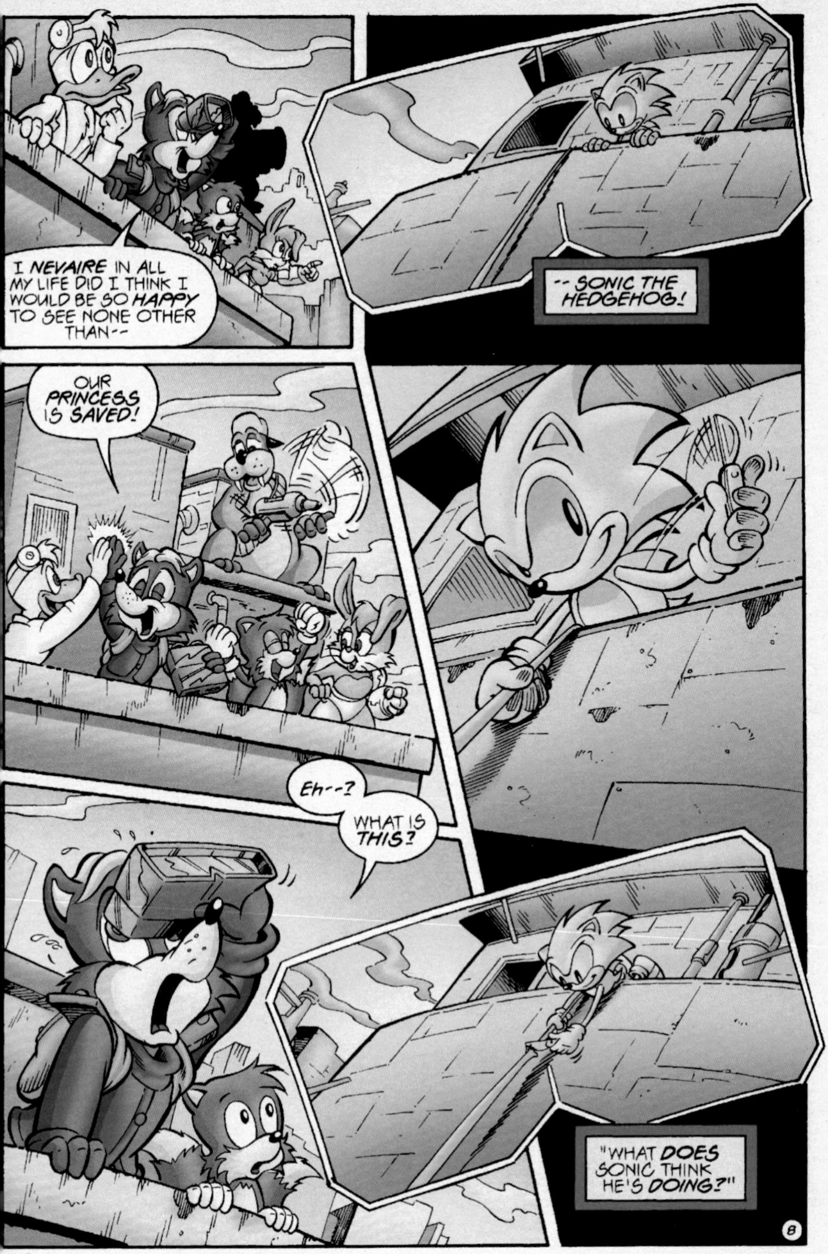

I NEVAIRE IN ALL MY LIFE DID I THINK I WOULD BE SO HAPPY TO SEE NONE OTHER THAN--
--SONIC THE HEDGEHOG!
OUR PRINCESS IS SAVED!
Eh--?
WHAT IS THIS?
"WHAT DOES SONIC THINK HE'S DOING?"

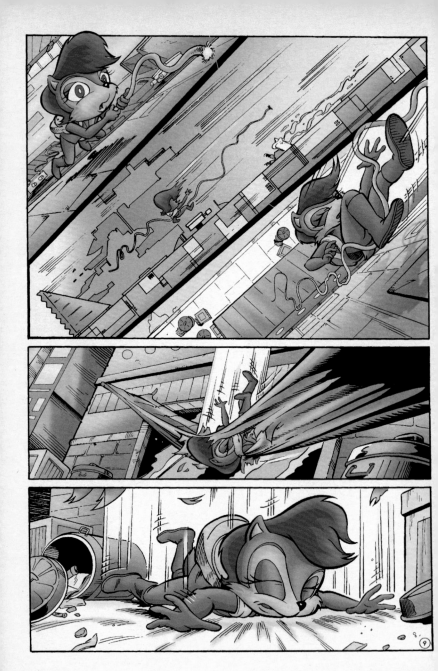

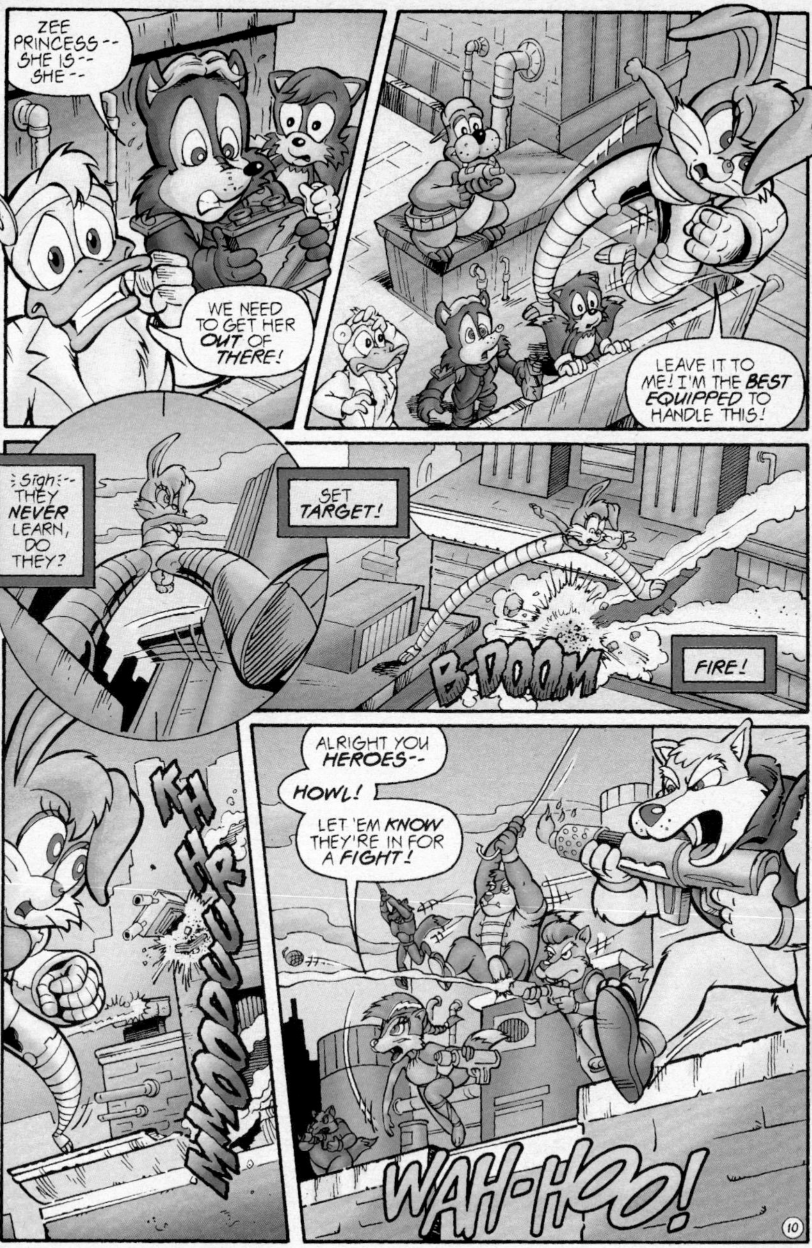

ZEE PRINCESS-- SHE IS-- SHE--
WE NEED TO GET HER OUT OF THERE!
LEAVE IT TO ME! I'M THE BEST EQUIPPED TO HANDLE THIS!
:Sigh:-- THEY NEVER LEARN, DO THEY?
SET TARGET!
B-DOOM
FIRE!
KHHR
WHOOOOOM
ALRIGHT YOU HEROES--
HOWL!
LET 'EM KNOW THEY'RE IN FOR A FIGHT!
WAH-HOO!

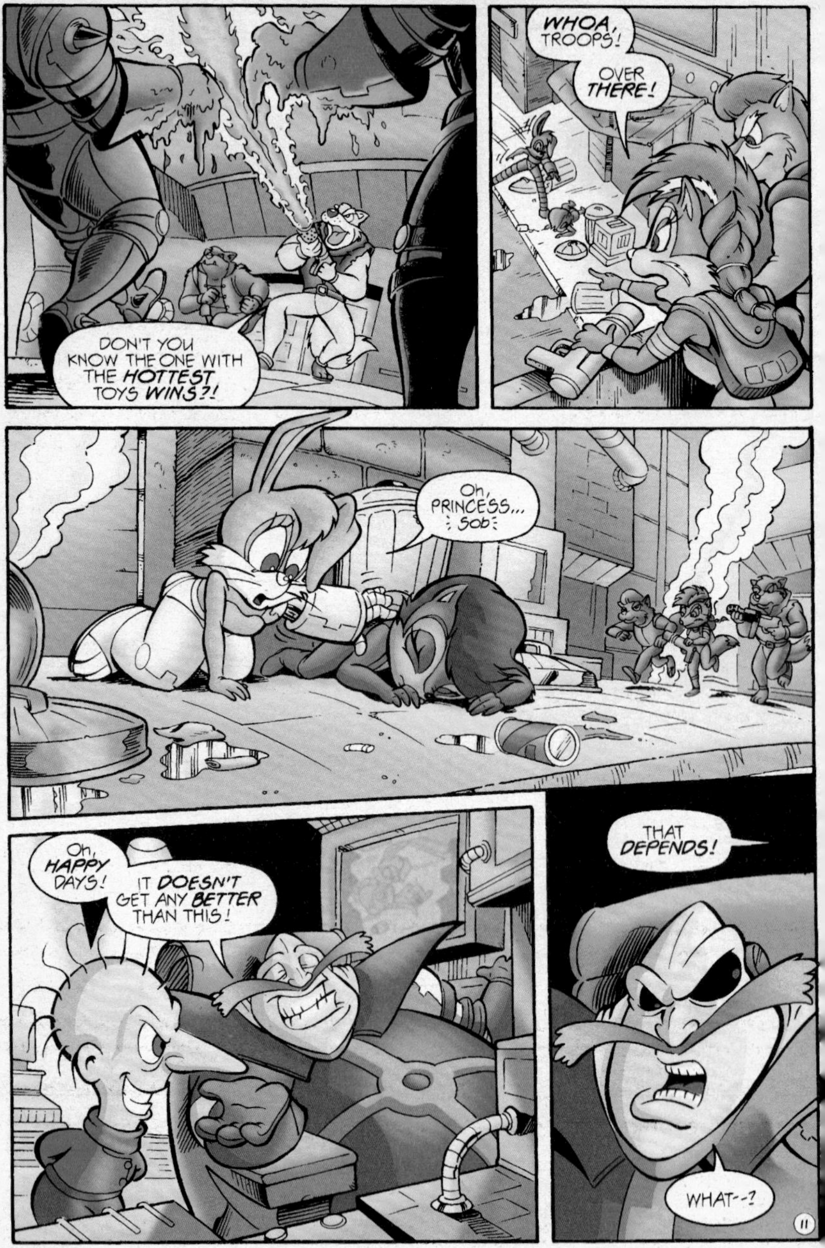
DON'T YOU KNOW THE ONE WITH THE HOTTEST TOYS WINS?!
WHOA, TROOPS!
OVER THERE!
Oh, PRINCESS... Sob
Oh, HAPPY DAYS!
IT DOESN'T GET ANY BETTER THAN THIS!
THAT DEPENDS!
WHAT--?

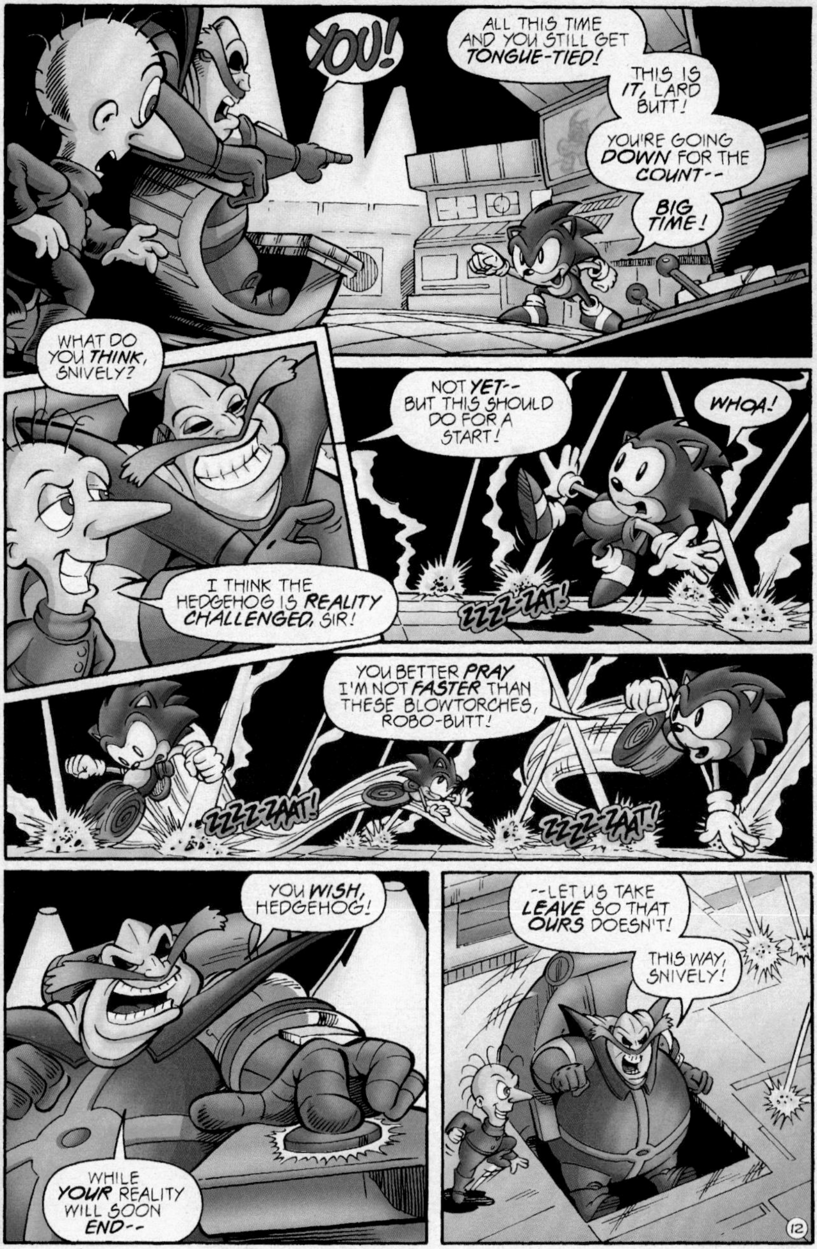
YOU!
ALL THIS TIME AND YOU STILL GET TONGUE-TIED!
THIS IS IT, LARD BUTT!
YOU'RE GOING DOWN FOR THE COUNT--
BIG TIME!
WHAT DO YOU THINK, SNIVELY?
I THINK THE HEDGEHOG IS REALITY CHALLENGED, SIR!
NOT YET--BUT THIS SHOULD DO FOR A START!
WHOA!
ZZZZ-ZAT!
YOU BETTER PRAY I'M NOT FASTER THAN THESE BLOWTORCHES, ROBO-BUTT!
ZZZZ-ZAAT!
ZZZZ-ZAAT!
YOU WISH, HEDGEHOG!
WHILE YOUR REALITY WILL SOON END--
--LET US TAKE LEAVE SO THAT OURS DOESN'T!
THIS WAY, SNIVELY!

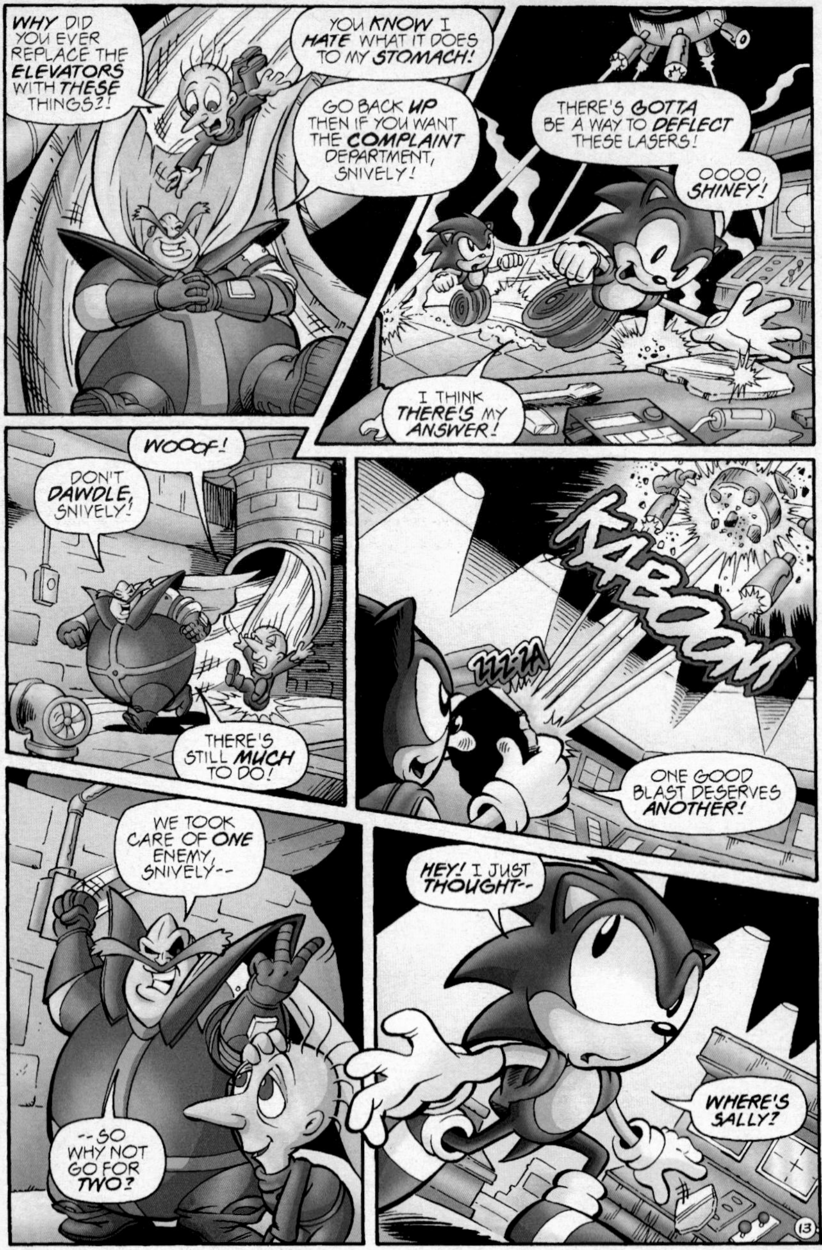
WHY DID YOU EVER REPLACE THE ELEVATORS WITH THESE THINGS?!
YOU KNOW I HATE WHAT IT DOES TO MY STOMACH!
GO BACK UP THEN IF YOU WANT THE COMPLAINT DEPARTMENT, SNIVELY!
THERE'S GOTTA BE A WAY TO DEFLECT THESE LASERS!
OOOO, SHINEY!
I THINK THERE'S MY ANSWER!
WOOOF!
DON'T DAWDLE, SNIVELY!
THERE'S STILL MUCH TO DO!
KABOOM
ZZZ-ZA
ONE GOOD BLAST DESERVES ANOTHER!
WE TOOK CARE OF ONE ENEMY, SNIVELY--
--SO WHY NOT GO FOR TWO?
HEY! I JUST THOUGHT--
WHERE'S SALLY?

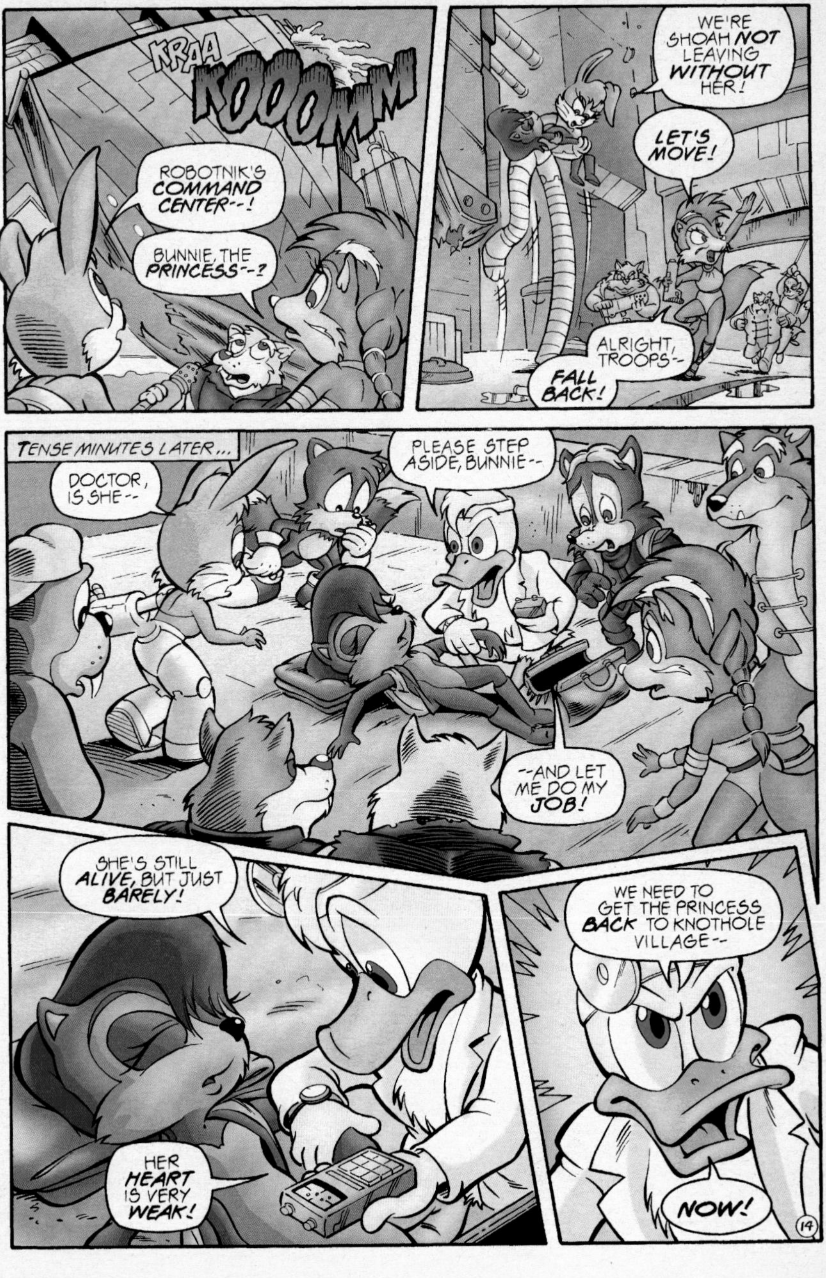
KRAA KOOOMM
ROBOTNIK'S COMMAND CENTER--!
BUNNIE, THE PRINCESS--?
WE'RE SHOAH NOT LEAVING WITHOUT HER!
LET'S MOVE!
ALRIGHT, TROOPS--
FALL BACK!
TENSE MINUTES LATER...
DOCTOR, IS SHE--
PLEASE STEP ASIDE, BUNNIE--
--AND LET ME DO MY JOB!
SHE'S STILL ALIVE, BUT JUST BARELY!
HER HEART IS VERY WEAK!
WE NEED TO GET THE PRINCESS BACK TO KNOTHOLE VILLAGE--
NOW!
14

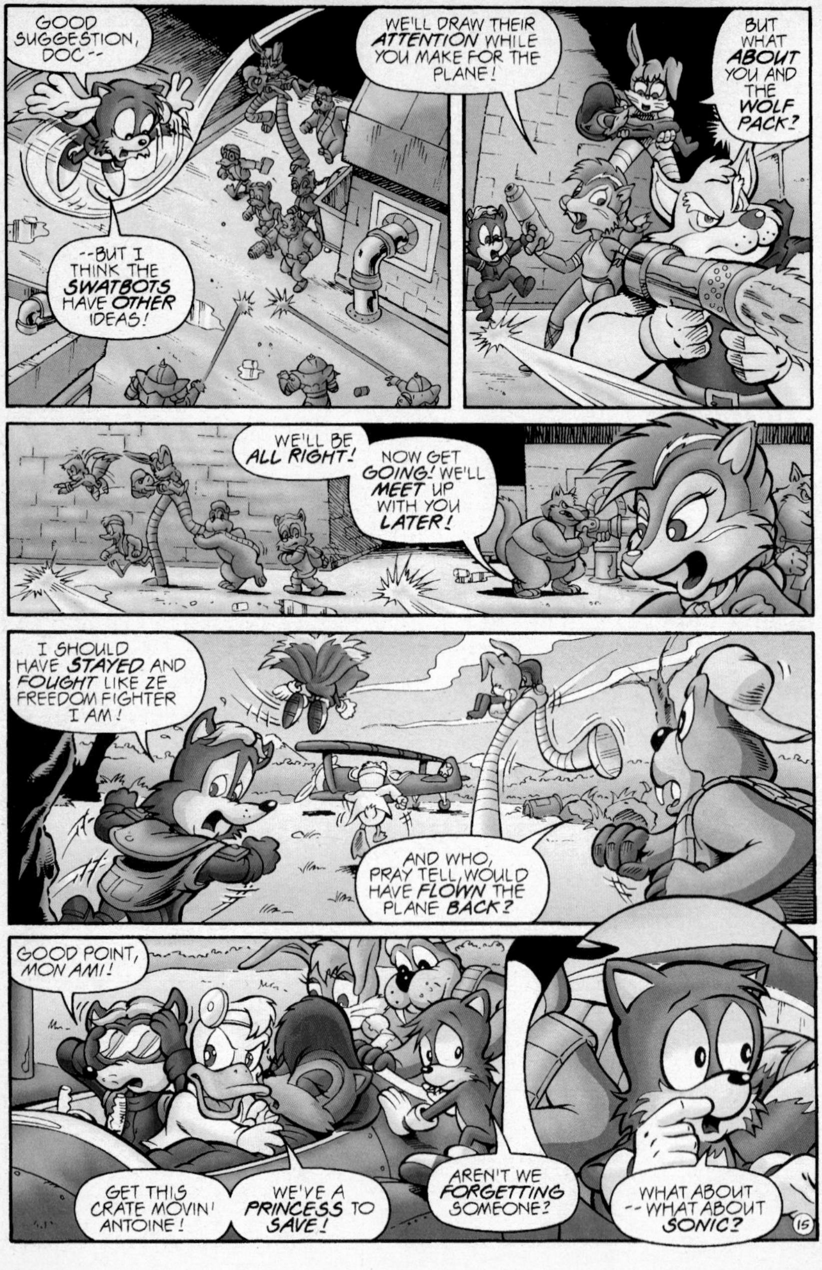
GOOD SUGGESTION, DOC--
--BUT I THINK THE SWATBOTS HAVE OTHER IDEAS!
WE'LL DRAW THEIR ATTENTION WHILE YOU MAKE FOR THE PLANE!
BUT WHAT ABOUT YOU AND THE WOLF PACK?
WE'LL BE ALL RIGHT!
NOW GET GOING! WE'LL MEET UP WITH YOU LATER!
I SHOULD HAVE STAYED AND FOUGHT LIKE ZE FREEDOM FIGHTER I AM!
AND WHO, PRAY TELL, WOULD HAVE FLOWN THE PLANE BACK?
GOOD POINT, MON AMI!
GET THIS CRATE MOVIN' ANTOINE!
WE'VE A PRINCESS TO SAVE!
AREN'T WE FORGETTING SOMEONE?
WHAT ABOUT --WHAT ABOUT SONIC?
15

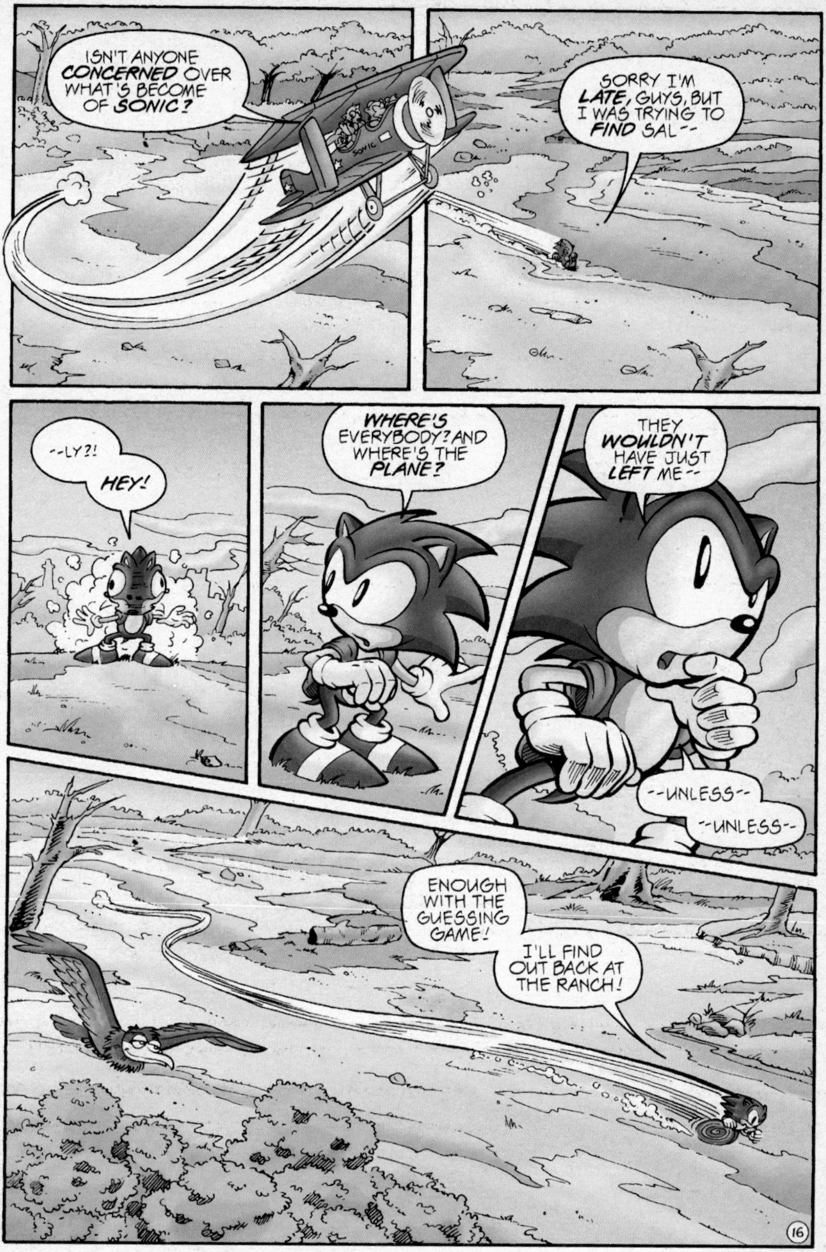
ISN'T ANYONE CONCERNED OVER WHAT'S BECOME OF SONIC?
SONIC
SORRY I'M LATE, GUYS, BUT I WAS TRYING TO FIND SAL--
--LY?!
HEY!
WHERE'S EVERYBODY? AND WHERE'S THE PLANE?
THEY WOULDN'T HAVE JUST LEFT ME--
--UNLESS--
--UNLESS--
ENOUGH WITH THE GUESSING GAME!
I'LL FIND OUT BACK AT THE RANCH!

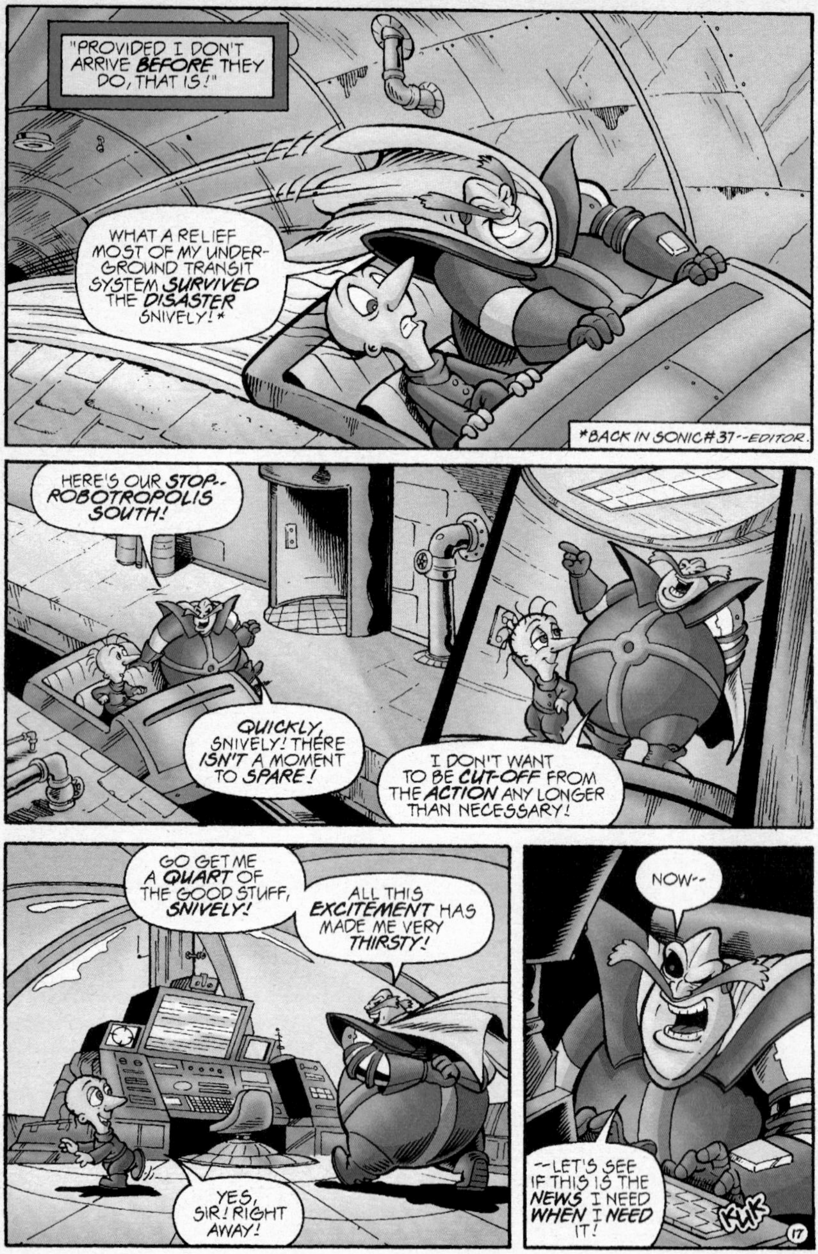
"PROVIDED I DON'T ARRIVE BEFORE THEY DO, THAT IS!"
WHAT A RELIEF MOST OF MY UNDER-GROUND TRANSIT SYSTEM SURVIVED THE DISASTER SNIVELY! *
*BACK IN SONIC #37--EDITOR.
HERE'S OUR STOP-- ROBOTROPOLIS SOUTH!
QUICKLY, SNIVELY! THERE ISN'T A MOMENT TO SPARE!
I DON'T WANT TO BE CUT-OFF FROM THE ACTION ANY LONGER THAN NECESSARY!
GO GET ME A QUART OF THE GOOD STUFF, SNIVELY!
ALL THIS EXCITEMENT HAS MADE ME VERY THIRSTY!
YES, SIR! RIGHT AWAY!
NOW--
--LET'S SEE IF THIS IS THE NEWS I NEED WHEN I NEED IT!
KLIK

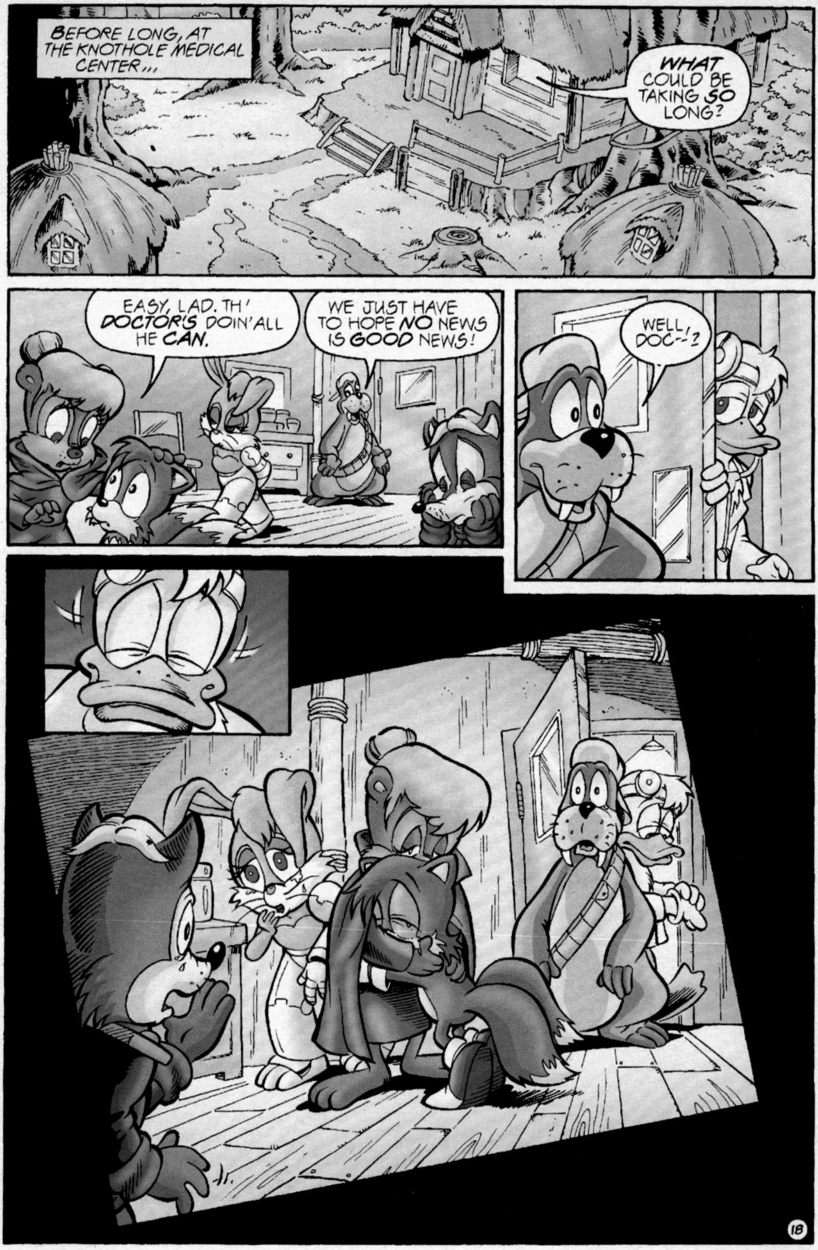
BEFORE LONG, AT THE KNOTHOLE MEDICAL CENTER...
WHAT COULD BE TAKING SO LONG?
EASY, LAD. TH' DOCTOR'S DOIN' ALL HE CAN.
WE JUST HAVE TO HOPE NO NEWS IS GOOD NEWS!
WELL, DOC--!?

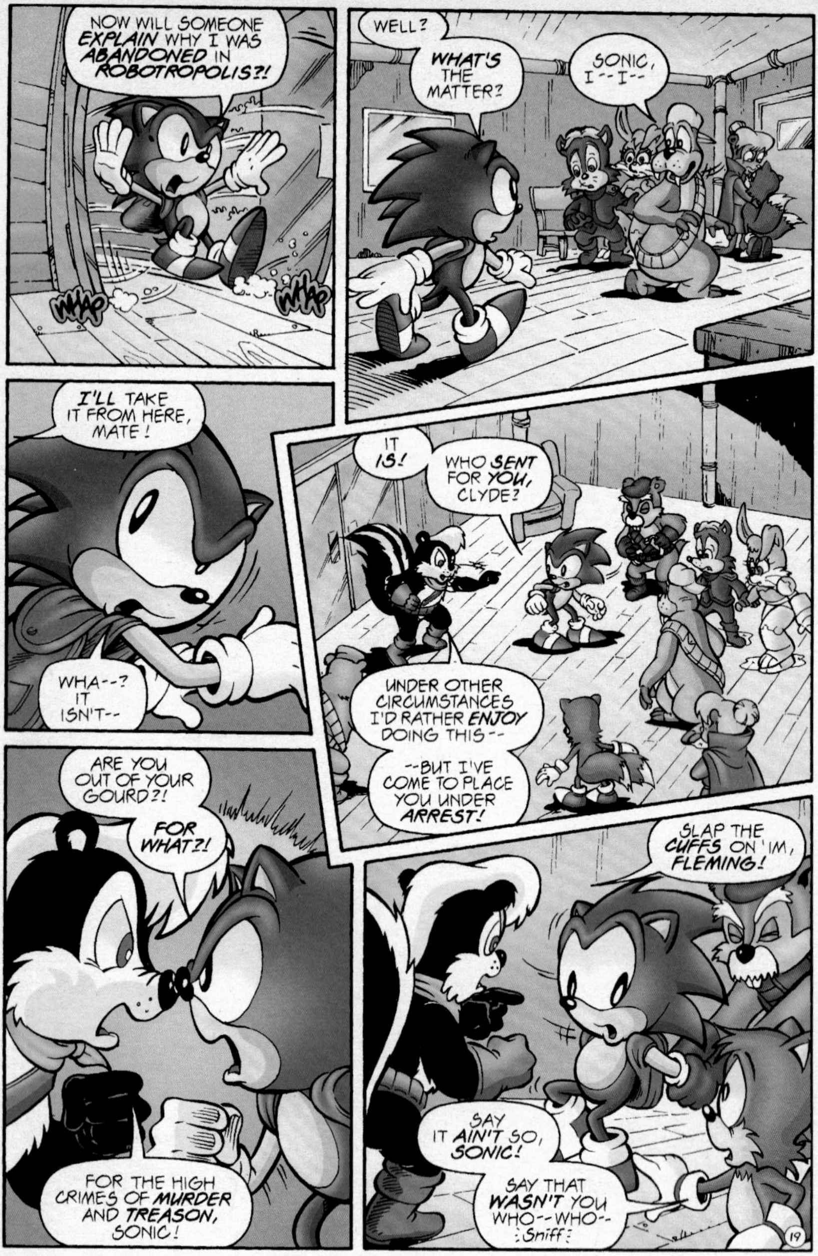
NOW WILL SOMEONE EXPLAIN WHY I WAS ABANDONED IN ROBOTROPOLIS?!
WHAP
WHAP
WELL?
WHAT'S THE MATTER?
SONIC, I--I--
I'LL TAKE IT FROM HERE, MATE!
WHA--? IT ISN'T--
IT IS!
WHO SENT FOR YOU, CLYDE?
UNDER OTHER CIRCUMSTANCES I'D RATHER ENJOY DOING THIS--
--BUT I'VE COME TO PLACE YOU UNDER ARREST!
ARE YOU OUT OF YOUR GOURD?!
FOR WHAT?!
FOR THE HIGH CRIMES OF MURDER AND TREASON, SONIC!
SLAP THE CUFFS ON 'IM, FLEMING!
SAY IT AIN'T SO, SONIC!
SAY THAT WASN'T YOU WHO--WHO--
:Sniff:

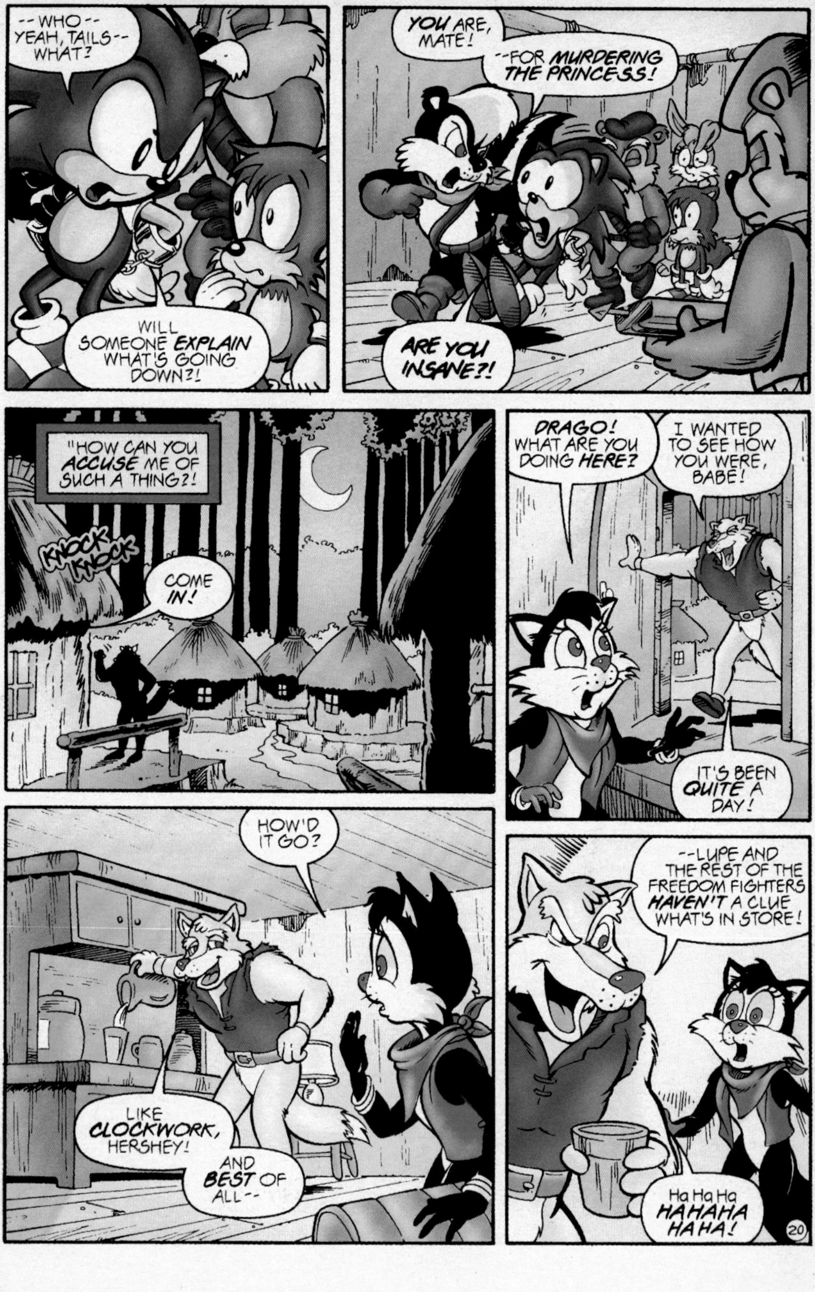
--WHO--
YEAH, TAILS--
WHAT?
WILL SOMEONE EXPLAIN WHAT'S GOING DOWN?!
YOU ARE, MATE!
--FOR MURDERING THE PRINCESS!
ARE YOU INSANE?!
"HOW CAN YOU ACCUSE ME OF SUCH A THING?!
KNOCK KNOCK
COME IN!
DRAGO! WHAT ARE YOU DOING HERE?
I WANTED TO SEE HOW YOU WERE, BABE!
IT'S BEEN QUITE A DAY!
HOW'D IT GO?
LIKE CLOCKWORK, HERSHEY!
AND BEST OF ALL--
--LUPE AND THE REST OF THE FREEDOM FIGHTERS HAVEN'T A CLUE WHAT'S IN STORE!
Ha Ha Ha HAHAHA HAHA!
20

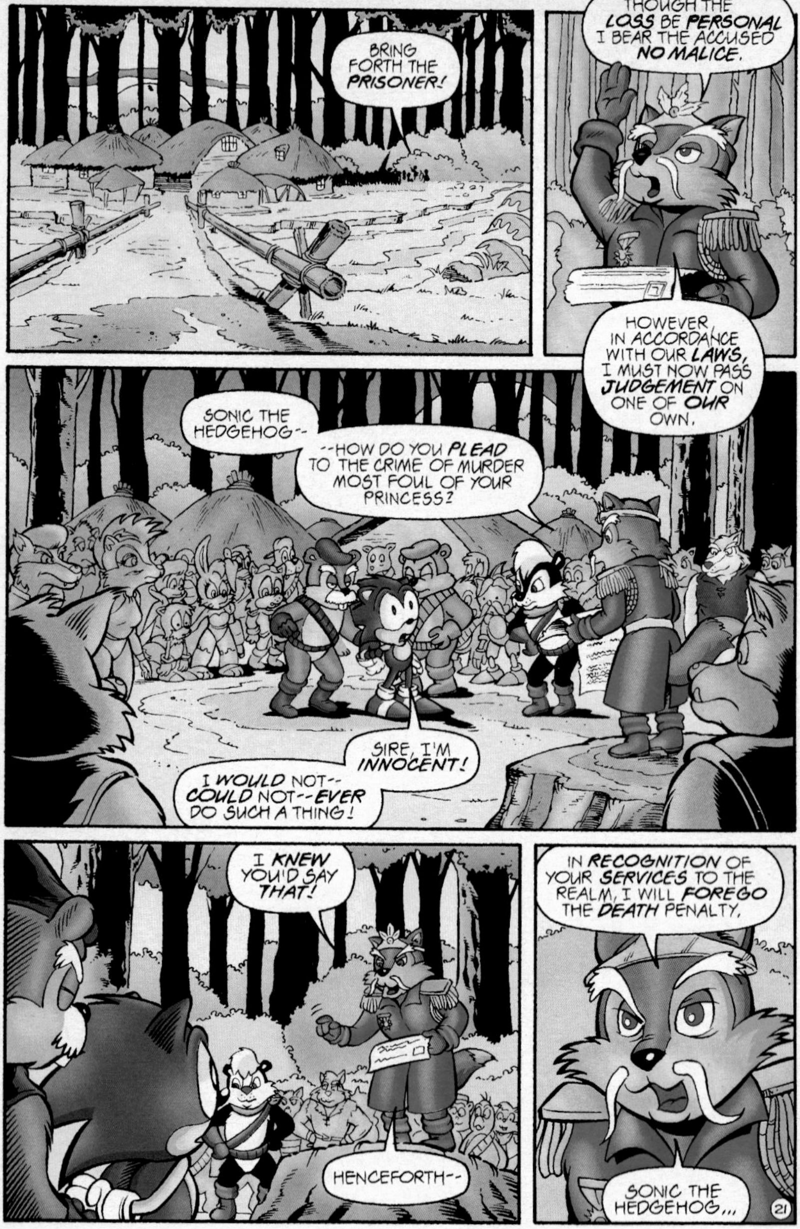
BRING FORTH THE PRISONER!
THOUGH THE LOSS BE PERSONAL I BEAR THE ACCUSED NO MALICE.
HOWEVER, IN ACCORDANCE WITH OUR LAWS, I MUST NOW PASS JUDGEMENT ON ONE OF OUR OWN.
SONIC THE HEDGEHOG--
--HOW DO YOU PLEAD TO THE CRIME OF MURDER MOST FOUL OF YOUR PRINCESS?
SIRE, I'M INNOCENT!
I WOULD NOT--COULD NOT--EVER DO SUCH A THING!
I KNEW YOU'D SAY THAT!
HENCEFORTH--
IN RECOGNITION OF YOUR SERVICES TO THE REALM, I WILL FOREGO THE DEATH PENALTY.
SONIC THE HEDGEHOG,,,
21

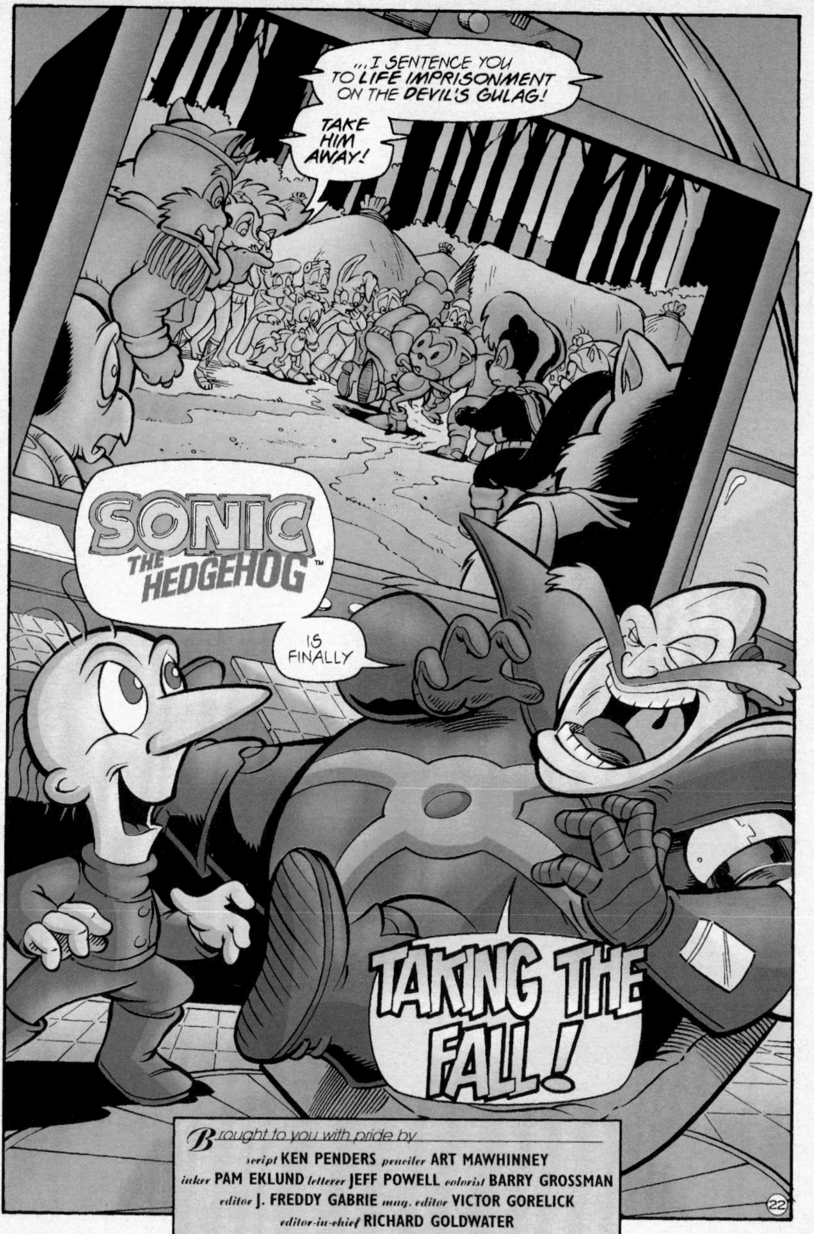

...I SENTENCE YOU TO LIFE IMPRISONMENT ON THE DEVIL'S GULAG!
TAKE HIM AWAY!
SONIC THE HEDGEHOG™
IS FINALLY
TAKING THE FALL!
Brought to you with pride by
script KEN PENDERS penciler ART MAWHINNEY
inker PAM EKLUND letterer JEFF POWELL colorist BARRY GROSSMAN
editor J. FREDDY GABRIE mng. editor VICTOR GORELICK
editor-in-chief RICHARD GOLDWATER
22

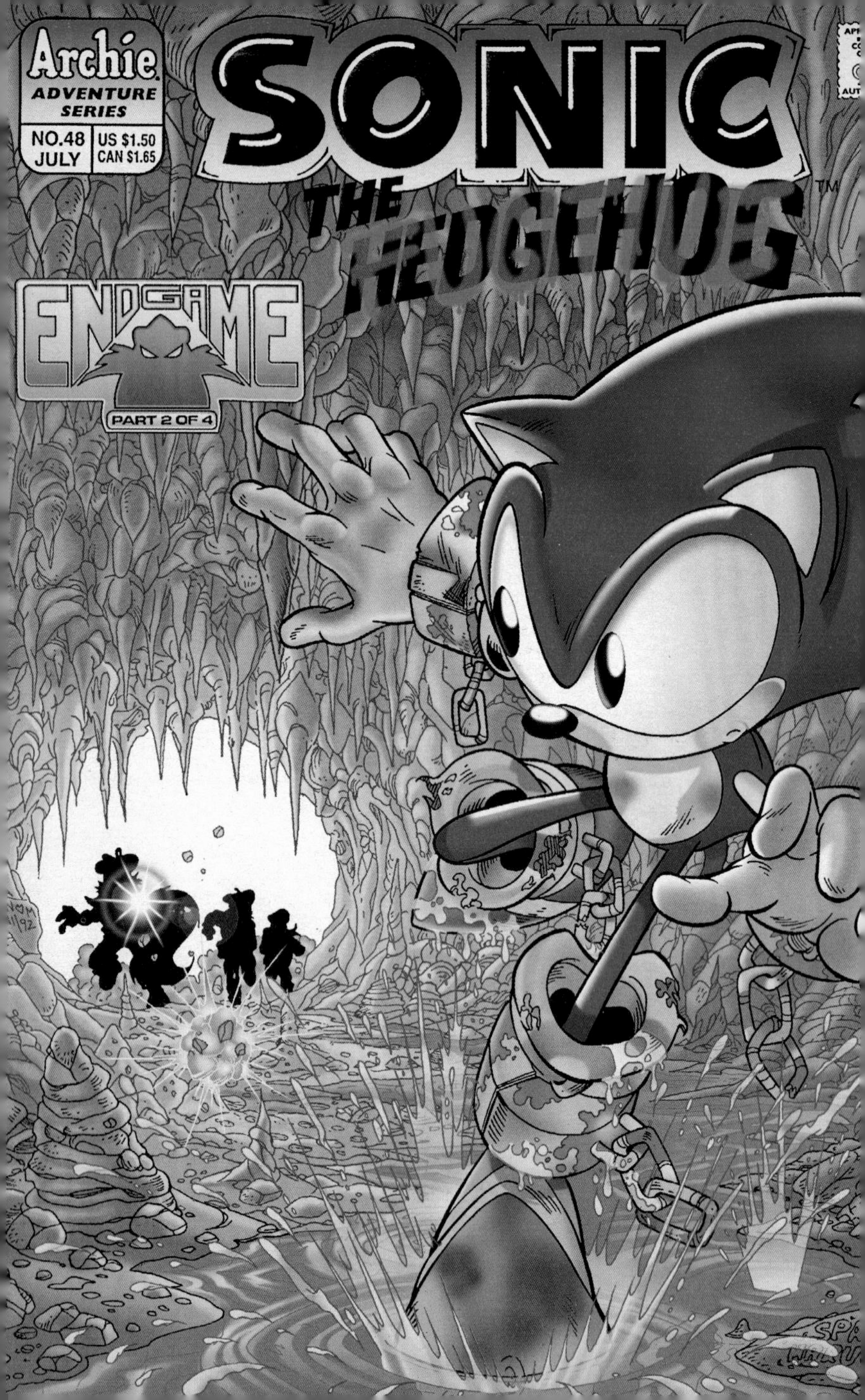
Archie
ADVENTURE SERIES
NO.48
JULY
US $1.50
CAN $1.65
SONIC THE HEDGEHOG™
ENDGAME
PART 2 OF 4

Years ago, most of the young residents of **Planet Mobius** were forced into war, defending themselves against the conspiracy of **Julian**, former **Warlord** of the **Kingdom of Acorn**. Most notable of these "Freedom Fighters" is a team led by the King's own daughter, and championed by the swiftest hero in the land. While their past efforts have been valiant, they have been a far cry from the total defeat of the rechristened **Dr. Robotnik**.

When their former sire staged a miraculous return to health, fortune seemed to shine on our stalwart heroes. The glistening hope of more experienced **leadership** paved the way for potential salvation.

Alas, it was not to be...

During their latest mission, **Princess Sally Acorn** met sudden tragedy. Returned to **Knothole Village**, she was pronounced **DEAD**. Almost as tragic was the revelation that she died at the hands of... **Sonic The Hedgehog** himself!

Pronouncing sentence, the king condemned the "former" hero to a life of imprisonment. While it is clear that treachery and deceit abound, it is equally unclear who all the conspirators are of this swift **injustice**. While it is certain that the dark forces of **Robotropolis** are preparing their next move, it is equally uncertain whether our heroes will rally, recreating the former glory of the once-gleaming city of **Mobotropolis**.

One thing cannot be disputed — no one will ever be the same...

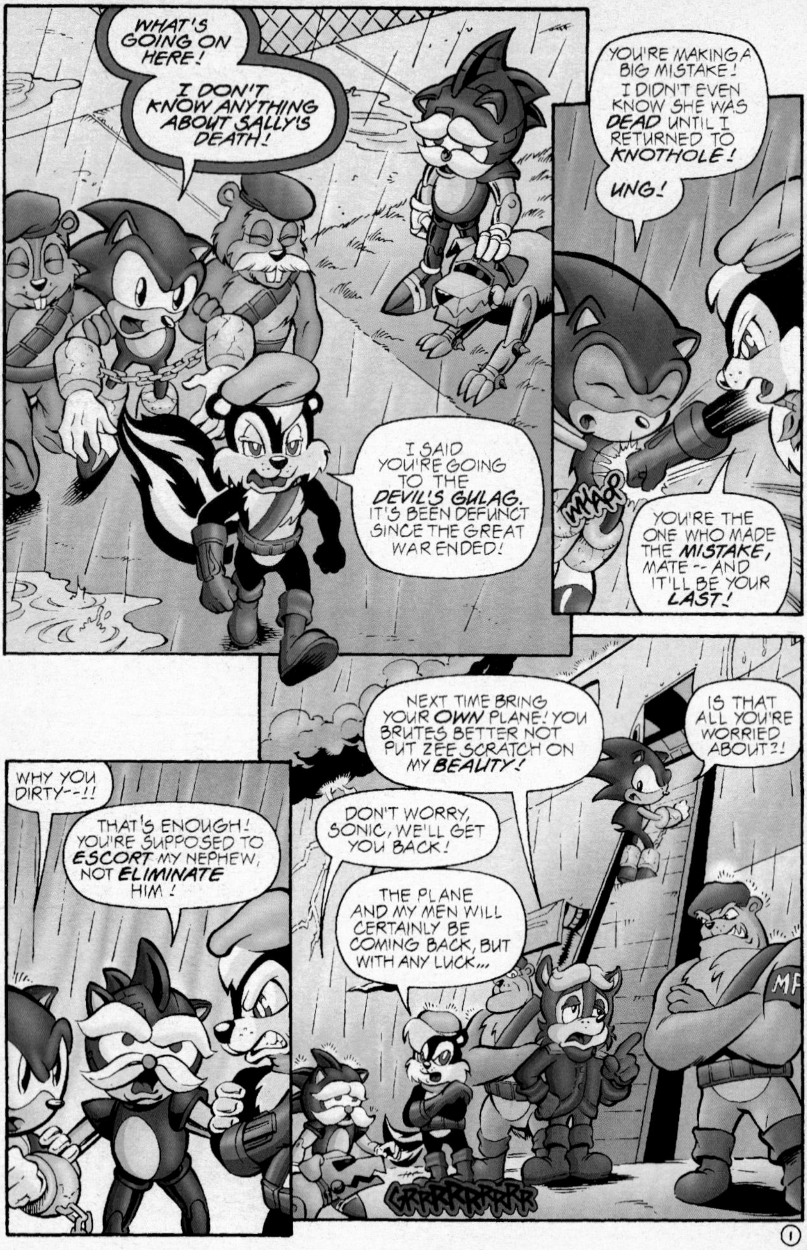
WHAT'S GOING ON HERE!
I DON'T KNOW ANYTHING ABOUT SALLY'S DEATH!
I SAID YOU'RE GOING TO THE DEVIL'S GULAG. IT'S BEEN DEFUNCT SINCE THE GREAT WAR ENDED!
YOU'RE MAKING A BIG MISTAKE! I DIDN'T EVEN KNOW SHE WAS DEAD UNTIL I RETURNED TO KNOTHOLE!
UNG!
WHAP
YOU'RE THE ONE WHO MADE THE MISTAKE, MATE -- AND IT'LL BE YOUR LAST!
WHY YOU DIRTY--!!
THAT'S ENOUGH! YOU'RE SUPPOSED TO ESCORT MY NEPHEW, NOT ELIMINATE HIM!
NEXT TIME BRING YOUR OWN PLANE! YOU BRUTES BETTER NOT PUT ZEE SCRATCH ON MY BEAUTY!
IS THAT ALL YOU'RE WORRIED ABOUT?!
DON'T WORRY, SONIC, WE'LL GET YOU BACK!
THE PLANE AND MY MEN WILL CERTAINLY BE COMING BACK, BUT WITH ANY LUCK...
MP
GRRRRRRRRR

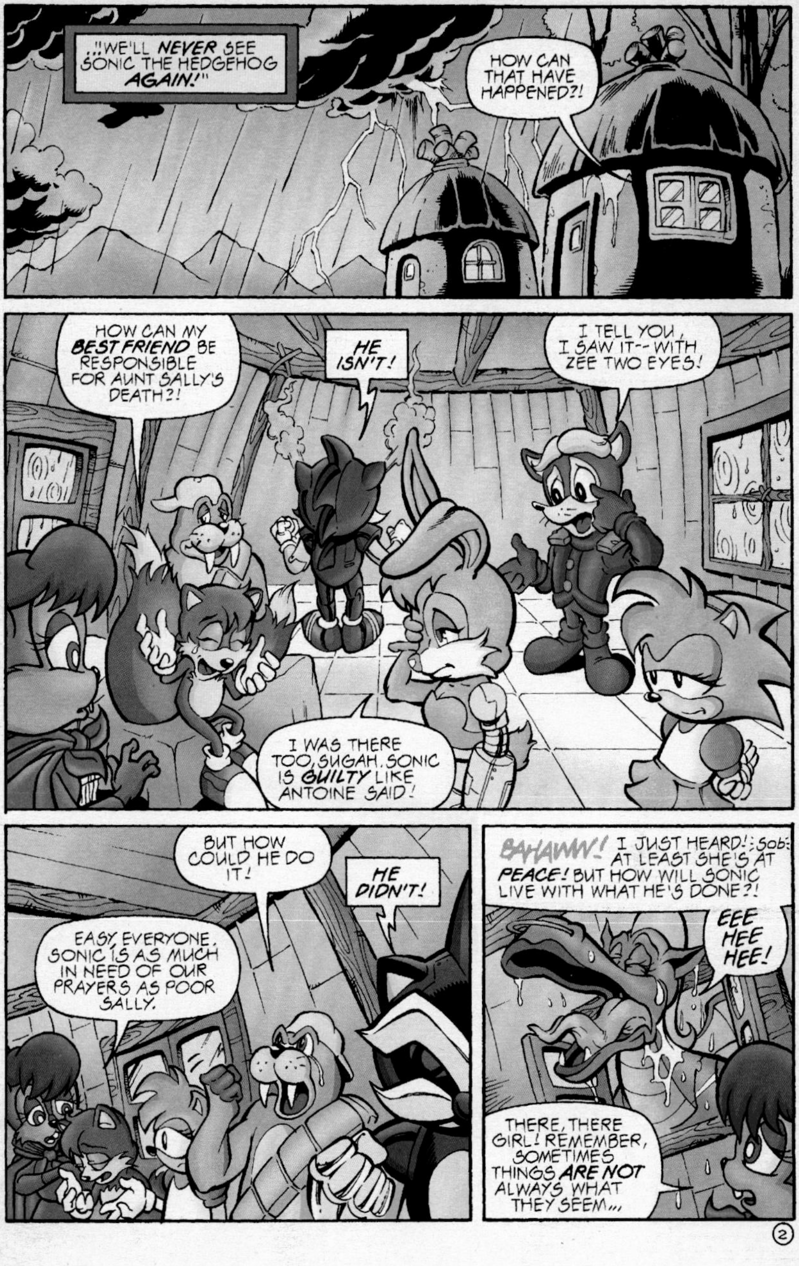
"...WE'LL NEVER SEE SONIC THE HEDGEHOG AGAIN!"
HOW CAN THAT HAVE HAPPENED?!
HOW CAN MY BEST FRIEND BE RESPONSIBLE FOR AUNT SALLY'S DEATH?!
HE ISN'T!
I TELL YOU, I SAW IT-- WITH ZEE TWO EYES!
I WAS THERE TOO, SUGAH. SONIC IS GUILTY LIKE ANTOINE SAID!
BUT HOW COULD HE DO IT!
HE DIDN'T!
EASY, EVERYONE. SONIC IS AS MUCH IN NEED OF OUR PRAYERS AS POOR SALLY.
BAHAWW! I JUST HEARD! :SOB: AT LEAST SHE'S AT PEACE! BUT HOW WILL SONIC LIVE WITH WHAT HE'S DONE?!
EEE HEE HEE!
THERE, THERE GIRL! REMEMBER, SOMETIMES THINGS ARE NOT ALWAYS WHAT THEY SEEM...

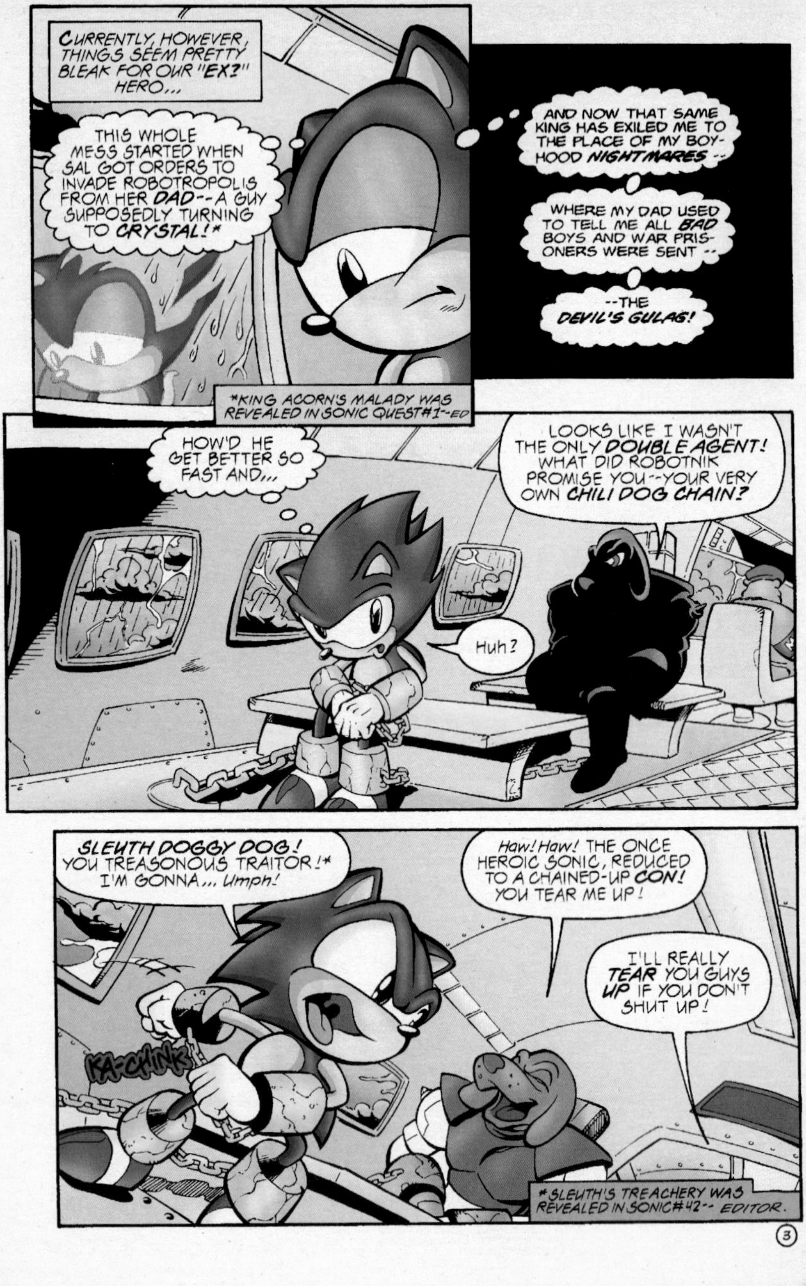

CURRENTLY, HOWEVER, THINGS SEEM PRETTY BLEAK FOR OUR "EX?" HERO...
THIS WHOLE MESS STARTED WHEN SAL GOT ORDERS TO INVADE ROBOTROPOLIS FROM HER DAD--A GUY SUPPOSEDLY TURNING TO CRYSTAL!*
AND NOW THAT SAME KING HAS EXILED ME TO THE PLACE OF MY BOYHOOD NIGHTMARES--
WHERE MY DAD USED TO TELL ME ALL BAD BOYS AND WAR PRISONERS WERE SENT--
--THE DEVIL'S GULAG!
*KING ACORN'S MALADY WAS REVEALED IN SONIC QUEST #1--ED
HOW'D HE GET BETTER SO FAST AND...
LOOKS LIKE I WASN'T THE ONLY DOUBLE AGENT! WHAT DID ROBOTNIK PROMISE YOU--YOUR VERY OWN CHILI DOG CHAIN?
Huh?
SLEUTH DOGGY DOG! YOU TREASONOUS TRAITOR!* I'M GONNA... Umph!
Haw! Haw! THE ONCE HEROIC SONIC, REDUCED TO A CHAINED-UP CON! YOU TEAR ME UP!
I'LL REALLY TEAR YOU GUYS UP IF YOU DON'T SHUT UP!
KA-CHINK
*SLEUTH'S TREACHERY WAS REVEALED IN SONIC #42-- EDITOR.

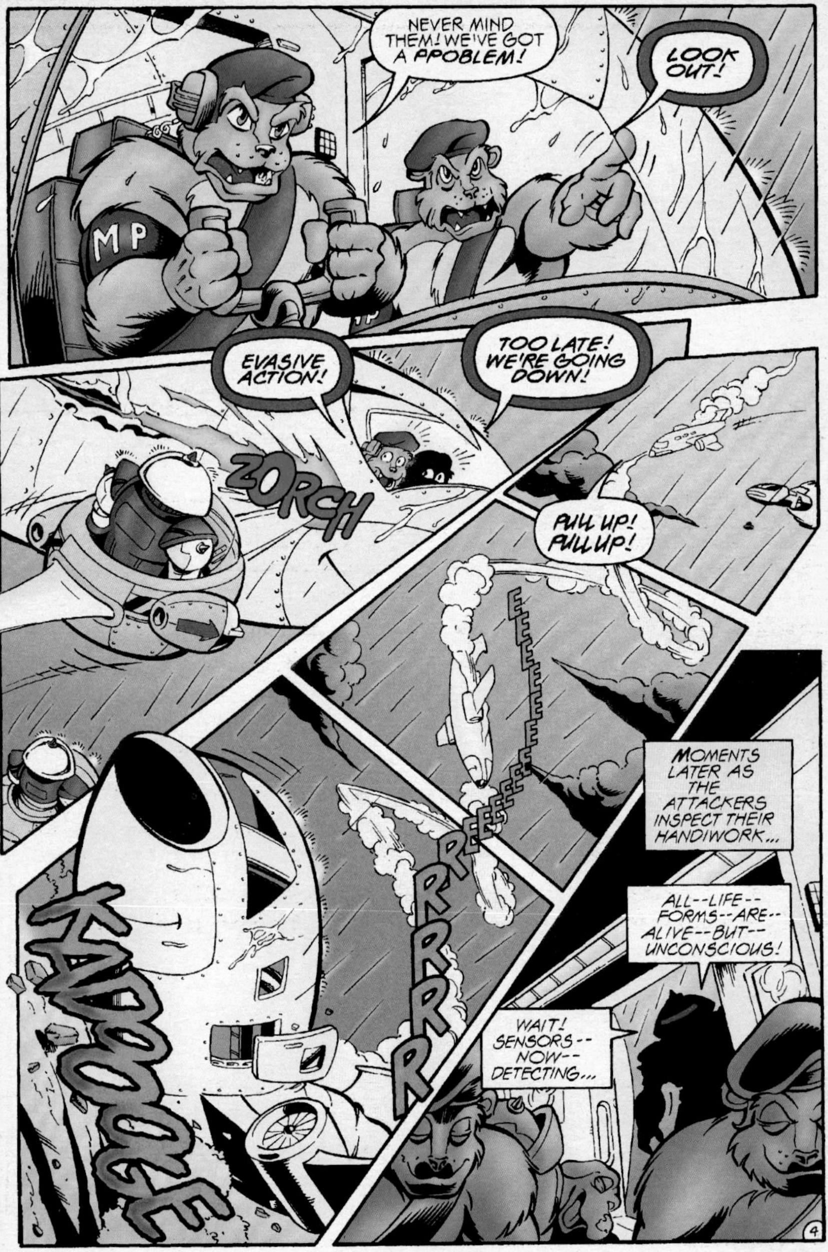
NEVER MIND THEM! WE'VE GOT A PPOBLEM!
LOOK OUT!
EVASIVE ACTION!
TOO LATE! WE'RE GOING DOWN!
ZORCH
PULL UP! PULL UP!
EEEEEEEEEEEEE
RRRRRR
KAPOOGE
MOMENTS LATER AS THE ATTACKERS INSPECT THEIR HANDIWORK...
ALL--LIFE--FORMS--ARE--ALIVE--BUT--UNCONSCIOUS!
WAIT! SENSORS--NOW--DETECTING...

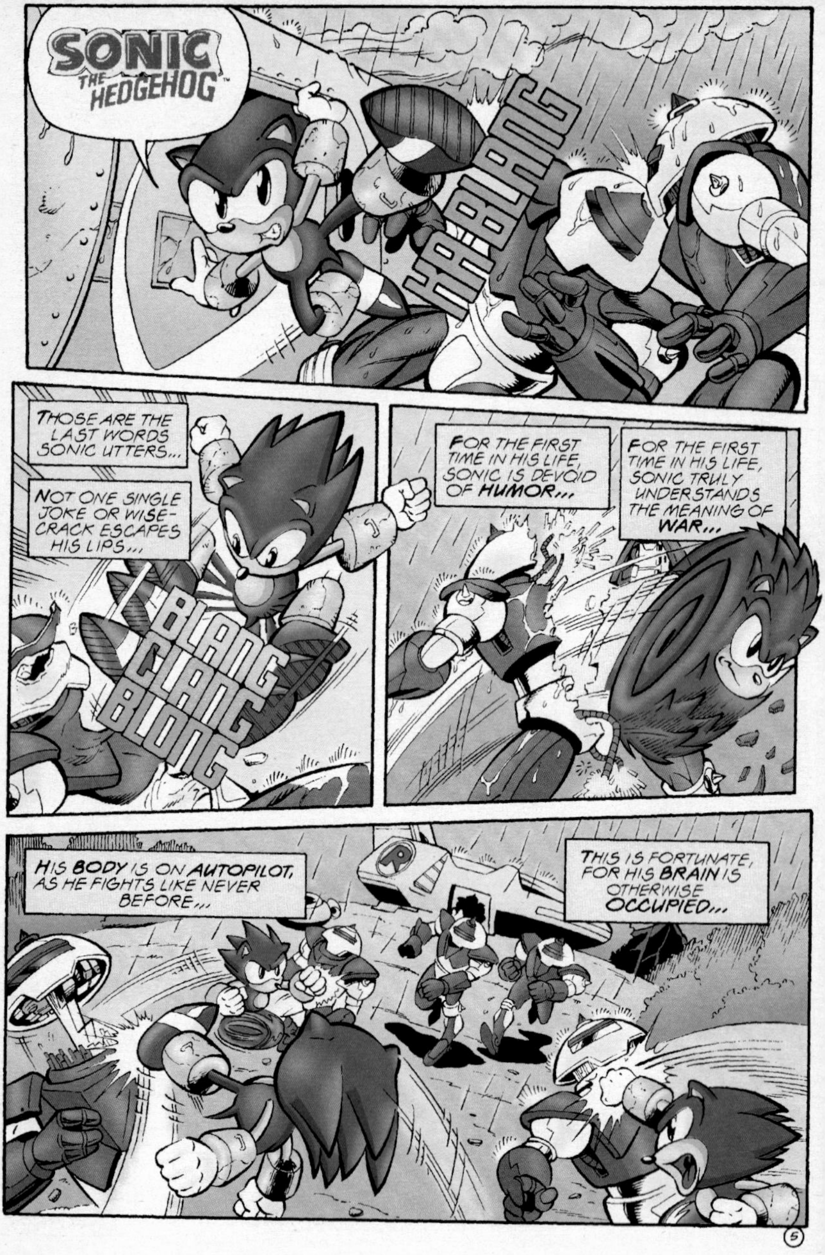
SONIC THE HEDGEHOG™
KA-BLANG
THOSE ARE THE LAST WORDS SONIC UTTERS...
NOT ONE SINGLE JOKE OR WISE-CRACK ESCAPES HIS LIPS...
BLANG CLANG BLONG
FOR THE FIRST TIME IN HIS LIFE, SONIC IS DEVOID OF HUMOR...
FOR THE FIRST TIME IN HIS LIFE, SONIC TRULY UNDERSTANDS THE MEANING OF WAR...
HIS BODY IS ON AUTOPILOT, AS HE FIGHTS LIKE NEVER BEFORE...
THIS IS FORTUNATE, FOR HIS BRAIN IS OTHERWISE OCCUPIED...

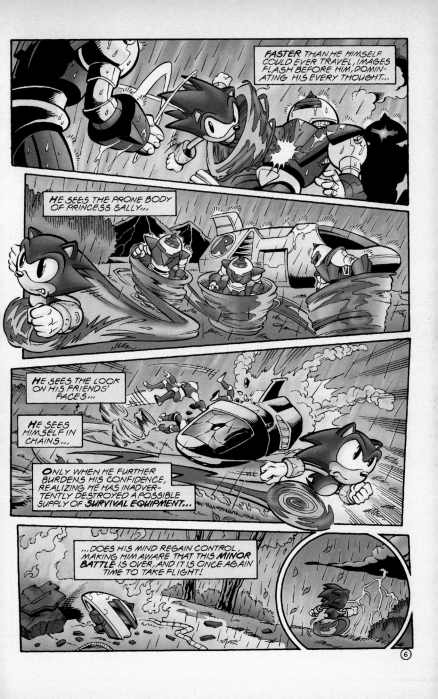

FASTER THAN HE HIMSELF COULD EVER TRAVEL, IMAGES FLASH BEFORE HIM, DOMINATING HIS EVERY THOUGHT...

HE SEES THE PRONE BODY OF PRINCESS SALLY...

HE SEES THE LOOK ON HIS FRIENDS' FACES...

HE SEES HIMSELF IN CHAINS...

ONLY WHEN HE FURTHER BURDENS HIS CONFIDENCE, REALIZING HE HAS INADVERTENTLY DESTROYED A POSSIBLE SUPPLY OF SURVIVAL EQUIPMENT...

...DOES HIS MIND REGAIN CONTROL, MAKING HIM AWARE THAT THIS MINOR BATTLE IS OVER, AND IT IS ONCE AGAIN TIME TO TAKE FLIGHT!

6

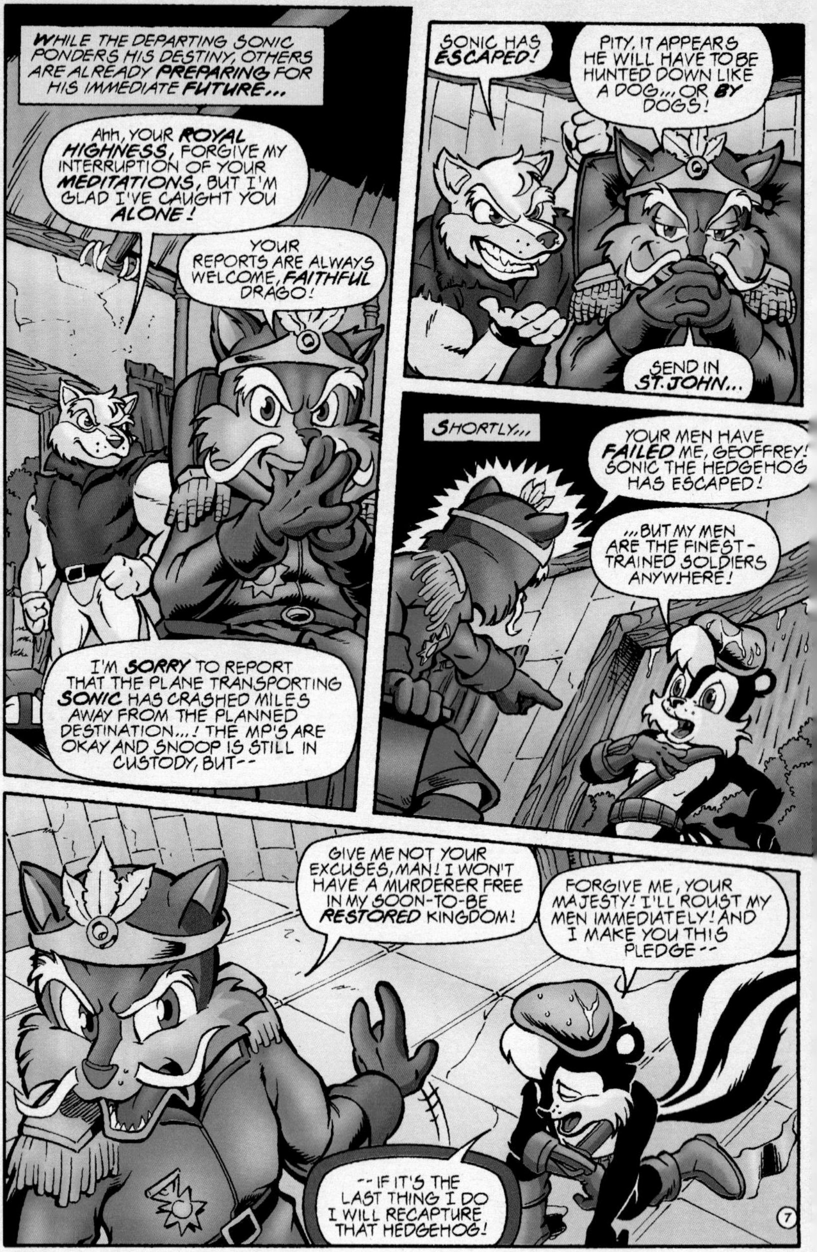
WHILE THE DEPARTING SONIC PONDERS HIS DESTINY, OTHERS ARE ALREADY PREPARING FOR HIS IMMEDIATE FUTURE...
Ahh, YOUR ROYAL HIGHNESS, FORGIVE MY INTERRUPTION OF YOUR MEDITATIONS, BUT I'M GLAD I'VE CAUGHT YOU ALONE!
YOUR REPORTS ARE ALWAYS WELCOME, FAITHFUL DRAGO!
I'M SORRY TO REPORT THAT THE PLANE TRANSPORTING SONIC HAS CRASHED MILES AWAY FROM THE PLANNED DESTINATION...! THE MP'S ARE OKAY AND SNOOP IS STILL IN CUSTODY, BUT--
SONIC HAS ESCAPED!
PITY. IT APPEARS HE WILL HAVE TO BE HUNTED DOWN LIKE A DOG,...OR BY DOGS!
SEND IN ST. JOHN...
SHORTLY...
YOUR MEN HAVE FAILED ME, GEOFFREY! SONIC THE HEDGEHOG HAS ESCAPED!
...BUT MY MEN ARE THE FINEST-TRAINED SOLDIERS ANYWHERE!
GIVE ME NOT YOUR EXCUSES, MAN! I WON'T HAVE A MURDERER FREE IN MY SOON-TO-BE RESTORED KINGDOM!
FORGIVE ME, YOUR MAJESTY! I'LL ROUST MY MEN IMMEDIATELY! AND I MAKE YOU THIS PLEDGE--
--IF IT'S THE LAST THING I DO I WILL RECAPTURE THAT HEDGEHOG!
7

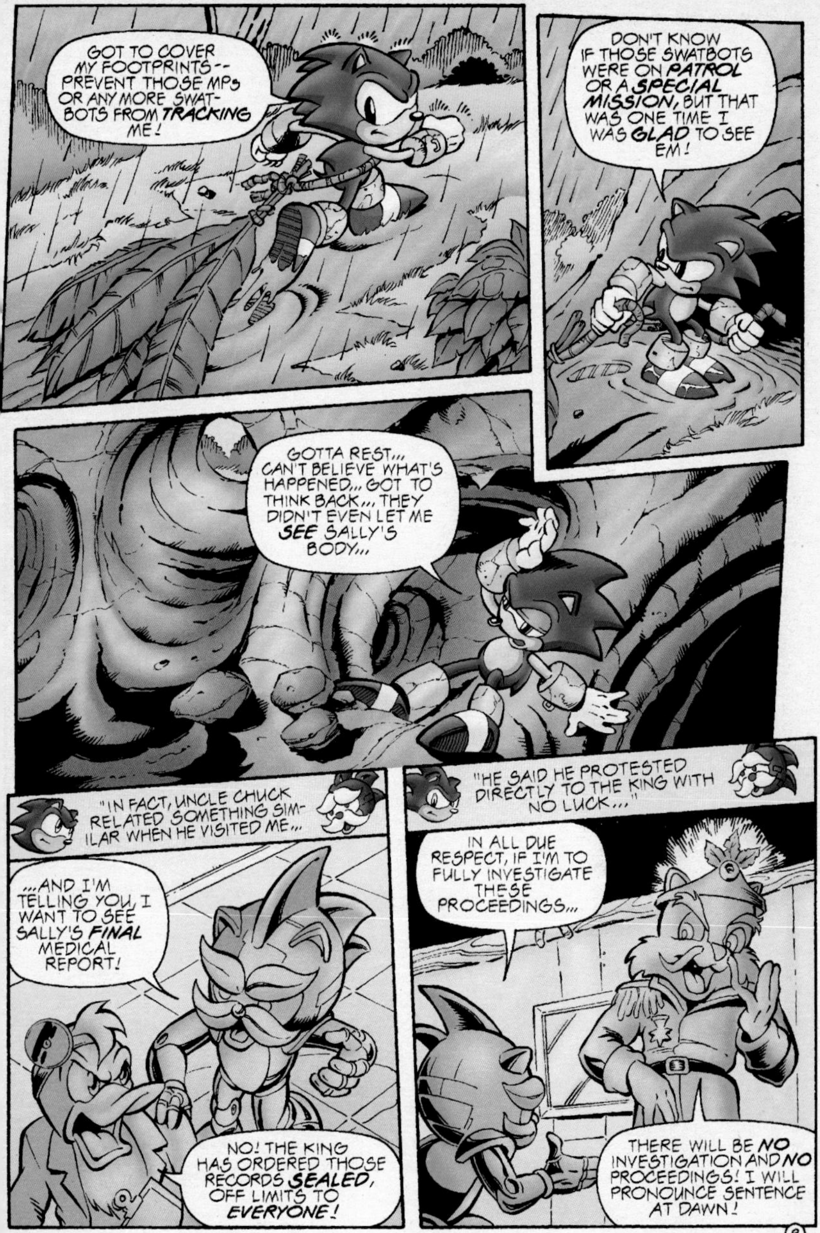

GOT TO COVER MY FOOTPRINTS-- PREVENT THOSE MPs OR ANY MORE SWAT-BOTS FROM TRACKING ME!
DON'T KNOW IF THOSE SWATBOTS WERE ON PATROL OR A SPECIAL MISSION, BUT THAT WAS ONE TIME I WAS GLAD TO SEE EM!
GOTTA REST... CAN'T BELIEVE WHAT'S HAPPENED... GOT TO THINK BACK... THEY DIDN'T EVEN LET ME SEE SALLY'S BODY...
"IN FACT, UNCLE CHUCK RELATED SOMETHING SIM-ILAR WHEN HE VISITED ME...
...AND I'M TELLING YOU, I WANT TO SEE SALLY'S FINAL MEDICAL REPORT!
NO! THE KING HAS ORDERED THOSE RECORDS SEALED, OFF LIMITS TO EVERYONE!
"HE SAID HE PROTESTED DIRECTLY TO THE KING WITH NO LUCK..."
IN ALL DUE RESPECT, IF I'M TO FULLY INVESTIGATE THESE PROCEEDINGS...
THERE WILL BE NO INVESTIGATION AND NO PROCEEDINGS! I WILL PRONOUNCE SENTENCE AT DAWN!

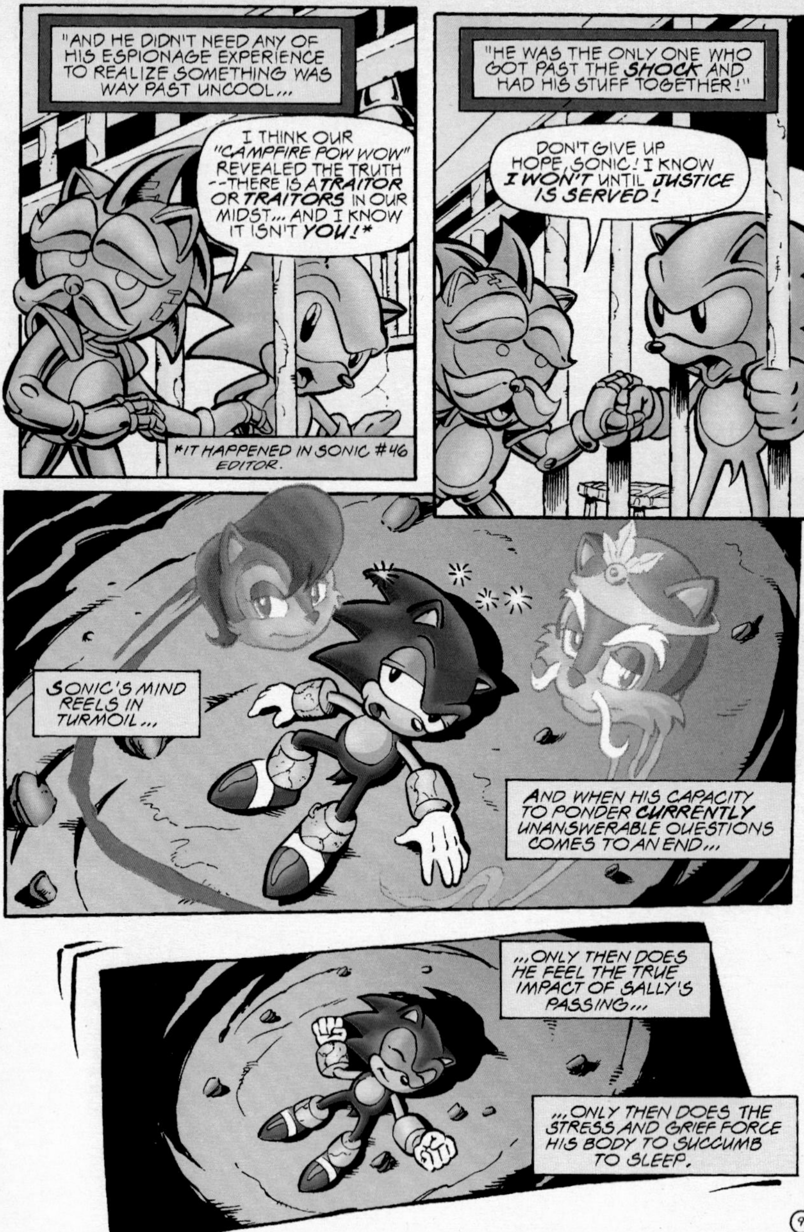
"AND HE DIDN'T NEED ANY OF HIS ESPIONAGE EXPERIENCE TO REALIZE SOMETHING WAS WAY PAST UNCOOL...
I THINK OUR "CAMPFIRE POW WOW" REVEALED THE TRUTH --THERE IS A TRAITOR OR TRAITORS IN OUR MIDST... AND I KNOW IT ISN'T YOU!*
*IT HAPPENED IN SONIC #46 EDITOR.
"HE WAS THE ONLY ONE WHO GOT PAST THE SHOCK AND HAD HIS STUFF TOGETHER!"
DON'T GIVE UP HOPE, SONIC! I KNOW I WON'T UNTIL JUSTICE IS SERVED!
SONIC'S MIND REELS IN TURMOIL...
AND WHEN HIS CAPACITY TO PONDER CURRENTLY UNANSWERABLE QUESTIONS COMES TO AN END...
...ONLY THEN DOES HE FEEL THE TRUE IMPACT OF SALLY'S PASSING...
...ONLY THEN DOES THE STRESS AND GRIEF FORCE HIS BODY TO SUCCUMB TO SLEEP.

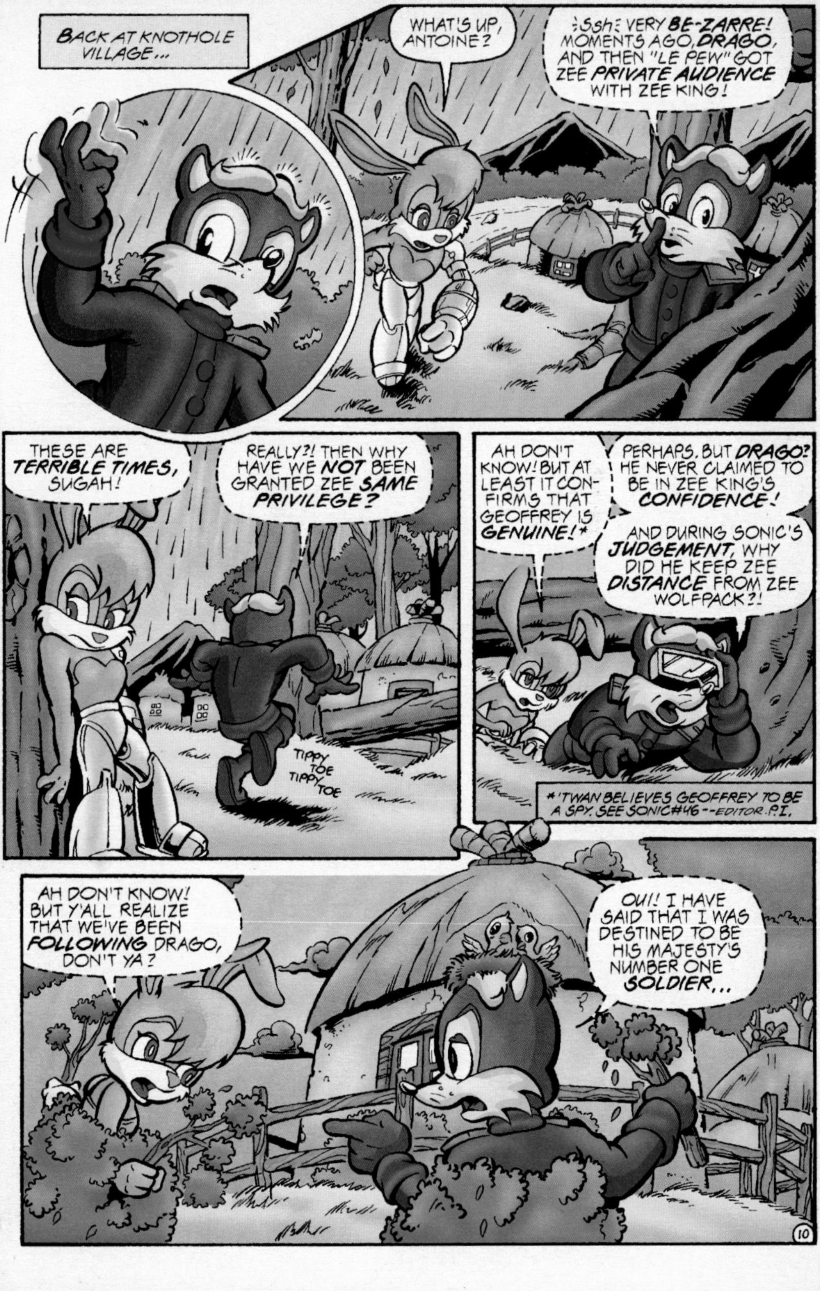
BACK AT KNOTHOLE VILLAGE...
WHAT'S UP, ANTOINE?
Ssh! VERY BE-ZARRE! MOMENTS AGO, DRAGO, AND THEN "LE PEW" GOT ZEE PRIVATE AUDIENCE WITH ZEE KING!
THESE ARE TERRIBLE TIMES, SUGAH!
REALLY?! THEN WHY HAVE WE NOT BEEN GRANTED ZEE SAME PRIVILEGE?
TIPPY TOE TIPPY TOE
AH DON'T KNOW! BUT AT LEAST IT CONFIRMS THAT GEOFFREY IS GENUINE!*
PERHAPS. BUT DRAGO? HE NEVER CLAIMED TO BE IN ZEE KING'S CONFIDENCE!
AND DURING SONIC'S JUDGEMENT, WHY DID HE KEEP ZEE DISTANCE FROM ZEE WOLFPACK?!
*'TWAN BELIEVES GEOFFREY TO BE A SPY. SEE SONIC #46 --EDITOR P.I.
AH DON'T KNOW! BUT Y'ALL REALIZE THAT WE'VE BEEN FOLLOWING DRAGO, DON'T YA?
OUI! I HAVE SAID THAT I WAS DESTINED TO BE HIS MAJESTY'S NUMBER ONE SOLDIER,...
10

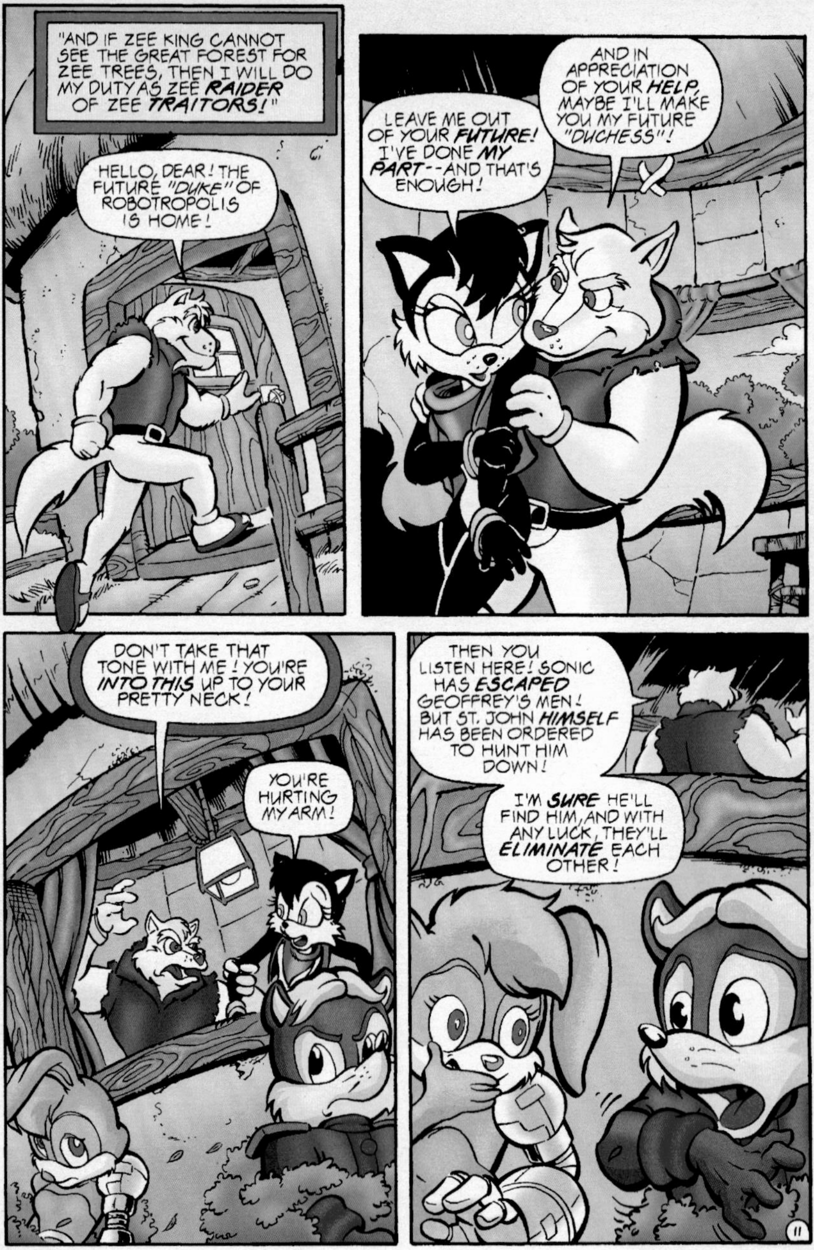
"AND IF ZEE KING CANNOT SEE THE GREAT FOREST FOR ZEE TREES, THEN I WILL DO MY DUTY AS ZEE RAIDER OF ZEE TRAITORS!"
HELLO, DEAR! THE FUTURE "DUKE" OF ROBOTROPOLIS IS HOME!
AND IN APPRECIATION OF YOUR HELP, MAYBE I'LL MAKE YOU MY FUTURE "DUCHESS"!
LEAVE ME OUT OF YOUR FUTURE! I'VE DONE MY PART--AND THAT'S ENOUGH!
DON'T TAKE THAT TONE WITH ME! YOU'RE INTO THIS UP TO YOUR PRETTY NECK!
YOU'RE HURTING MY ARM!
THEN YOU LISTEN HERE! SONIC HAS ESCAPED GEOFFREY'S MEN! BUT ST. JOHN HIMSELF HAS BEEN ORDERED TO HUNT HIM DOWN!
I'M SURE HE'LL FIND HIM, AND WITH ANY LUCK, THEY'LL ELIMINATE EACH OTHER!
11

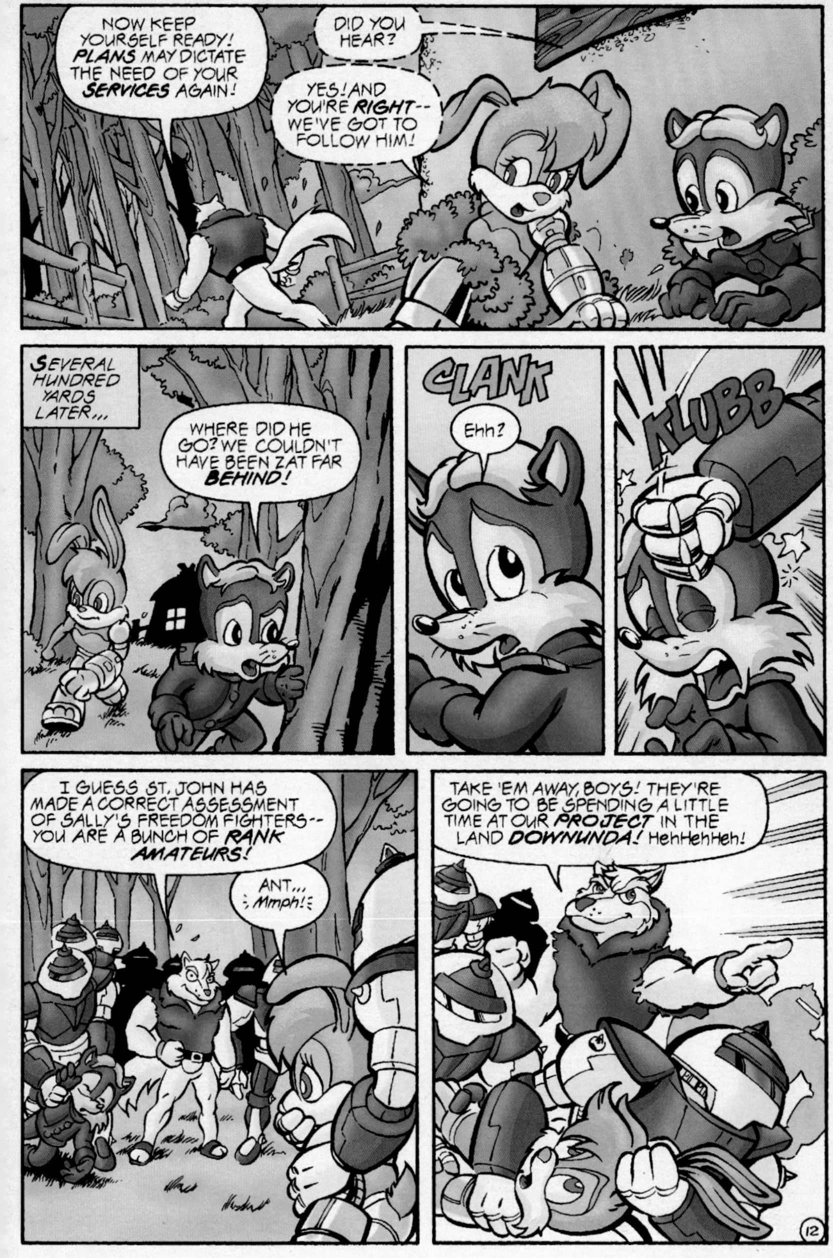
NOW KEEP YOURSELF READY! PLANS MAY DICTATE THE NEED OF YOUR SERVICES AGAIN!
DID YOU HEAR?
YES! AND YOU'RE RIGHT-- WE'VE GOT TO FOLLOW HIM!
SEVERAL HUNDRED YARDS LATER...
WHERE DID HE GO? WE COULDN'T HAVE BEEN ZAT FAR BEHIND!
CLANK
Ehh?
KLUBB
I GUESS ST. JOHN HAS MADE A CORRECT ASSESSMENT OF SALLY'S FREEDOM FIGHTERS-- YOU ARE A BUNCH OF RANK AMATEURS!
ANT... Mmph!
TAKE 'EM AWAY, BOYS! THEY'RE GOING TO BE SPENDING A LITTLE TIME AT OUR PROJECT IN THE LAND DOWNUNDA! HehHehHeh!

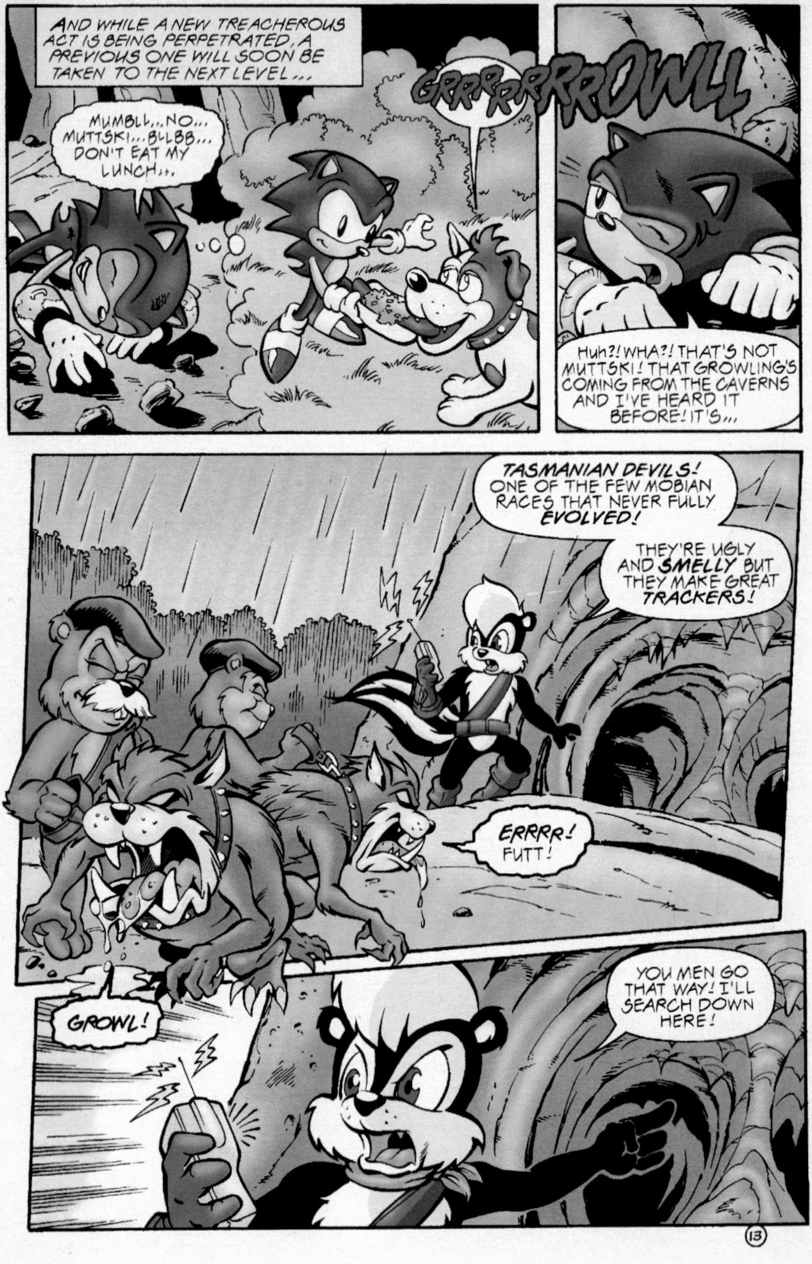
AND WHILE A NEW TREACHEROUS ACT IS BEING PERPETRATED, A PREVIOUS ONE WILL SOON BE TAKEN TO THE NEXT LEVEL...
MUMBLL...NO... MUTTSKI...BLLBB... DON'T EAT MY LUNCH...
GRRRRRRRROWLL
Huh?! WHA?! THAT'S NOT MUTTSKI! THAT GROWLING'S COMING FROM THE CAVERNS AND I'VE HEARD IT BEFORE! IT'S...
TASMANIAN DEVILS! ONE OF THE FEW MOBIAN RACES THAT NEVER FULLY EVOLVED!
THEY'RE UGLY AND SMELLY BUT THEY MAKE GREAT TRACKERS!
ERRRR! FUTT!
GROWL!
YOU MEN GO THAT WAY! I'LL SEARCH DOWN HERE!

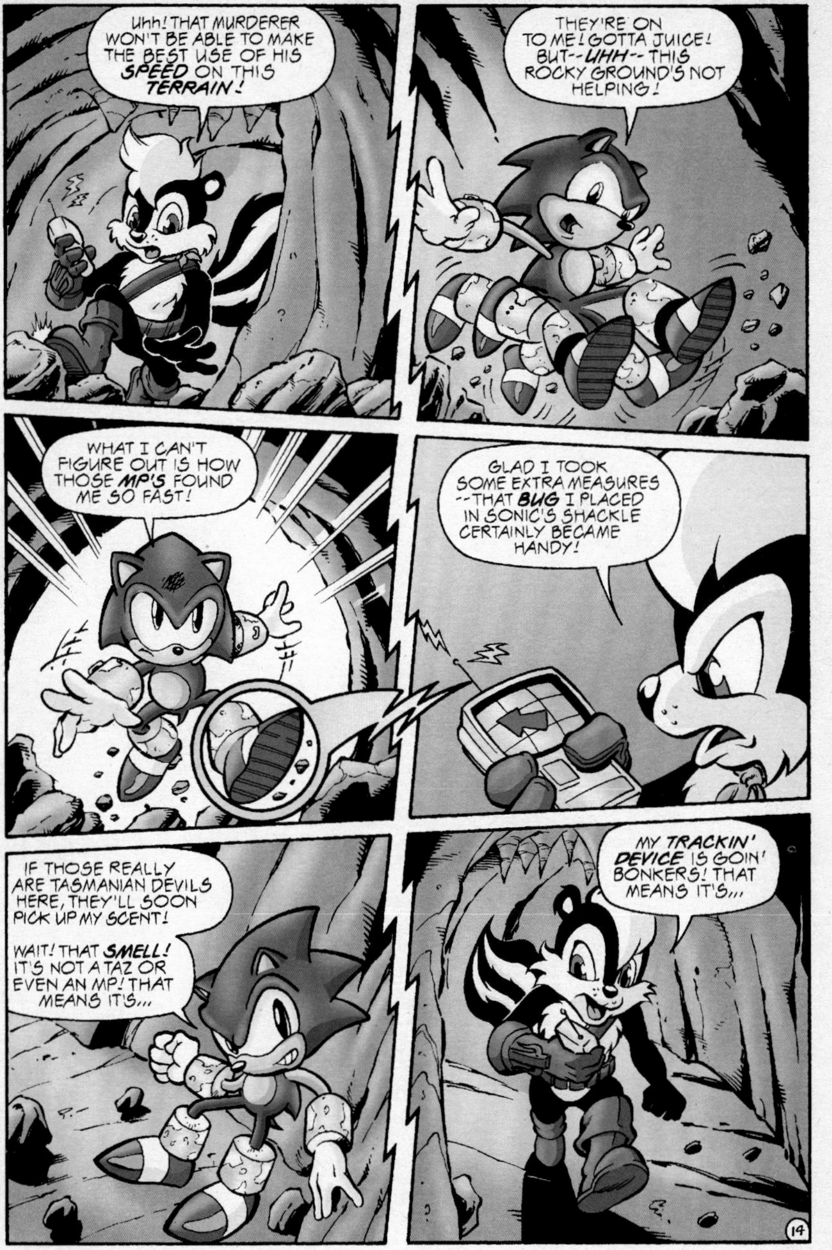
Uhh! THAT MURDERER WON'T BE ABLE TO MAKE THE BEST USE OF HIS SPEED ON THIS TERRAIN!
THEY'RE ON TO ME! GOTTA JUICE! BUT--UHH--THIS ROCKY GROUND'S NOT HELPING!
WHAT I CAN'T FIGURE OUT IS HOW THOSE MP'S FOUND ME SO FAST!
GLAD I TOOK SOME EXTRA MEASURES --THAT BUG I PLACED IN SONIC'S SHACKLE CERTAINLY BECAME HANDY!
IF THOSE REALLY ARE TASMANIAN DEVILS HERE, THEY'LL SOON PICK UP MY SCENT!
WAIT! THAT SMELL! IT'S NOT A TAZ OR EVEN AN MP! THAT MEANS IT'S...
MY TRACKIN' DEVICE IS GOIN' BONKERS! THAT MEANS IT'S...

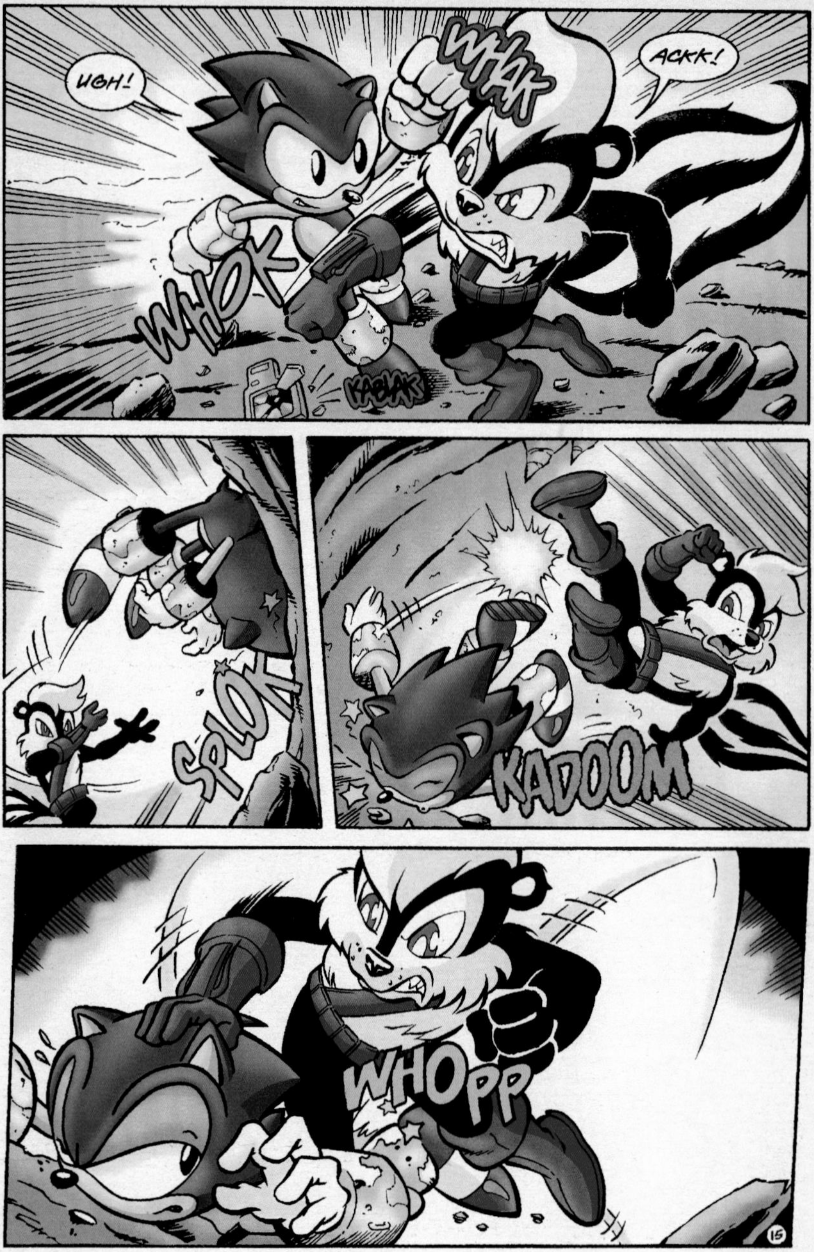
UGH!
WHAK
ACKK!
WHOK
KABLAK
SPLOK
KADOOM
WHOPP

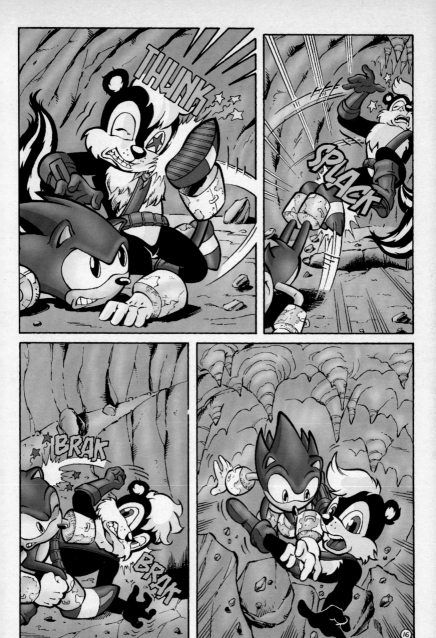

THUNK

SPLACK

BRAK

BRAK

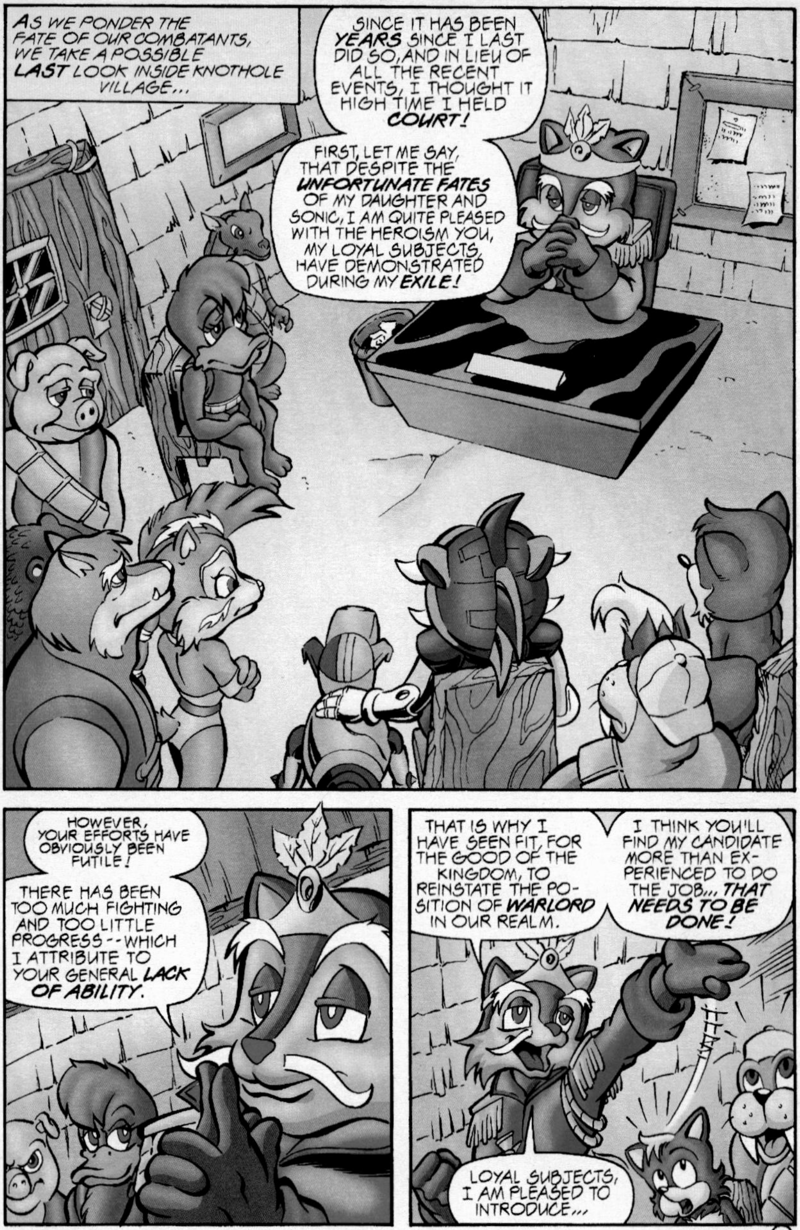
AS WE PONDER THE FATE OF OUR COMBATANTS, WE TAKE A POSSIBLE LAST LOOK INSIDE KNOTHOLE VILLAGE...
SINCE IT HAS BEEN YEARS SINCE I LAST DID SO, AND IN LIEU OF ALL THE RECENT EVENTS, I THOUGHT IT HIGH TIME I HELD COURT!
FIRST, LET ME SAY, THAT DESPITE THE UNFORTUNATE FATES OF MY DAUGHTER AND SONIC, I AM QUITE PLEASED WITH THE HEROISM YOU, MY LOYAL SUBJECTS, HAVE DEMONSTRATED DURING MY EXILE!
HOWEVER, YOUR EFFORTS HAVE OBVIOUSLY BEEN FUTILE!
THERE HAS BEEN TOO MUCH FIGHTING AND TOO LITTLE PROGRESS--WHICH I ATTRIBUTE TO YOUR GENERAL LACK OF ABILITY.
THAT IS WHY I HAVE SEEN FIT, FOR THE GOOD OF THE KINGDOM, TO REINSTATE THE PO-SITION OF WARLORD IN OUR REALM.
I THINK YOU'LL FIND MY CANDIDATE MORE THAN EX-PERIENCED TO DO THE JOB... THAT NEEDS TO BE DONE!
LOYAL SUBJECTS, I AM PLEASED TO INTRODUCE...

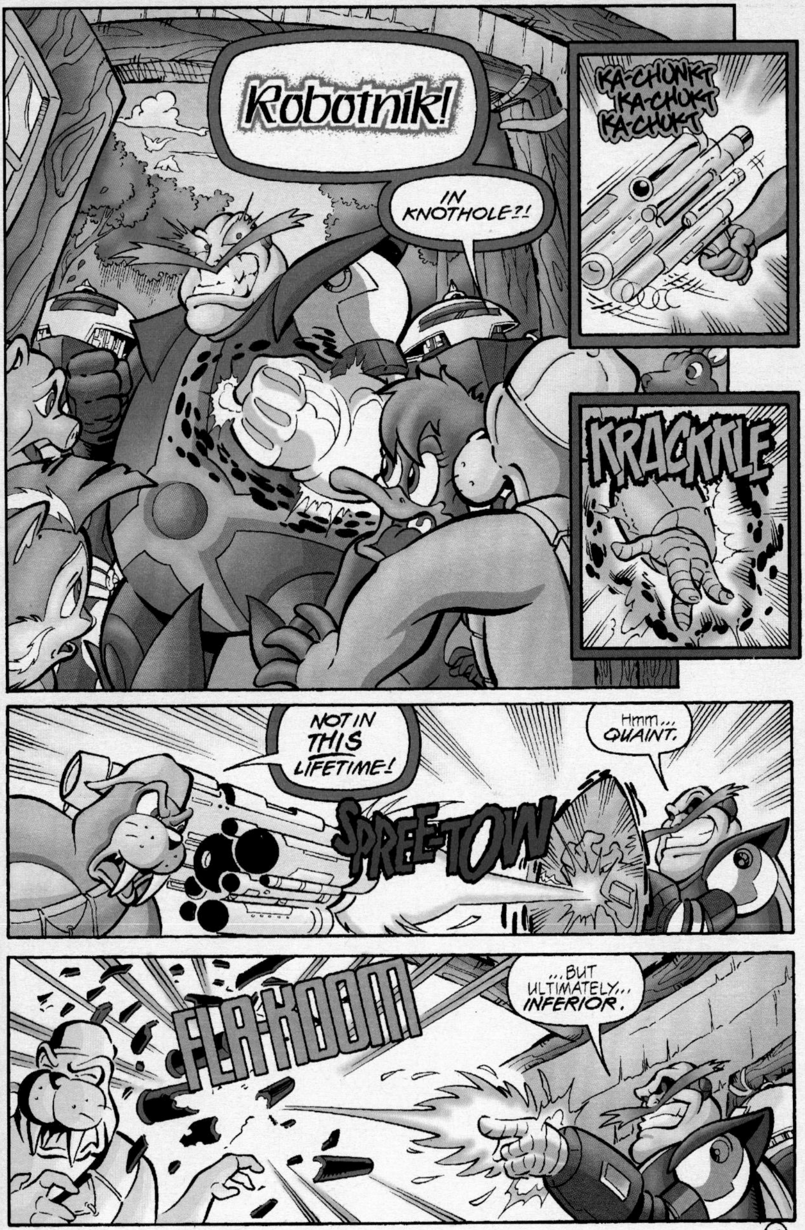
Robotnik!
IN KNOTHOLE?!
KA-CHUNK! KA-CHUK! KA-CHUK!
KRACKKLE
NOT IN THIS LIFETIME!
SPREE-TOW
Hmm... QUAINT.
FLA-KOOM
...BUT ULTIMATELY... INFERIOR.

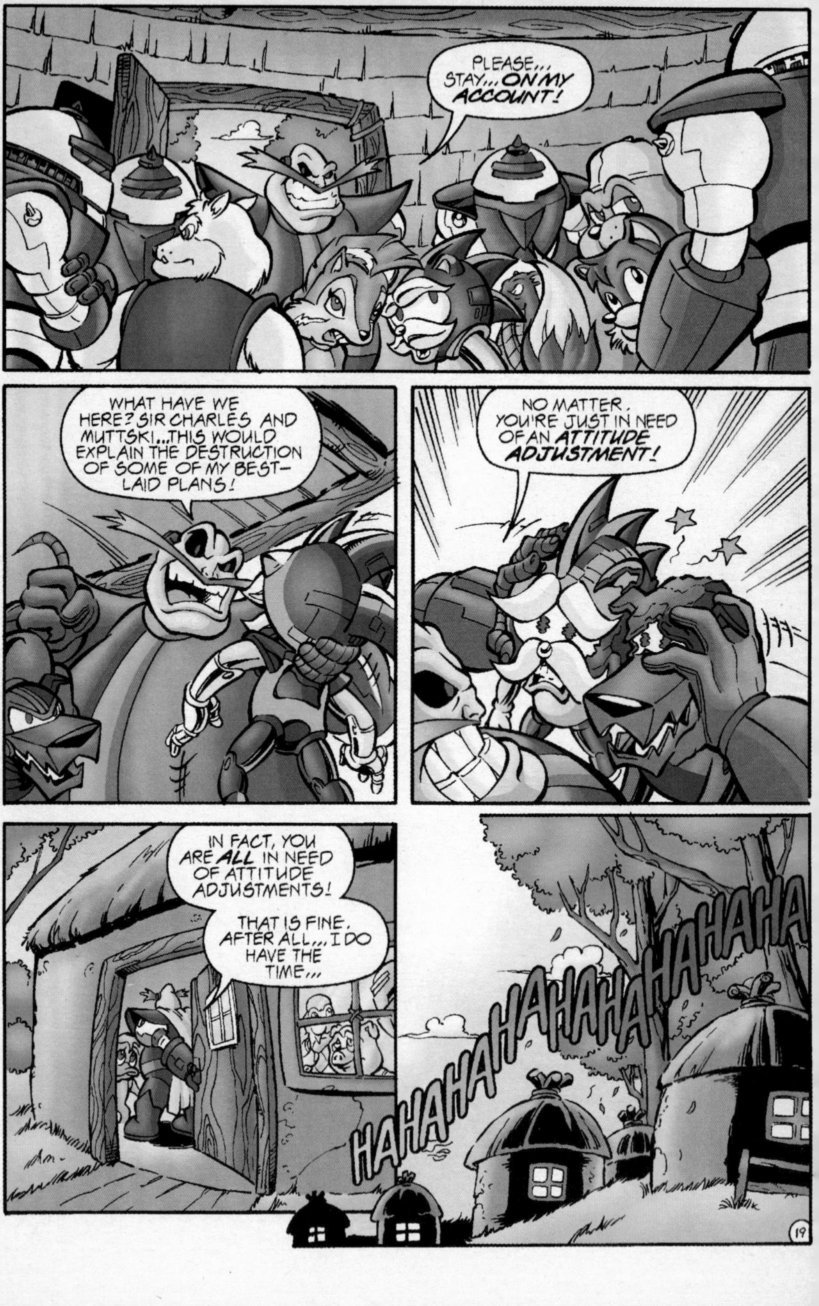
PLEASE... STAY... ON MY ACCOUNT!
WHAT HAVE WE HERE? SIR CHARLES AND MUTTSKI...THIS WOULD EXPLAIN THE DESTRUCTION OF SOME OF MY BEST-LAID PLANS!
NO MATTER. YOU'RE JUST IN NEED OF AN ATTITUDE ADJUSTMENT!
IN FACT, YOU ARE ALL IN NEED OF ATTITUDE ADJUSTMENTS!
THAT IS FINE. AFTER ALL... I DO HAVE THE TIME...
HAHAHAHAHAHAHAHAHAHAHAHA

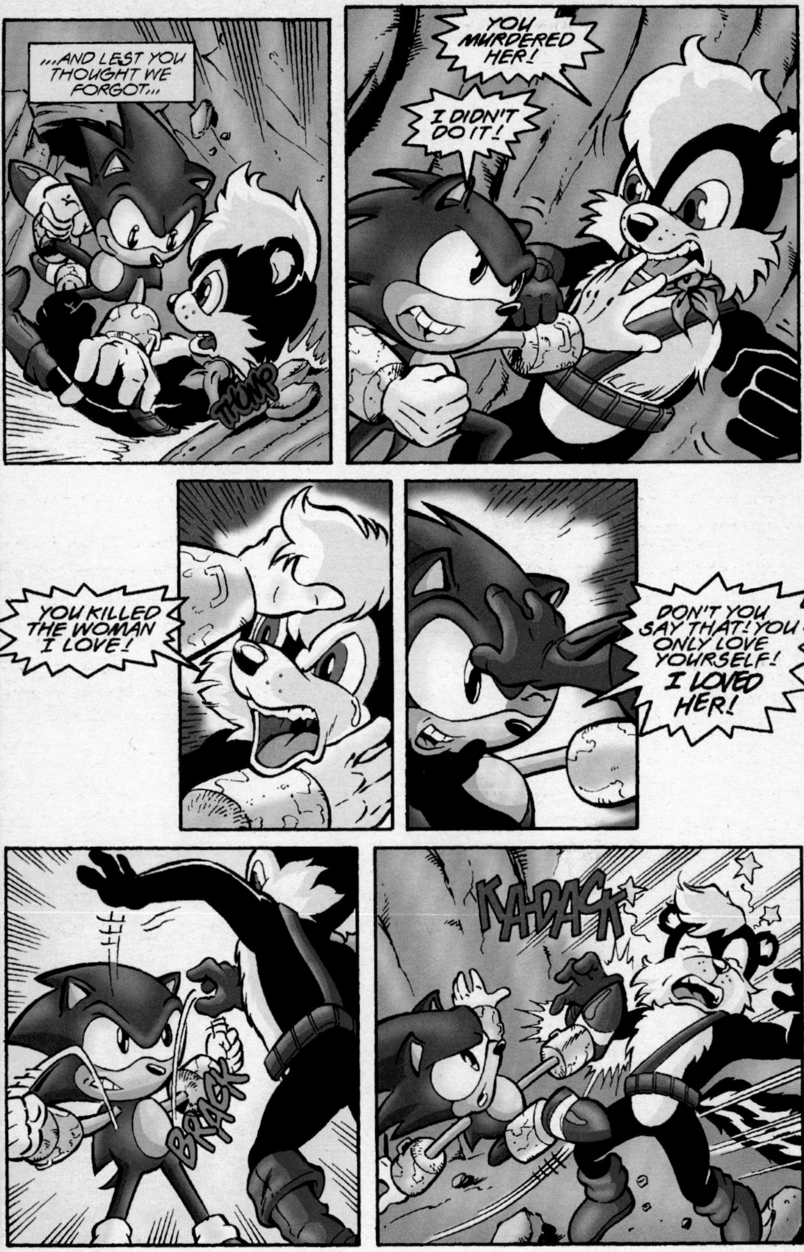
...AND LEST YOU THOUGHT WE FORGOT...
THOMP
YOU MURDERED HER!
I DIDN'T DO IT!
YOU KILLED THE WOMAN I LOVE!
DON'T YOU SAY THAT! YOU ONLY LOVE YOURSELF! I LOVED HER!
BRACK
KA-DACK

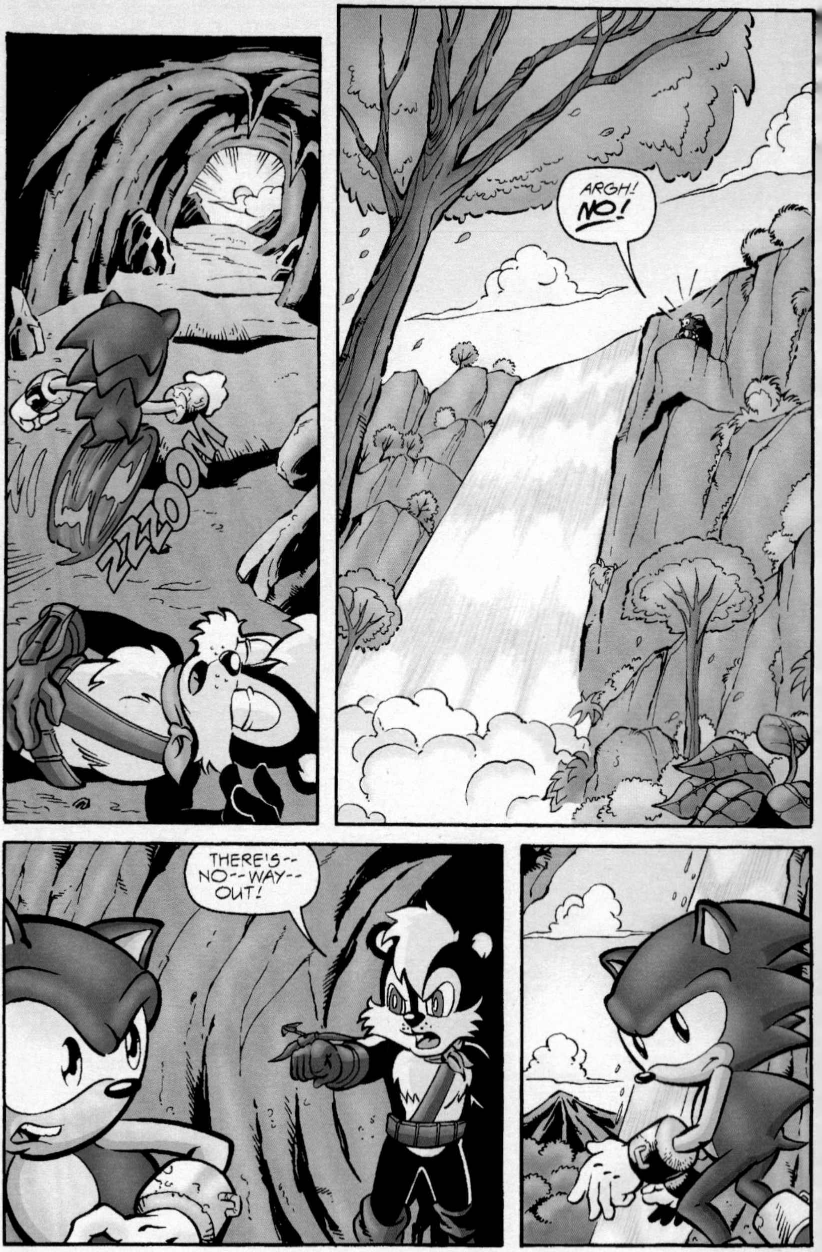
ZZZOOM
ARGH! NO!
THERE'S-- NO--WAY-- OUT!

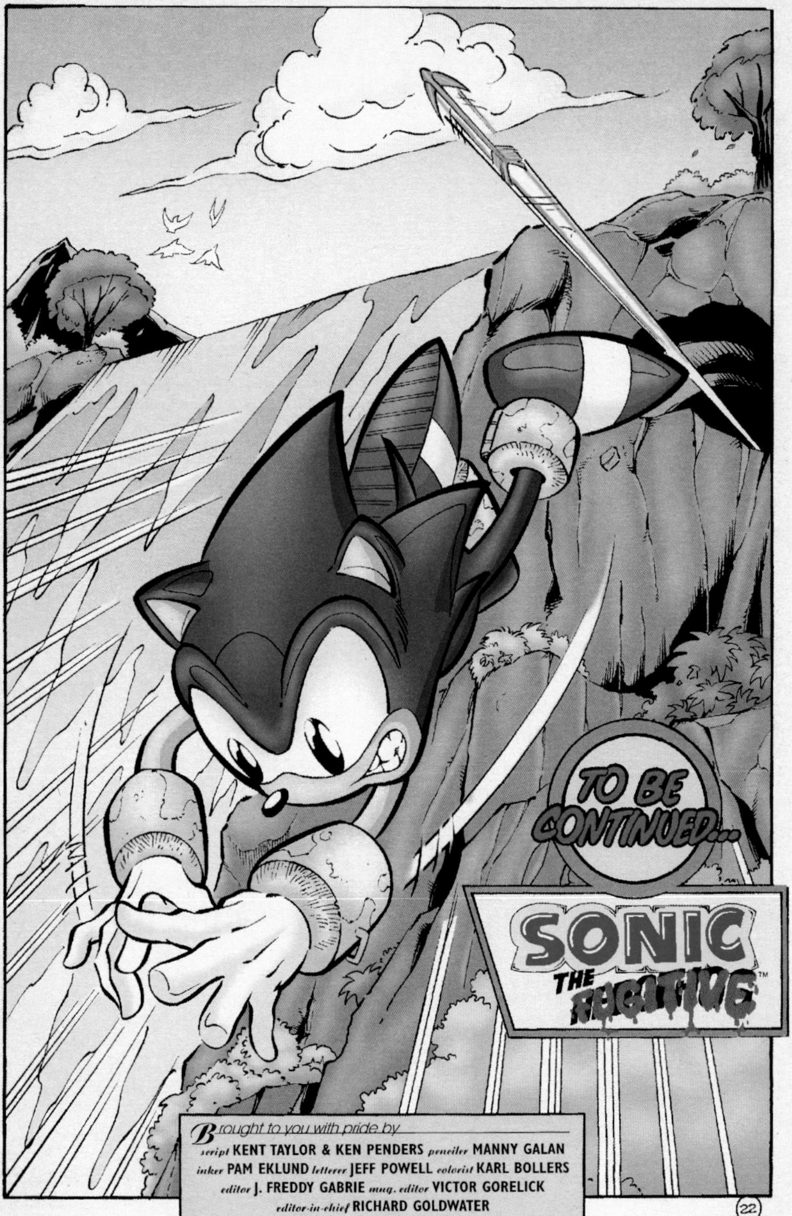
TO BE CONTINUED...
SONIC THE FUGITIVE™
Brought to you with pride by
script KENT TAYLOR & KEN PENDERS penciler MANNY GALAN
inker PAM EKLUND letterer JEFF POWELL colorist KARL BOLLERS
editor J. FREDDY GABRIE mng. editor VICTOR GORELICK
editor-in-chief RICHARD GOLDWATER

SONIC THE HEDGEHOG ™

Welcome to a brief who's who
of the Sonic universe.
You have just read some
of the earliest
and most loved stories from the
Sonic comic. We thought
you'd like to learn a little extra
about a few of your
favorite Sonic characters.

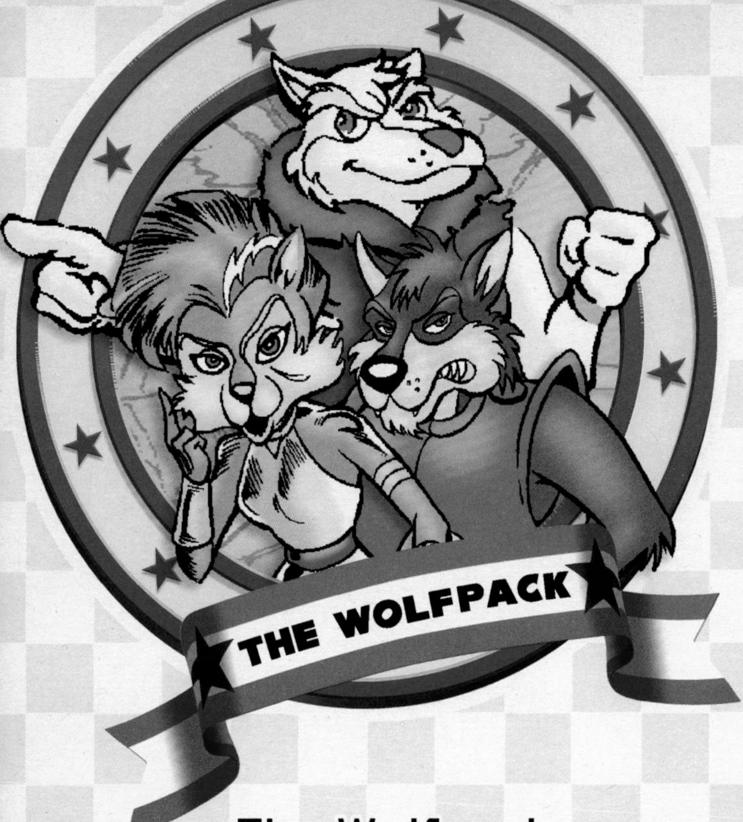
THE WOLFPACK

The Wolfpack

A noble band of wolves scattered from their homeland by Dr. Robotnik. Led by the courageous Lupe, they've linked up with the Knothole Freedom Fighters to help fight the mad doctor's tyranny!

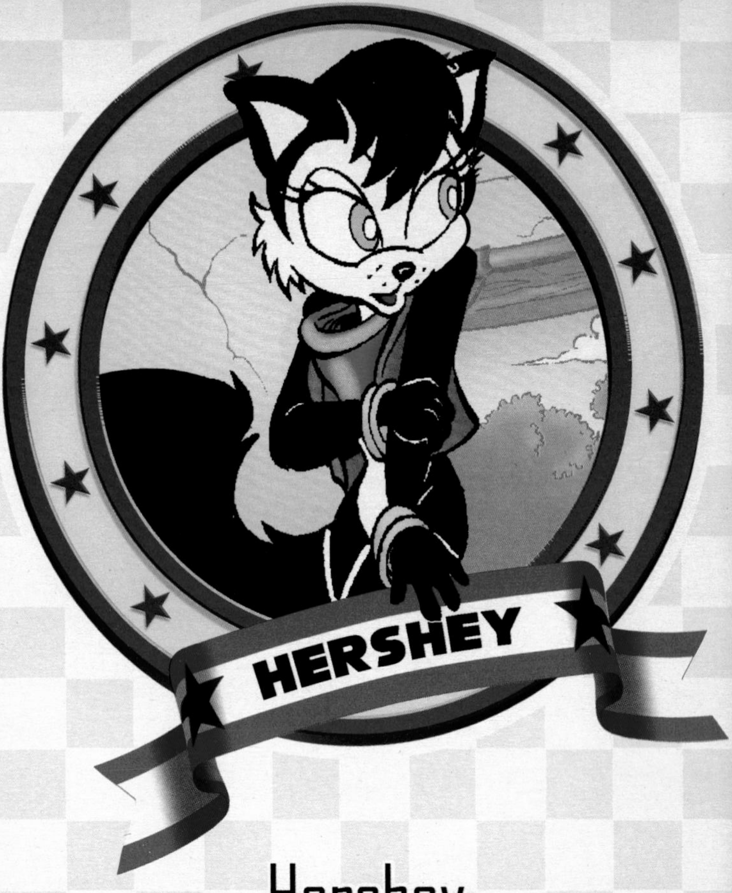
HERSHEY

Hershey

A sweet girl with a bad habit of picking the wrong guy! What does she see in Drago Wolf? And what part does she play in Dr. Robotnik's newest sinister plot?

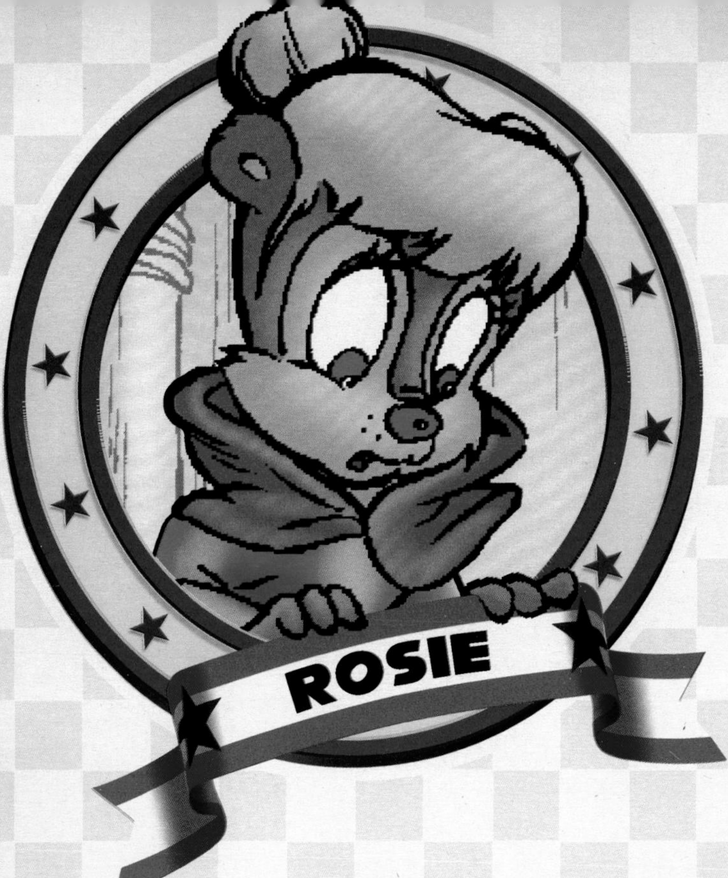
ROSIE

Rosie

The kindly matron of Knothole Village who looks after the war orphans. She helped raise the Freedom Fighters into the heroes they are today!

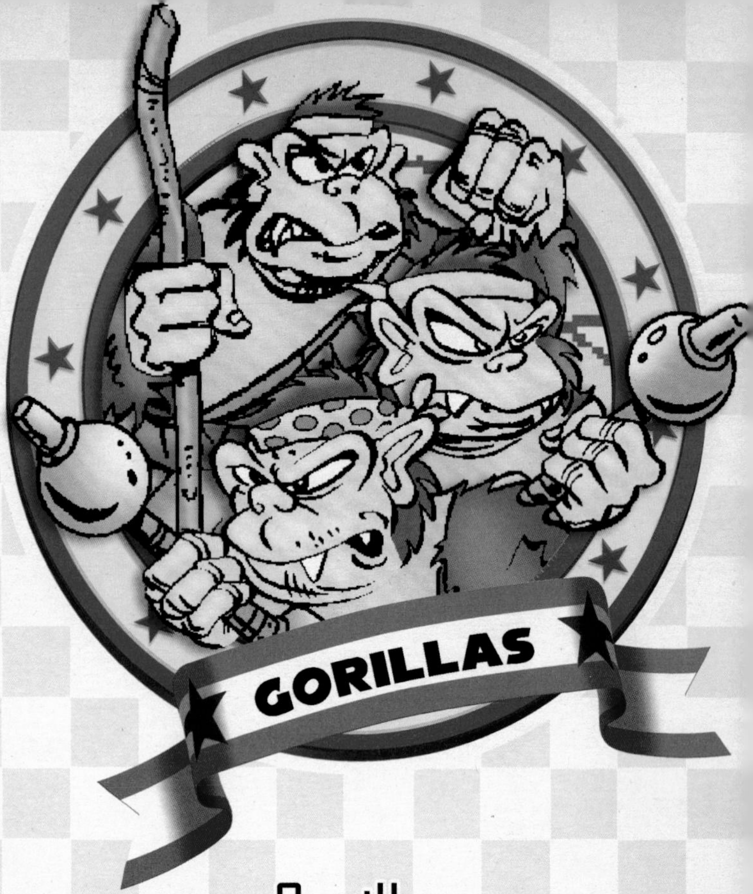
GORILLAS

Gorillas

Once a peaceful family troupe, they had to militarize to fight back against Dr. Robotnik. Can Sonic show them the path back to peace?

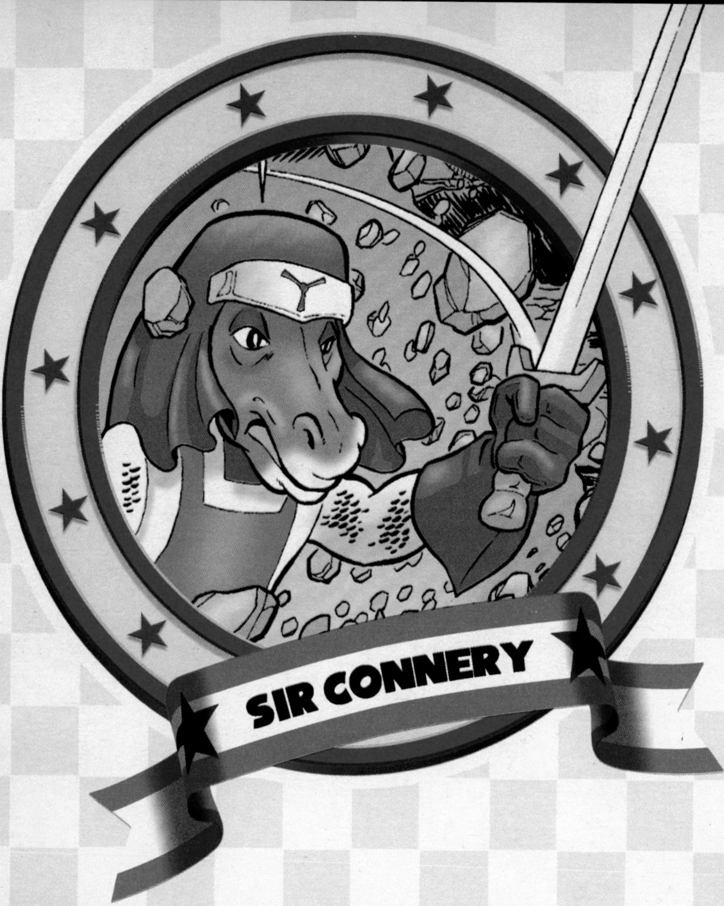
SIR CONNERY

Sir Connery

A paladin knight who once served King Acorn. He was sent on a quest by the Ancient Walkers to rid the world of dark magic with the mystical Sword of Light.

SORCERER & ENCHANTRESS

Sorcerer & Enchantress

A pair of dark magic users hiding out on Angel Island. Black Death used many trinkets and potions to bully his way to power, while the Enchantress used her powers to enslave men's minds!

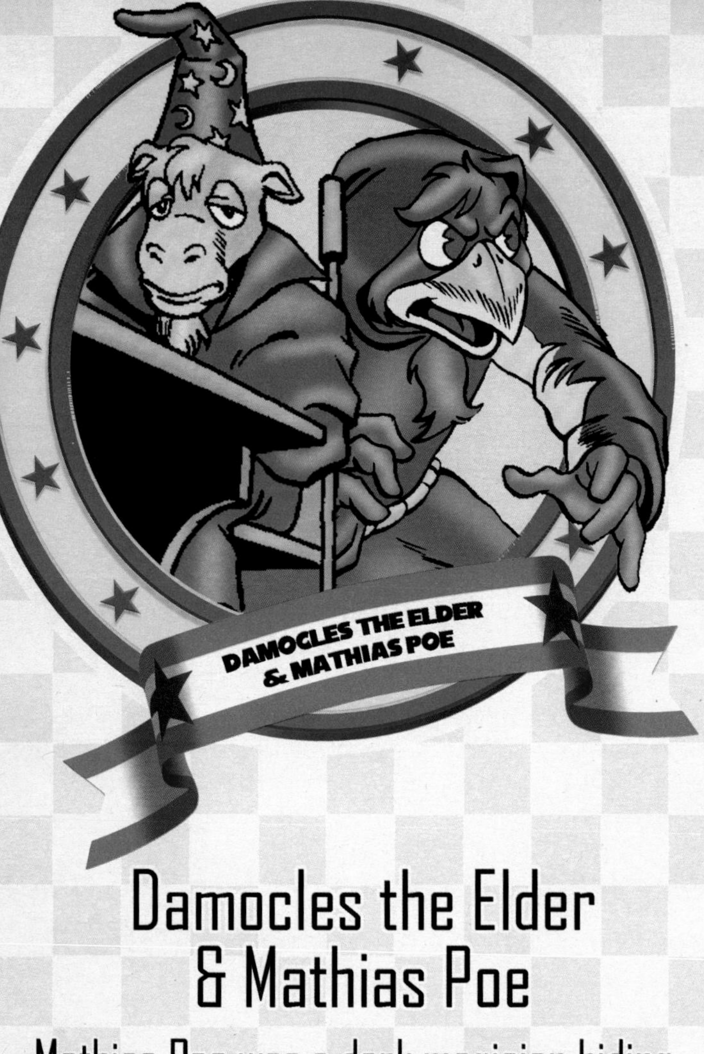
DAMOCLES THE ELDER
& MATHIAS POE

Damocles the Elder & Mathias Poe

Mathias Poe was a dark magician hiding out on Angel Island, using the Sword of Acorns to power his magic. He hid it in a double of Damocles – another prominent wizard. But where is the real Damocles?

SONIC THE HEDGEHOG™

Welcome to a brief what's what of the Sonic universe. You have just read some of the earliest and most loved stories from the Sonic comic. We thought you'd like to learn a little extra about a few of the items and places that make the Sonic universe so awesome!

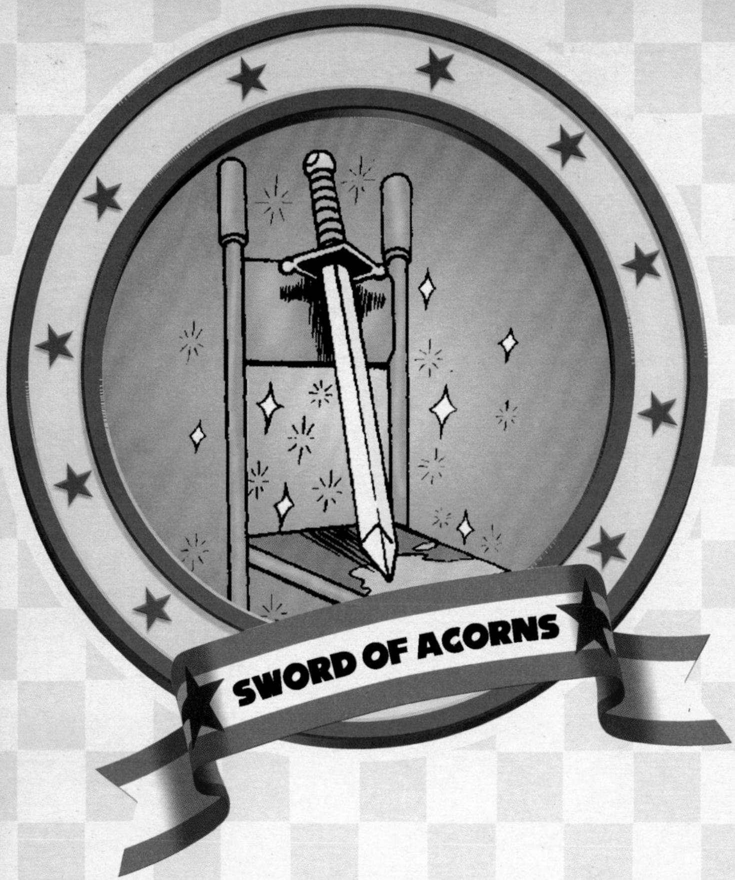
SWORD OF ACORNS

Sword of Acorns

A magical sword forged from the Source of All. It holds a mystic link with King Acorn, and it can super-charge a magic-user's powers!